The Ghost Quartet

The Ghost Quartet

EDITED BY MARVIN KAYE

A TOM DOHERTY ASSOCIATES BOOK · NEW YORK

THE GHOST QUARTET

Introduction copyright © 2008 by Marvin Kaye
"The Place of Waiting" copyright © 2008 by Brian Lumley
"Hamlet's Father" copyright © 2008 by Orson Scott Card
"The Haunted Single Malt" copyright © 2008 by Marvin Kaye
"Strindberg's Ghost Sonata" copyright © 2008 by Tanith Lee

Interior illustrations copyright © 2008 by Stephen Hickman

A Tor Book
Published by Tom Doherty Associates, LLC
175 Fifth Avenue
New York, NY 10010

www.tor-forge.com

Tor® is a registered trademark of Tom Doherty Associates, LLC.

ISBN-13: 978-0-7653-1251-8
ISBN-10: 0-7653-1251-4

First Edition: September 2008

Printed in the United States of America

0 9 8 7 6 5 4 3 2 1

CONTENTS

Do you believe in ghosts?

Drew Beltane, psychic investigator of *A Cold Blue Light,* a haunted-house novel Parke Godwin and I cowrote, answered this question with a counter-query:

"Do *you* believe in Grand Central Station?"

On the other hand, archy, Don Marquis's cockroach *auteur*, responded in this savvy fashion:

of course i do not believe in them
if you had known
as many of them as i have
you would not
believe in them either

But do *I* believe in them?

In the early years of my life, I wasn't sure. I was certainly interested, though. I tried, unsuccessfully, to finish reading my first novel (*Dracula,* what else?), but before that, I did manage to get all the way through August Derleth's revengeful (*and* protective) ghostly cover story of the March 1947 issue of *Weird Tales*, "Mr. George," published under Derleth's pseudonym, Stephen Grendon.

Even that early exposure was predated by my screening of one of the scariest ghost films ever made: Val Lewton/Robert Wise's *The Body Snatcher*. I saw it in 1945, when I was seven years old. My mother never would have approved the choice, so thanks belatedly to my cousin Norman Sporn, of Richmond, Virginia, for sneaking me in with him, instead of going to the new Danny Kaye movie that we were supposed to see. (I *was* torn; Kaye was one of my favorites, as my surname might suggest.)

So all my life, I've been attracted to ghost stories, both the "real" ones and the fictitious. Fantasy literature in general has always interested me, and to a lesser extent, science fiction and murder mysteries, but more than vampires or werewolves or miscellaneous monsters, my imagination always has been captivated by haunted houses, ditto rooms, *double* ditto lives . . . whose dilemma Maxwell Anderson captured in his verse tragedy, *Winterset*—

> In all these turning lights I find no clue
> Only a masterless night, and in my blood
> No certain answer. Yet is my mind my own,
> Yet is my heart a cry toward something dim

To my mind, ghost stories are a vital tool in that search.

There is a celebrated opinion advanced by Stanley Kubrick while he was filming Stephen King's *The Shining:* "Anything that says there's something after death is an optimistic story." A valid idea, but the inevitable pain and loss of being human makes the notion of life after this one not all that appealing. I've seen buttons at science fiction conventions that declare, "*Life sucks, and then—you die.*" They got it wrong; here's how I'd word it: *Life sucks, and then—you live.*"

However ghost stories impinge upon or contradict one's philosophy, they are very effective in doing so. One reason they are, I think, is because they are more frightening—*because they are more plausible*—than ghouls, vampires, Frankenstein monsters, mummies, werewolves, zombies, or even murderers who resemble Peter Lorre (OK, those *do* come close!). I have never met anyone who saw a mummy move, but in more than one roomful of 100 people, I've discovered that 80 percent of the audience either have their own ghostly experience to recount, or at least one that happened to a family member or close friend.

Psychic investigators have more than a few theories concerning what does or does not constitute a haunting. Is it actually someone who died who now "endures" on another plane? Is it merely blind psychic energy, the effluent of emotions soaked up by the bricks and mortar of the place where it happened? Or is it a fragmented sliver of personality not altogether dissipated by death? (The latter theory was proposed by Drew Beltane, fictional spokesperson for author Parke Godwin.)

The afterlife is probably as complicated as the life we're currently stuck in. Which means that all the disparate theories may be to some extent right (and, therefore, to some extent wrong).

So—do *I* believe in ghosts?

I used to argue with myself about this. I wanted to believe, for the reason Stanley Kubrick put forth. But accepting any answer based on my personal need to believe in said answer has always distanced me from my own wishes; as I once wrote, "The need to believe is an almost inescapable trap of the ego."

Yet my opinion on ghosts has definitely changed over time. Three events made this happen:

* The first was back in the mid-60s when I was a newspaperman in Pennsylvania. I was assigned to write an article on the Joseph Priestley home in Northumberland, a town situated at the divergence of the Susquehanna River (it divides there into its northern and western branches). Priestley, a Quaker minister, political theorist, philosopher and discoverer of oxygen, was a friend of Thomas Jefferson. By moving to Pennsylvania, Priestley attained his own variety of religious freedom. His home and laboratory still stand in Northumberland along the banks of the Susquehanna and are open to the public as an historic site and museum.

When I visited the Priestley House, no one told me it was haunted, but the vibes there suggested it might be. When I mentioned this to the newspaper's family editor, he nodded vigorously. One of Priestley's descendants, who at that time still managed the house, told him, "Joseph still putters about in his laboratory at night."

By the way, this is the only *pleasant* haunting I've experienced. At the Priestley house, I had a strong sense of someone friendly looking over my shoulder. (Well, after all, he *was* a member of the Society of Friends!)

* The second paranormal experience in my life was terrifying. It was in the early '70s. I lived in New York and was public relations director of the Light Opera of Manhattan, which chiefly existed to produce Gilbert & Sullivan operettas . The producer thought his production of *The Pirates of Penzance* was haunted, for odd things tended to happen when that show was up and running.

But *Pirates* wasn't running on the hot July night I am about to describe. The set for *H.M.S. Pinafore* was up. It was late; the show was over. I was in the office at the rear of the theatre writing one of my nonfiction books. The theatre was locked up. Suddenly I heard a loud crash from center stage. My first thought was that the work light had come loose and smashed to the floor. But when I went out to see what was wrong, I saw the work light was still on. Nothing seemed out of place.

And then (though I saw nothing), from the stage itself I felt a presence that resented my being there. Wave after wave of cold hatred swept up the aisle, washing over and *into* me. My heart began beating fast. I swiftly packed up my things—something seemed to be telling me that I had a *time limit* to get out!

I was supposed to turn off the air conditioner. But the control button was onstage. No way was I going up there! Outside, on East 74th Street, the July night air made me sweat, yet I still felt dreadfully cold, as if body heat had been drained from within, as perhaps it was.

The next morning the house manager chastised me for leaving the air conditioner running. I explained what happened; he said, "Well, I'll tell the landlord . . . *but* . . . " But a few minutes later, he returned, amazed. For the landlord told him, "Oh, yes, of course . . . *you must get out when that happens!*"

So they were well aware of their resident ghosts.

Here's the sequel: next morning, the house manager approached and said, "Marvin! It happened to *me* last night! I let myself into the theatre around midnight to get my tape recorder and heard a loud bang. When I went into the aisle, I felt the same waves of hate you told me about. But I got this thought, sort of like, 'Well, you didn't know . . . you have a time limit . . . get out!'"

A *time limit*—a detail I hadn't shared with him.

* Going to Edinburgh was the third experience that modified my crumbling skepticism concerning ghosts. After two

months in Scotland, I had to acknowledge the existence of something that for want of a better definition must be labelled *ghost.*

What happened in Scotland? Some of the details may be found in "The Haunted Single Malt," elsewhere in this volume.

The Ghost Quartet began with a suggestion from my dear friend Tanith Lee. I've never actually met Tanith. Our friendship is "across the pond," i.e., the Atlantic Ocean. Tanith is responsible for the major change in the nature of my anthologies. I've edited many collections for The Science Fiction Book Club; they consisted of approximately fifty stories apiece, some public domain, some written by midlist (i.e., underappreciated) genre authors, and some by famous or should-be-famous writers. Tanith's reprinted works distinguished some of my earlier anthologies . . . but then she suggested I edit an anthology called *The Vampire Sextette* and promised that if I did, she would like to be one of the six authors whose stories, at least in her case, would include vampirism, sexuality, and music (?!).

The book did quite well . . . now let's fast-forward several spin-offs: *The Dragon Quintet, The Fair Folk,* both of which featured splendid new fiction by Tanith.

And then came her new suggestion: *The Ghost Quartet.* If I sold this, she said she would be one of the four contributors, for she wished to write a story based on August Strindberg's play, *The Ghost Sonata.* She also hoped that I might write one of the other three tales . . . "My blushes, Watson!"

I confess that I tried to meet Tanith's challenge by writing a sequel to my novel, *Fantastique,* but then one afternoon as I was either approaching or leaving The Parlour, my favorite pub in Manhattan, the phrase popped into my mind: *The Haunted Single Malt.* I was taken by it as a title, but wondered if I could come up with a plot to justify it. Tanith thinks I did . . . hope you do!

Inviting Brian Lumley to be part of the quartet was a no-brainer. The third issue of *H.P. Lovecraft's Magazine of Horror,* which I edit, is devoted to him and includes a biography, a bibliography, and two brilliant new stories by Brian.

What I didn't know, but soon learned, is that Brian is one of the *fastest* writers in the business! He sent me "The Place of Waiting" even before I delivered the contract to his agent!

Tor Books made the final choice for this quartet: they wanted Orson Scott Card, which suited me fine, as I'd bought two superb stories from him in the past. I hadn't realized that, like yours truly, Scott is a Shakespeare teacher and scholar. A new twist on *Hamlet* distinguishes his highly original peek beyond the scenes of Elsinore.

So that's how *The Ghost Quartet* was assembled. Now let's return to my original question—

Do *you* believe in ghosts?

Well, of course you do! Otherwise, why would you be reading this?

MARVIN KAYE
New York City, 2007

The Place of Waiting

BRIAN LUMLEY was born in a British coal-mining town and spent more than twenty years in the British military, serving as a sergeant of the Royal Military Police. Though he began his writing career with humorous science fiction, he discovered horror fiction while he was stationed in Berlin in the early 1960s. He was especially taken by the works of H. P. Lovecraft and himself became a renowned contributor to the Cthulhu Mythos tales begun by "HPL," writing both shorter fiction and novels in that genre. A recent issue of *H. P. Lovecraft's Magazine of Horror* was specially devoted to him, and included two new stories as well as a bibliographical history and interview with Mr. Lumley.

"The Place of Waiting" is a ghost story set mostly in the outdoors, though its situs–Dartmoor and vicinity–is so unsettlingly spooky that Arthur Conan Doyle employed it in what has been called the only Sherlock Holmes story where the locale dominates the detective: *The Hound of the Baskervilles.*

by BRIAN LUMLEY

I sit here by our swimming pool, with one eye on my son in the water and the other on the seagulls lazily drifting, circling on high. Actually they're not just drifting; they're climbing on thermals off the nearby fields, spiralling up to a certain height from which they know they can set off south across the bay on their long evening glide to Brixham to meet the fishing boats coming in to harbour. And never once having beaten a wing across all those miles, just gliding, they'll be there in plenty of time to beg for sprats as the fish are unloaded.

It's instinct with those birds; they've been doing it for so long that now they don't even think about it, they just do it. It's like at ant-flying time, or flying-ant time, if you prefer: those two or three of the hottest days of summer when all of a sudden the ant queens make up their minds to fly and establish new hives or whatever ant nesting sites are called. Yes, for the gulls know all about that, too.

The crying of gulls: plaintive, sometimes painful, often annoying, especially when they're flight-training their young. But this time of year—well you can always tell when it's ant-flying time. Because that's just about the *only* time when the seagulls are silent. And you won't see a one in the sky until the queen ants stream up in their thousands from all the Devon gardens, all at the same time—like spawning corals under the full moon—as if some telepathic message had gone out into an ant aether, telling them, "It's time! It's time!"

Time for the seagulls, too. For suddenly, out of nowhere, the sky is full of them. And their silence is because they're eating. Eating ants, yes. And I amuse myself by imagining that the gulls have learned how to interpret ant telepathy, when in all probability it's only a matter of timing and temperature: Ma Nature as opposed to insect (or avian) ESP.

And yet . . . there are stranger things in heaven and earth—and between the two—and I no longer rule out anything . . .

My son cries out, gasps, gurgles, and shrieks . . . but only with joy, thank God, as I spring from my deck chair! Only with joy—the sheer enjoyment of the shallow end of the pool. Not that it's shallow enough (it's well out of his depth in fact, for he's only two and a half), but he's wearing his water-wings and his splashing and chortling alone should have told me that all was well.

Except I wasn't doing my duty as I should have been; I was paying too much attention to the seagulls. And well—

—Well, call it paranoia if you like. But I watch little Jimmy like a hawk when he is in the water, and I've considered having the pool filled in. But his mother says no, that's just silly, and whatever it was that I *think* happened to me out on the moors that time, I shouldn't let it interfere with living our lives to the fullest. And anyway she loves our pool, and so does little Jimmy, and so would I, except . . .

Only three weeks ago a small child drowned in just such a pool right here in Torquay, less than a mile away. And to me—

especially to me—that was a lot more than a tragic, if simple, accident. It was a beginning, not an end. The beginning of something that can *never* end, not until there are no more swimming pools. And even then it won't be the end for some poor, unfortunate little mite.

But you don't understand, right? And you never will until you know the full story. So first let me get little Jimmy out of the pool, dried, and into the house, into his mother's care, and then I'll tell you all about it . . .

Have you ever wondered about haunted houses? Usually very old houses, perhaps Victorian or older still? Well, probably not, because in this modern technological society of ours we're not much given to considering such unscientific things. And first, of course, you would have to believe in ghosts: the departed, or not quite departed, revenants of folks dead and long since buried. But if so, if you have wondered, then you might also have begun to wonder why it's these *old* houses which are most haunted, and only very rarely new ones.

And, on the same subject, how many so-called old wives' tales have you heard, ghost stories, literally, about misted country crossroads where spectral figures are suddenly caught in a vehicle's headlights, lurching from the hedgerows at midnight, screaming their silent screams with their ragged hands held out before them? Well, let me tell you: such stories are legion! And now I know why.

But me, I didn't believe in ghosts. Not then, anyway . . .

My mother died in hospital here in Torbay some four and a half years ago. And incidentally, I'm glad about that; not about her dying, no, of course not, but that she did it in hospital. These days lots of people die in hospital, which is natural enough.

Anyway, it hit me really badly, more so because I had only recently lost someone else: my wife, when we'd divorced simply
because we no longer belonged together. It had taken us eleven
years to find that out: the fact that right from the start, we hadn't
really belonged together. But while our parting was mutually acceptable and even expedient, still it was painful. And I would
like to think it hurt both of us, for I certainly felt it: a wrenching
inside, like some small but improbably necessary organ was no
longer in there, that it was missing, torn or fallen out. And at the
time I'd thought that was the end of it; what was missing was
gone forever; I wouldn't find anyone else and there would be no
family, no son to look up to me as I had looked up to my father.
A feeling of . . . I don't know, discontinuity?

But I had still had my mother—for a little while, anyway. My
poor dear Ma.

Now, with all this talk of ghosts and death and whatnot, don't
anyone take it that I was some kind of odd, sickly mother's-boy
sort of fellow like Norman Bates, the motel keeper in that Hitch-
cock film. No, for that couldn't be further from the truth. But after my father had died (also in hospital, for they had both been
heavy smokers) it had been my Ma who had sort of clung to
me . . . quite the other way round, you see? Living not too far
away, she had quickly come to rely on me. And no, that didn't
play a part in our divorce. In fact by then it had made no difference at all; our minds were already made up, Patsy's and mine.

Anyway, Patsy got our house—we'd agreed on that, too—for
it had made perfectly good sense that I should go and live with
Ma. Then, when it was her time (oh my Good Lord, as if we had
been anticipating it!) her house would come to me. And so
Patsy's and my needs both would be catered for, at least insofar
as we wouldn't suffer for a roof over our heads . . .

Ma painted, and I like to think I inherited something of her not inconsiderable talent. In fact, that was how I made a living: my work was on show in a studio in Exeter where I was one of a small but mainly respected coterie of local artists, with a somewhat smaller, widespread band of dedicated, affluent collectors. I thank my lucky stars for affluent collectors! And so, with the addition of the interest on monies willed to me by my father, I had always managed to eke out a living of sorts.

Ma painted, yes, and always she looked for the inspiration of drama. The more dramatic her subject, the finer the finished canvas. Seascapes on the Devon coast, landscapes on the rolling South Hams, the frowning ocean-hewn cliffs of Cornwall; and of course those great solemn tors on the moor . . . which is to say Dartmoor: the location for Sherlock Holmes'—or rather Arthur Conan Doyle's—famous (or infamous) *Hound of the Baskervilles*.

Ah, that faded old film! My mother used to say, "It's not like that, you know. Well, it *is* in some places, and misty, too. But not *all* the time! Not like in that film. And I've certainly never seen the like of that fearsome old tramp that Basil Rathbone made of himself! Not on Dartmoor, God forbid! Yes, I know it was only Sherlock Holmes in one of his disguises, but still, I mean . . . Why, if the moors were really like *that* I swear I'd never want to paint there again!"

I remember that quite clearly, the way she said: "It's not *like* that, you know," before correcting herself. For in fact it is like that—and too much like that—in certain places . . .

After she'd gone I found myself revisiting the locations where we had painted together: the coastlines of Cornwall and our own Devon, the rolling, open countryside, and eventually Dartmoor's great tors, which my dictionary somewhat inadequately describes as hills or rocky heights. But it was the Celts who called them tors or torrs, from which we've derived tower, and some of them do indeed "tower" on high. Or it's possible the name comes from the Latin: the Roman *turris*. Whichever, I'll get to the tors in a moment. But first something of Dartmoor itself:

All right, so it's not like that faded old Basil Rathbone *Hound of the Baskervilles* film. Not entirely like that, anyway; not *all* the time. In fact in the summer it's glorious, and that was mainly when I would go there; for I was still attempting to paint there despite that it had become a far more lonely business . . . often utterly lonely, on my own out there on the moors.

But glorious? Beautiful? Yes it certainly was, and for all that I don't go there any more, I'm sure it still is. Beautiful in a fashion all its own. Or perhaps the word I'm searching for is unique. Uniquely dramatic . . . gloriously wild . . . positively neolithic, in its outcrops and standing stones, and prehistoric in the isolation and sometimes desolation of its secret, if not sacred, places.

As for outcrops, standing stones and such: well, now we're back to the tors.

On Eastern Dartmoor my mother and I had painted that amazing jumble of rocks, one of the largest outcrops in the National Park, known as Hound Tor (no connection to Doyle's hound, at least not to my knowledge). But along with a host of other gigantic stacks, such as the awesome Haytor Rock or Vixen Tor, the Hound hadn't been one of Ma's favourites. Many a lesser pile or tranquil river location had been easier to translate to canvas, board, or art paper. It wasn't that we were idle, or lacking in skill or patience—certainly not my mother, whose true-to-life pictures were full of the most intricate detail—but that the necessities of life and the endless hours required to trap such monsters simply didn't match up to our limited time. One single significant feature of any given rock could take Ma a whole day to satisfactorily transcribe in oils! And because I only rarely got things right at the first pass, they sometimes took me even longer. Which is why we were satisfied to paint less awesome or awkward subjects, and closer to home whenever possible.

Ah, but when I say "closer to home" . . . surely Dartmoor is *only* a moor? What's a few miles between friends? Let me correct you:

Dartmoor is three hundred and fifty square miles of mists, mires, woodlands, rushing rivers, tors carved in an age of ice, small villages, lonely farmsteads, and mazy paths; all of which forms the largest tract of unenclosed land in southern England. The landscape may range in just a few miles from barren, naked summits—several over five hundred metres in height—through heather-clad moorland, to marsh and sucking bog. There, in four national nature reserves and numerous protected sites, Dartmoor preserves an astonishing variety of plants and wildlife; all of this a mere twenty miles from Plymouth to the south, and a like distance from Exeter to the east.

Parts of the moor's exposed heath contain the remains of Bronze and Iron Age settlements, now home to the hardy Dartmoor ponies; but the River Dart's lush valley—cut through tens of thousands of years of planetary evolution—displays the softer side of rural Devon, where thatched cottages, tiny villages, and ancient inns seem almost hidden away in the shady lee of knolls or protective hollows.

Dartmoor is, in short, a fascinating fantasy region, where several of the tors have their own ghosts—which is only to be expected in such a place—but I fancy their ectoplasm is only a matter of mist, myth, and legend. Most of them. Some of them, certainly . . .

I won't say where I went that first time—which is to say the first time anything peculiar happened—for reasons which will become amply apparent, but it was close to one of our favourite places. Close to, but not the precise spot, for that would have meant feeling my mother's presence. Her memory, or my memory *of* her, in that place, might have interfered with my concentration. And I'm not talking about ghosts here, just memories, nostalgia if you like: a sentimental longing for times spent with someone who had loved me all of her life, now gone forever. And if that makes me seem weak, then explain to me how even strong men find themselves still crying over a pet dog dead for months and even years, let alone a beloved parent.

And there is no paradox here, in my remembering yet needing to hold the memories to some degree at bay. I missed my Ma, yes, but I knew that I couldn't go on mourning her for the rest of my life.

Anyway, it was in the late summer—in fact August, this time of year—when less than an hour's drive had taken me onto the moor and along a certain second-class road, to a spot where I parked my car in a lay-by near a crossroads track leading off across the heather. Maybe a quarter-mile away there was a small domed hill, which faced across a shaded shallow depression, one of Dartmoor's more accessible tors: an oddly unbalanced outcrop that looked for all the world as if it had been built of enormous, worn and rounded dominoes by some erratic Titan infant and was now trying hard not to topple over. An illusion, naturally, because it was entirely possible that this was just one massive rock, grooved by time and the elements into a semblance of many separate horizontal layers.

And here I think I had better give the stack a name—even one of my own coining—rather than simply call it a tor. Let's call it Tumble Tor, if only because it looked as if at any moment it just might!

My mother and I had tried to paint Tumble Tor on a number

of occasions, never with any great success. So maybe I could do it now and at least finish a job that we had frequently started and just as often left unresolved. That was the idea, my reason for being there, but as stated I would not be painting from any previously occupied vantage point. Indeed, since the moors seem to change from day to day and (obviously) more radically season to season, it would be almost impossible to say precisely where those vantage points had been. My best bet was to simply plunk myself down in a spot which felt totally strange, and that way be sure that I'd never been there before.

As for painting: I wouldn't actually be doing any, not on this, my first unaccompanied visit to Tumble Tor. Instead I intended to prepare a detailed pencil sketch, and in that way get as well acquainted as possible with the monolith before attempting the greater familiarity of oils and colour. In my opinion, one has to respect one's subjects.

It had been a long hot summer and the ground was very hard underfoot, the soil crumbling as I climbed perhaps one third of the way up the knoll to a stone-strewn landing where the ground levelled off in a wide ledge. The sun was still rising in a mid-morning sky, but there in the shade of the summit rising behind me I seated myself on a flat stone and faced Tumble Tor with my board and paper resting comfortably on my knees. And using various grades of graphite I began to transpose my oddly staggered subject onto paper.

Time passed quickly . . .

Mid-afternoon, I broke for a ham sandwich with mayonnaise, washed down with a half thermos of bitter coffee. I had brought my binoculars with me; now and then I trained them on my car to ensure that it remained safe and hadn't attracted the attention of any overly curious strangers. The glasses were also handy as a means of bringing Tumble Tor into greater resolution, making it easy to study its myriad bulges and folds before committing them to paper.

As I looked again at that much-wrinkled rock, a lone puff of cloud eased itself in front of the sun. Tumble Tor fell into shade, however temporarily, and suddenly I saw a figure high in one of the outcrop's precipitous shoulders: the figure of a man leaning against the rock there, peering in a furtive fashion—or so it seemed to me—around the shoulder and across the moor in the general direction of the road. Towards my car? Perhaps.

The puff of cloud persisted, slowly moving, barely drifting, across what was recently an empty, achingly blue sky, and I was aware of the first few wisps of a ground mist in the depression between my knoll and Tumble Tor. I glanced again at the sky and saw that the cloud was the first of a string of cotton-wool puffs reaching out toward Exeter in a ruler-straight line. Following this procession to its source, I was able to pick out the shining silver speck that had fashioned the aerial trail: a jet aircraft, descending toward Exeter airport. Its long vapour trail—even as it broke up into these small "clouds"—seemed determined to track across the face of the sun.

I looked again at Tumble Tor, and adjusted the focus of my binoculars to bring the lone climber—the furtive observer of some near-distant event?—into sharper perspective. He hadn't moved except to turn his head in my direction, and I had little doubt but that he was now looking at me. At a distance of something less than four hundred and fifty yards, I must be visible to him as he was to me. But of course I had the advantage of my glasses . . . or so I thought.

He was thin and angular, a stick of a man, with wild hair blowing in a wind I couldn't feel, some current of air circulating around his precarious position. He wore dark clothing, and as I once again refocused I saw that indeed he carried binoculars around his neck. Though he wasn't using them, still I felt he gazed upon me. I tried to get a clearer view of his face but the image was blurred, trembling with the movement of my hands. However, when finally I did manage to get a good look . . . it was his narrow eyes that left a lasting impression.

They seemed to glow in the shade of the rock with that so-called "red-eye" complication of amateur photography: an illusion—a trick of the light—obviously. But the way they were fixed upon me, those eyes, was somehow disconcerting. It was as if he was spying on me, and not the other way around.

But spying? Feeling like some kind of voyeur, I lowered my glasses and looked away.

Meanwhile, having swung across the sky, the sun had found me; soon my hollow in the side of the hill, rather than providing shade, was going to become a sun-trap. And so I reckoned it was time to call it a day and head for home. Before I could put my art things aside, however, a tall shadow fell across me and a deep voice said, "Aye, and ye've picked the perfect spot for it. What a grand picture the auld tor makes frae here, eh?"

Momentarily startled, I jerked myself around to look up at the speaker. He was a dark silhouette, blocking out the sun.

"Oh dear!" he said, himself startled. "Did I make ye jump just then? Well, I'm sorry if I've disturbed ye, and more so if I've broken yer mood. But man, ye must hae been concentratin' verra hard not tae hear me comin' down on ye."

"Concentrating?" I answered. "Actually I was watching that fellow on the tor there. He must be a bit of a climber. Myself, I don't have much of a head for heights."

"On the tor, ye say?" Shading his eyes and standing tall, he peered at Tumble Tor, now bright once more in full sunlight. "Well then, he must hae moved on, gone round the back. I cannae see anyone on the rock right now, no frae here." Then, stepping down level with me, he crouched to examine my drawing close up. And in my turn—now that the sun was out of my eyes—I could look more closely at him.

A big, powerful man, I judged him to be in his mid-fifties. Dressed in well-worn tweeds, good walking boots, and carrying a knobbed and ferruled stick, he could well have been a gamekeeper—and perhaps he was.

"I . . . I do hope I'm not trespassing here," I finally mumbled. "I mean, I hope this isn't private ground."

"Eh?" he cocked his head a little, then smiled. "What? Do ye take me for a gillie or somethin'? No, no, I'm no that. And as far as I ken this ground's free for us all. But a trespasser? Well, if ye are then so am I, and hae been for some twenty years!" He nodded at the unfinished drawing in my lap. "That's a bonny piece of work. Will ye no finish it? Ye'll excuse that I'm pokin' my nose in, but I sense ye were about tae leave."

"Was and am," I answered, getting to my feet and dusting myself off. "The sun's to blame . . . the shadows on the tor are falling all wrong now. Also, the back of my neck was getting a bit warm." I stooped, gathered up my art things, and looked at the drawing. "But I thank you for your comment because this is just—"

"—A preliminary sketch?"

"Oh?" I said. "And how did you know that?"

Again he smiled, but most engagingly. "Why, there's paint under yer fingernails. And ye've cross-hatched all the areas that are the selfsame colour as seen frae here . . . stone grey, that is. Ye'll be plannin' a painting—am I no right?"

I studied him more closely. He had tousled brown hair—a lot of it for a man of his years—a long weathered face, brown, friendly eyes over a bulbous nose, and a firm mouth over a jut of a chin. His accent revealed his nationality, and he made no attempt to disguise it. The Scots are proud of themselves, and they have every right to be. This one looked as much a part of the moors as . . . well, as Tumble Tor itself.

Impulsively, I stuck my hand out. "You're right, I'm planning a painting. I'm Paul Stanard, from Torquay. I'm pleased to meet you."

"Andrew Quarry," he came back at once, grasping my hand. "Frae a mile or two back there." A jerk of his head indicated the knoll behind us. "My house is just off the Yelverton road, set back a wee in a copse. But—did ye say Stanard?"

"Paul Stanard, yes." I nodded.

"Hmm," he mused. "Well, it's probably a coincidence, but there's a picture in my house painted by one Mary May Stanard: it's a moors scene that I bought in Exeter."

"My mother," I told him, again nodding. "She sold her work through various art shops in Exeter and elsewhere. And so do I. But she . . . she died some nine months ago. Lung cancer."

"Oh? Well, I'm sorry for ye," he answered. "What, a smoker was she? Aye, it's a verra bad business. Myself, I gave my auld pipe up years ago. But her picture—it's a bonny thing."

I smiled, however sadly. "Oh, she knew how to paint! But I doubt if it will ever be worth any more than you paid for it."

"Ah, laddie," he said, shaking his head. "But I didnae buy it for what others might reckon its value. I bought it because I thought it might look right hangin' in my livin'room. And so it does."

Andrew Quarry: he was obviously a gentleman, and so open—so down-to-earth—that I couldn't help but like him. "Are you by chance going my way?" I enquired. "That's my car down on the road there. Maybe we can walk together?"

"Most certainly!" he answered at once. "But only if I can pre-vail upon ye tae make a little detour and drop me off on the

Yelverton road. It'll be a circular route for ye but no too far out of ye're way, I promise ye."

As I hesitated he quickly added, "But if ye're in a hurry, then dinnae fret. The walkin's good for a man. And me: I must hae tramped a thousand miles over these moors, so a half-dozen more willnae harm me."

"Not at all," I answered. "I was just working out a route, that's all. For while I've crossed Dartmoor often enough, still I sometimes find myself confused. Maybe I don't pay enough attention to maps and road signs, and anyway my sense of direction isn't up to much. You might have to show me the way."

"Oh, I can do that easily enough," Quarry answered. "And I know what ye mean. I walk these moors freely in three out of four seasons, but in the fourth I go verra carefully. When the snow is on the ground, oh it's beautiful beyond a doubt—ah, but it hides all the landmarks! A man can get lost in a blink, and then the cold sets in." As we took off down the steep slope he asked: "So then, how did ye come here?"

"I'm sorry?"

"Yer route, frae the car tae here."

"Oh. I followed the path—barely a track, really—but I walked where many feet have gone before: around that clump of standing stones there, and so on to the foot of this hill where I left the track, climbed through the heather, and finally arrived at this grassy ledge."

"I see." He nodded. "Ye avoided the more direct line frae yer vehicle tae the base of the tor, and frae the tor tae the knoll. Verra sensible."

"Oh?"

"Aye. Ye see those rushes?" He pointed. "Between the knoll and yon rock? And those patches of red and green, huggin' close tae the ground? Well those colours hint of what lies underfoot, and it's marshy ground just there. Mud like that'll suck yer shoes off! It would make a more direct route as the crow flies, true enough, but crows dinnae hae tae walk!"

"You can tell all that from the colour of the vegetation? The state of the ground, that is?" He obviously knew his Dartmoor, this man.

He shrugged. "Did I no say how I've lived here for twenty years? A man comes tae understand an awfy lot in twenty years." Then he laughed. "Oh, it's no great trick. Those colours: they indicate mosses, sphagnum mosses. And together with the rushes, that means boggy ground."

We had reached the foot of the knoll and set off following the rough track, making a detour wide of the tor and the allegedly swampy ground; which is to say we reversed and retraced my incoming route. And Quarry continued talking as we walked:

"Those sphagnums . . ." he said, pausing to catch his breath. ". . . That's peat in the makin'. A thousand years from now, it'll be good burnin' stuff, buried under a couple of feet of softish earth. Well, that's if the moor doesnae dry out—as it's done more than its share of this last verra hot summer. Aye, climatic change and all that."

I was impressed. "You seem to be a very knowledgeable man. So then, what are you, Mr. Quarry? Something in moors conservation? Do you work for the National Park Authority? A botanist, perhaps?"

"Botany?" He raised a shaggy eyebrow. "My profession? No laddie, hardly that. I *was* a veterinary surgeon up in Scotland a good long spell ago—but I dinnae hae a profession, not any more. Ye see, my hands got a wee bit wobbly. Botany's my hobby now, that's all. All the green things . . . I enjoy tae identify them, and the moor has an awfy lot tae identify."

"A Scotsman in Devon," I said. "I should have thought the

highlands would be just as varied ... just as suitable to your needs."

"Aye, but my wife was a Devon lass, so we compromised."

"Compromised?"

He grinned. "She said she'd marry me, if I said I'd come live in Devon. I've no regretted it." And then, more quietly, "She's gone now, though, the auld girl. Gone before her time. Her heart gave out. It was most unexpected."

"I'm sorry to hear it," I said. "And so you live alone?"

"For quite some time, aye. Until my Jennie came home frae America. So now's a nice time for me. Jennie was studyin' architectural design; she got her credentials—top of the class, too— and now works in Exeter."

We were passing the group of tall stones, their smoothed and rounded sides all grooved with the same horizontal striations. I nodded to indicate them. "They look like the same hand was at work carving them."

"And so it was," said Quarry. "The hand of time—of the ice age—of the elements. But all the one hand when ye think it through. This could well be the tip of some buried tor, like an iceberg of stone in a sea of earth."

"There's something of the poet in you," I observed.

He smiled. "Oh, I'm an auld lad of nature, for a fact!"

And, once again on impulse, I said, "Andrew, if I may call you that, I'd very much like you to have that drawing—that's if you'd care to accept it. It's unfinished, I know, but—"

"—But I would be delighted!" he cut in. "Now tell me: how much would ye accept for it?"

"No," I said. "I meant as a gift."

"A gift!" He sounded astonished. "But why on earth would a body be givin' all those hours of work away?"

"I really don't know." I shook my head and shrugged. "And

anyway, I haven't worked on it all that long. Maybe I'd like to think of it on your wall, beside my mother's painting."

"And so it shall be—if ye're sure? . . ."

"I am sure."

"Then I thank ye kindly."

Following which we were quiet, until eventually we arrived at the car. There, as I let Quarry into the passenger's seat, I looked back at the sky and Tumble Tor. The puffs of cloud were still there, but dispersing now, drifting, breaking up. And on that strange high rock, nothing to be seen but the naked stone. Yet for some reason that thin, pale face with its burning eyes continued to linger in my own mind's eye . . .

Dartmoor is crisscrossed by many paths, tracks, roads . . . none of which are "major" in the sense of motorways, though many are modern, metalled, and with sound surfaces. Andrew Quarry directed me expertly by the shortest route possible, through various crossroads and turns, until we'd driven through Two Bridges and Princetown. Shortly after that, he bade me stop at a stile in a hazel hedge. Beyond the stile a second hedge, running at right angles to the road, sheltered a narrow footpath that paralleled a brook's meandering contours. And some twenty-five yards along this footpath, in a fenced copse of oaks and birch trees, there stood Quarry's house.

It was a good sized two-storied place, probably Victorian, with oak-timbered walls of typical red Devon stone. In the high gables, under terra-cotta pantiles, wide windows had been thrown open; while on the ground floor, the varnished or polished oak frames of several more windows were barely visible, shining in the dapple of light falling through the trees. In one of these lower windows, I could only just make out the upper third of a raven-haired female figure busy with some task.

"That's Jennie," said Quarry, getting out of the car. "Ye can-nae mistake that shinin' head of hair. She's in the kitchen there, preparin' this or that. I never ate so well since she's been back. Will ye no come in for a cup of tea, Paul, or a mug of coffee, per-haps?"

"Er, no," I said, "I don't think so. I've a few things to do at home, and it's time I was on my way. But thanks for offering. I do appreciate it."

"And I appreciate ye're gift," he said. "Perhaps I'll see ye some other time? Most definitely, if ye're out there paintin' on the knoll. In fact, I shall make it my business to walk that way now and then."

"And I'll be there," I told him. "Not every day, but on occa-sion, at least until my painting is finished. I'll look forward to talking to you again."

"Aye," he nodded, "and so we shall." With which he climbed the stile with my rolled-up drawing under his arm, looked back and waved, then disappeared around a curve in the hedge.

The forecast was rain for the next day or two. I accepted the weatherman's verdict, stayed at home, and worked on other paintings while waiting for the skies to clear; which they did eventually. Then I returned to the knoll and Tumble Tor.

I got there early morning when there was some ground mist still lingering over from the night. Mists are a regular feature of Devon in August through December, and especially on the moors. As I left the car I saw four or five Dartmoor ponies at the gallop, their manes flying, kicking up their heels as they crossed the road. They must have known where they were headed, the nature of the uneven ground; either that or they were heedless of the danger, for with tendrils of mist swirling halfway up their gleaming legs they certainly couldn't see where their hooves were falling! They looked like the fabulous hippocampus, I thought—like sea-horses, braving the breakers—as they ran off across the moor and were soon lost in the poor visibility.

Poor visibility, yes . . . and I had come here to work on my painting! (Actually, to begin the second phase: this time using watercolours.) But the sun was well up, its rays already working on the mist to melt it away; Tumble Tor was mainly visible, for all that its foot was lost in the lapping swell; a further half hour should set things to right, by which time I would be seated on my ledge in the lee of the knoll.

Oh really? But unfortunately there was something I hadn't taken into account: namely that I wasn't nearly as sure-footed or knowledgeable as those Dartmoor ponies! Only leave the road and less than ten paces onto the moor I'd be looking and feeling very foolish, tripping over the roots of gorse and heather as I tried to find and follow my previous route. So then, best to stay put for now and let the sun do its work.

Then, frustrated, leaning against the car and lighting one of my very infrequent cigarettes, I became aware of a male figure approaching up the road. His legs wreathed in mist, he came on, and soon I could see that he was a "gentleman of the road," in short a tramp, but by no means a threat. On the contrary, he seemed rather time- and care-worn: a shabby, elderly, somewhat pitiful member of the brotherhood of wayfarers.

Only a few paces away he stopped to catch his breath, then seated himself upon one of those knee-high white-painted stones that mark the country verges. Oddly, he didn't at first seem to have noticed me; but he'd seen my car and appeared to be frowning at it, or at least eyeing it disdainfully.

As I watched him, wondering if I should speak, he took out a tobacco pouch and a crumpled packet of cigarette papers, only to toss the latter aside when he discovered it empty. Which was

when I stepped forward. And: "By all means, have one of these,"
I said, proferring my pack and shaking it to loosen up a cigarette.

"Eh?" And now he looked at me.

He could have been anything between fifty-five and seventy
years of age, that old man. But his face was so lined and wrin-
kled, so lost in the hair of his head, his beard, and moustache—
all matted together under a tattered, floppy hat—it would have
been far too difficult if not impossible to attempt a more accurate assessment. I looked at his hunched, narrow shoulders, his
spindly arms in a threadbare jacket, his dark gnarled hands with
liver spots and purple veins, and simply had to feel sorry for him.
Rheumy eyes gazed back at me, through curling wisps of shaggy
eyebrow, and lips that had been fretted by harsh weather trembled when he spoke:

"That's kind of you. I rarely begged but they often gave." It
was as if with that last rather odd sentence he was talking to himself.

"Take another," I told him, "for later."

"I didn't mean to take advantage of you," he answered, but
he took a second cigarette anyway. Then, looking at the pair of
small white tubes in his hand, he said, "But I think I'll smoke
them later, if you don't mind. I've had this cough, you see?"

"Not at all," I said. "I don't usually smoke myself, until the
evening. And then I sometimes fancy one with a glass of . . ." But
there I paused. He probably hadn't tasted brandy in a long, long
time—if ever.

He apparently hadn't noticed my almost-gaffe. "It's one of
my few pleasures," he said, placing the cigarettes carefully in his
tobacco pouch, drawing its string tight, fumbling it into a
leather-patched pocket. Then:

"But we haven't been properly introduced!" he said, making
an effort to stand, only to slump back down again. "Or could it

be—I mean, is it possible—that I once knew you?" He seemed unable to focus on me; it was as if he looked right through me. "I'm sorry . . . it's these poor old eyes of mine. They can't see you at all clearly."

"We've never met," I told him. "I'm Paul."

"Or, it could be the car," he said, going off at a tangent again and beginning to ramble. "Your car, that is. But the very car? . . . No, I don't think so. Too new."

"Well, I have parked here before," I said, trying my best to straighten out the conversation. "But just the once. Still, if you passed this way a few days ago you might well have seen it here."

"Hmmm!" he mused, blinking as he peered hard, studying my face. Then his oh-so-pale eyes opened wider. "Ah! *Now* I understand! You must have been trying very hard to see someone, and you got me instead. I'm Joe. Old Joe, they called me."

And finally I understood, too. The deprivations of a life on the road—of years of wandering, foraging, sleeping rough through filthy weather and hungry nights—had got to him. His body wasn't the only victim of his "lifestyle." His mind, too, had suffered. Or perhaps it was the other way around, and that was the cause, not the effect. Perhaps he had always been "not altogether there," as I've heard it said of such unfortunates.

And because I really didn't have very much to say—also because I no longer knew quite *what* to say, exactly—I simply shrugged and informed him, "I . . . I'm just waiting, that's all. And when this mist has cleared a bit, I'll be moving on."

"I'm waiting, too," he answered. "More or less obliged to wait. Here, I mean."

At which I simply had to ask: "Waiting? I didn't know this was a bus route? And if it is they're very infrequent. Or maybe you're waiting for a friend, some fellow, er, traveller? Or are you looking for a lift—in a car, I mean?" (Lord, I hoped not! Not that he smelled bad or anything, not that I'd noticed, anyway, but I should really hate to have to refuse him if he asked me.) And how stupid of me: that I should have mentioned a lift in the first place! For after all I was there to paint, not to go on mercy missions for demented old derelicts!

"Buses?" he said, cocking his head a little and frowning. "No, I can't say I've seen too many of those, not here. But a car, yes. That's a real possibility. Better yet, a motorcycle! Oh, it's a horrid, horrid thought—but it's my best bet by a long shot . . ."

And my best bet, I thought, would be to end a very pointless conversation and leave him sitting there on his own! Yes, and even as I thought it I saw that I could do just that, for the mist was lifting, or rather melting away as the sun sailed higher yet. And so:

"You'll excuse me," I said, with a glance across the moor at Tumble Tor, "but I'm afraid it's time . . ." And there I paused, snapping my head round to stare again at the ancient stack; at its grainy, grooved stone surfaces, all damply agleam, and its base still wreathed in a last few tendrils of mist. ". . . Afraid it's time to go."

And the reason I had frozen like that, albeit momentarily? Because he was there again: the climber on the tor. And despite that from this angle I could see only his head and shoulders, I knew at once that it was the same person I'd seen the last time I was here: the observer with the binoculars—perched so precariously on that same windy ledge—who once again seemed to be observing me! The sunlight reflected blindingly from the lenses of his glasses . . .

"I paid my way with readings," said the old tramp from his roadside stone, as if from a thousand miles away. "Give me your hand and I'll do one for you."

Distracted, I looked at him. "What? You'll do one?"

"A reading." He nodded. "I'll read your palm."

"I really don't—" I began, glancing again at Tumble Tor.

"—Oh, go on!" He cut me off. "Or you'll leave me feeling I'm in your debt."

But the man on the rock had disappeared, slipped away out of sight, so I turned again to Old Joe. He held out a trembling hand, and however reluctantly I gave him mine. Then:

"There," he said. "And look here, you have clearly defined lines! Why, it's just like reading a book!" He traced the lines in my palm with a slightly grimy forefinger, but so gently that I barely felt his touch. And in a moment:

"Ah!" He gasped. "An only son—that's you, I mean—and you were so very close to her. Now you're alone but she's still on your mind; every now and then you forget she's gone, and you look up expecting to see her. Yes, and those are the times when you're most likely to see what you ought *not* to be seeing!" Now he looked up at me, his old eyes the faded blue of the sky over a grey sea, and said, "She's moved on, your mother, Paul. She's safe and you can stop searching now."

Spiders with icy feet ran up and down my spine! I snatched my hand away, backed off, said, "W-w-what?"

"I'm sorry, so sorry!" he said, struggling to his feet. "I see too much, but so do you!" And as he went off, hobbling away in the same direction he'd come from, he paused to look back at me and called out, "You shouldn't look so hard, Paul." And once again after a short, sharp glance at Tumble Tor: "You shouldn't look so hard!"

Moments later a swell of mist like some slow-motion ocean rose up, deepening around him and obscuring him. His silhouette was quickly swallowed up in grey opacity, and having lost sight of him I once again turned my gaze on Tumble Tor. The moors can be very weird: mist in the one direction, clarity in the other! The huge outcrop continued to steam a little in the sun, but my route over the uneven ground was clearly visible. And of course the knoll was waiting.

Recovering from the shock Old Joe had supplied, determined to regain my composure, I collected my art things from my car's boot and set off on my semicircular route around Tumble Tor. Up there on the knoll twenty-five minutes later, I used my binoculars to scan the winding road to the north of the tor. Old Joe couldn't have got too far, now could he? But there was no mist, and there was no sign of Joe. Well then, he must have left the road and gone off across the moor along some track or other. Or perhaps someone had given him a lift after all. But neither had I seen any vehicles.

There was no sign of anyone on Tumble Tor either, but that didn't stop me from looking. And despite what Old Joe had said, I found myself looking pretty hard at that . . .

I couldn't concentrate on my work. It was the morning's strangeness, of course. It was Old Joe's rambling on the one hand, and his incredibly accurate reading on the other. I had always been aware that there were such people, certainly; I'd watched their performances on television, read of their extraordinary talents in various books and magazines, knew that they allegedly assisted the police in very serious investigations, and that séances were a regular feature in the lives of plenty of otherwise very sensible people. Personally, however, I'd always been sceptical of so-called psychic or occult phenomena, only rarely allowing that it was anything other than fake stage magic and "supernatural hocus-pocus."

Now? Well, what was I to think now? Or had I, like so many others (in my opinion) simply allowed myself to be sucked in by self-delusion, my own gullibility?

Perhaps the old tramp hadn't been so crazy after all. What if he'd merely used a few clever, well-chosen words and phrases and left me to fill in the blanks: a very subtle sort of hypnotism? And what if I had only imagined that he'd said the things he said? For of course my mother, comparatively recently passed on, was never far from my mind . . . anyone who ever lost someone will surely understand that the word "she"—just that single, simple word—would at once conjure her image, more especially now that there was no other "she" to squeeze her image aside.

Psychology? Was that Old Joe's special ability? Well, what or whichever, he'd certainly found my emotional triggers easily enough! Maybe I had worn a certain distinctive, telltale look; perhaps there had been some sort of forlorn air about me, as if I were lost, or as if I were looking for someone. But alone, out on the moors? Who could I possibly have been seeking out there? Someone who couldn't possibly be found, obviously. And Old Joe had simply extrapolated.

Stage magic, definitely . . . or maybe? I still couldn't make up my mind! And so couldn't concentrate. I managed to put a few soft pencilled guidelines onto the paper and a preliminary wash of background colour. But nothing looked right and my frustration was mounting. I couldn't seem to get Old Joe's words out of my head. And what of his warning, if that's what it was, that I shouldn't look so hard? I was looking "too hard," he'd said and I was "seeing too much"—seeing what I ought not to be seeing. Now what on earth had he been trying to convey, if anything, by that? One thing for sure: I'd had a very odd morning!

Too odd—and far too off-putting—so that when a mass of dark cloud began to spread across the horizon, driven my way by a rising wind out of the southwest, I decided to let it go and return to Torquay. Back at the car I saw something at the roadside, lying on the ground at the foot of the verge marker where Old Joe had seated himself. Two somethings in fact: cigarettes, my brand, apparently discarded, just lying there. But hadn't he said something about not wanting to be in my debt?

A peculiar old coot, to say the very least. And so, trying to put it all to the back of my mind, I drove home . . .

Then for the next three days I painted in my attic studio, listening to the sporadic patter of rain on my skylight while I worked on unfinished projects. And gradually I came to the conclusion that my chance encounter with Old Joe—more properly with his rambling, indirect choice of words and vague warnings—had been nothing more than a feeble, dazed old man's mumbo-jumbo, to which on a whim of coincidental, empathic emotions I had mistakenly attached far too much meaning.

And how, you might ask, is that possible? In the same way that if someone suddenly shouts, "Look out!" you jump . . . despite that nothing is coming! That's how. But now I ask myself: what if you *don't* jump? And what if something *is* coming?

Early in September, at the beginning of what promised to be an extended Indian summer, I ventured out onto Dartmoor yet again, this time fully determined to get to grips with Tumble Tor. It was a matter of pride by then: I wasn't about to let myself be defeated by a knob of rock, no matter how big it was!

That was my motive for returning to the moor, or so I tried to tell myself; but in all honesty, it was not the only reason. During the last ten days my sleep had been plagued by recurrent dreams: of a stick-thin, red-eyed man, gradually yet menacingly approaching me through a bank of dense swirling mist. Sometimes Tumble Tor's vague silhouette formed a backdrop to this relentless stalking; at other times there was only the crimson glare of

Hallowe'en eyes, full of rabid animosity and a burning evil—
such evil as to bring me starting awake in a cold sweat.

Determined to exorcise these nightmares, and since it was
quite obvious that Tumble Tor was their source—or that they
were the outcrop's evil *geniuses loci*, its spirits of place?—I supposed the best place to root them out must be on Dartmoor itself. So there I was once again, parking my car in the same spot,
the place where a dirt track crossed the road, with the open
moor and misshapen outcrop close at hand on my left, and in the
near distance the steep-sided hill or knoll.

And despite that my imagination conjured up an otherwise
intangible aura of—but of what? Of something lurking, waiting
there?—still I insisted on carrying out my plans; come what may
I was going to commence working! Whatever tricks the moor
had up its sleeve, I would simply ignore or defy them.

To be absolutely sure that I would at least get something done,
I had taken along my camera. If I experienced difficulty getting
started, then I would take some pictures of Tumble Tor from
which—in the comfort of my own home, at my leisure—I might
work up some sketches, thus reacquainting myself with my subject.

As it turned out, it was as well that I'd planned it that way; for
weather forecasts to the contrary, there was little or no sign of an
Indian summer on Dartmoor! Not yet, anyway. There was dew
on the yellow gorse and coarse grasses, and a carpet of ground
mist that the morning sun hadn't quite managed to shift; indeed
the entire scene seemed drab and uninspiring, and Tumble Tor
looked as gaunt as a lopsided skull, its dome shiny where wan
sunlight reflected from its damp surface.

Staring at it, I found myself wondering why the hell I had
wanted to paint it in the first place! But . . .

My usual route across the moorland's low-lying depression to
the knoll was well known to me by now; and since the ankle-

lapping mist wasn't so dense as to interfere with my vision at close range, I took up my camera and art things, made my way to the knoll, and climbed it to my previous vantage point. Fortunately, aware now of the moor's capriciousness, I had brought an old plastic raincoat with me to spread on the ground. And there I arranged the tools of my business as usual.

But when it came to actually starting to work . . . suddenly there was this weariness in me—not only a physical thing but also a numbing mental malaise—that had the effect of damping my spirits to such a degree that I could only sit there wondering what on earth was wrong with me. An uneasy expectancy? Some sort of foreboding or precognition? Well, perhaps . . . but rather than becoming aware, alert, on guard, I felt entirely fatigued, barely able to keep my eyes open.

A miasma then: some unwholesome exhalation spawned in the mist? Unlikely, but not impossible. And for a fact the mist was thicker now in the depression between the knoll and Tumble Tor, and around the base of the outcrop itself; while in the sky the sun had paled to a sickly yellow blob behind the grey overcast.

But once again—as twice before—as I looked at Tumble Tor I saw something other than wet stone and mist. Dull my mind and eyes might be, but I wasn't completely insensible or blind. And there he was where I had first seen him: the climber on the tor, the red-eyed observer on the rock.

And I remember thinking: "Well, so much for exorcism!" For this was surely the weird visitant of my dreams. Not that I saw him as a form of evil incarnate in himself, not then (for after all, what was he in fact but a man on an enormous boulder?) but that his activities—and his odd looks, of course—had made such an impression on me as to cause my nightmares in the first place.

These were the thoughts that crept through my numb mind

as I strove to fight free of both my mental and physical lethargy. But the swirling of the mist seemed hypnotic, while the unknown force working on my body—even on my head, which was gradually nodding lower and lower—weighed me down like so much lead. Or rather, to more accurately describe my perceptions, I felt that I was being *sucked* down as in a quagmire.

I tried one last time to focus my attention on the figure on Tumble Tor. Indeed, and before succumbing to my inexplicable faint, I even managed to take up my oh-so-heavy camera and snap a few shaky pictures. And between each period of whirring—as the film wound slowly forward and I tried to refocus—I could see that the man was now climbing down from the rock . . . but so very *quickly!* Impossibly quickly! Or perhaps it was simply that I was moving so slowly.

And now . . . now he had clambered down into the mist, and I somehow knew that my nightmare was about to become reality. For as in my dreams he was coming—he was now on his way to me—and the mental quagmire continued to suck at me.

Which was when everything went dark . . .

"What's this?" (At first, a voice from far, far away which some kind of mental red shift rapidly enhanced, making it louder and bringing it closer.) "Asleep on the job, are ye? Twitchin' like ye're havin' a fit!" And then, much more seriously: "Man, but I hope ye're *not* havin' a fit!"

"Eh?" I gave a start. "W-what?" And lifting my head, jerking awake, I straightened up so quickly that I came very close to toppling over sideways.

And there I was, still seated on my plastic mac, blinking up into the half-smiling, half-frowning, wholly uncertain features of Andrew Quarry. "G-*God*, I was dreaming!" I told him. "A nightmare. Just lately I . . . I've been plagued by them!"

"Then I'm glad I came along," he answered. "It was my hope tae find ye here, but when I saw ye sittin' there—jerkin' and moanin' and what-all—I thought it was best I speak out."

"And just as well that you did." I got my breath, finding it hard to breathe properly, and even harder to get to my feet. Quarry took my elbow, assisted me as, by way of explanation, I continued: "I . . . haven't been sleeping too well."

"No sleepin'?" He looked me straight in the eye. "Aye, I can see that. Man, ye're lookin' exhausted, so ye are! And tae fall asleep here—this early in the mornin'—now, that's no normal."

I could only agree with him, as for the first time I actually felt exhausted. "Maybe it was the mist." I searched for a better explanation. "Something sickening in the mist? Some kind of—I don't know—some kind of miasma maybe?"

He looked surprised, glanced across the moorland this way and that, in all directions. "The mist, ye say?"

I looked, too, across the low-lying ground to where Tumble Tor stood tall for all that it seemed to slump; tall, and oddly foreboding now, *and dry as a bone in the warm morning sunshine!*

At which I could only shake my head and insist: "But when I sat down there was a mist, and a thick mist at that! Wait . . ." And I looked at my watch—which was proof of nothing whatever, for I couldn't judge the time.

"Well?" Quarry studied my face, curiously I thought.

"So maybe I was asleep longer than I thought," I told him, lamely. "I must have been, for the mist to clear up like that."

His frown lifted. "Maybe not." He shrugged. "The moor's as changeable as a young girl's mind. I've known the mist tae come up in minutes and melt away just as fast. Anyway, ye're lookin' a wee bit steadier now. So will ye carry on, or what?"

"Carry on?"

"With ye're paintin'—or drawin'—or whatever."

"No, not now," I answered, shaking my head. "I've had more than enough of this place for now."

As he helped me to gather up my things, he said, "Then may I make a wee suggestion?"

"A suggestion?" We started down the hillside.

"Aye. Paul, ye look like ye could use some exercise. Ye're way too pale, too jumpy, and too high strung. Now then, there's this beautiful wee walk—no so wee, actually—frae my place along the beck and back. Now I'm no just lookin' for a lift, ye ken, but we could drive there in yer car, walk and talk, take in some verra nice autumn countryside while exercisin' our legs, and maybe finish off with a mug of coffee at my place before ye go on back tae Torquay. What do ye say?"

I almost turned him down, but . . . the fact was I was going short on company. Since the breakdown of my marriage (it seemed an awfully long time ago, but in fact had been less than eighteen months) all my friends had drifted away. Then again, since they had been mainly couples, maybe I should have expected that I would soon be cast out, to become a loner and outsider.

So now I nodded. "We can do that if you like. But—"

"Aye, but?"

"Is your daughter home? Er, Jennie?" Which was a blunt and stupid question whichever way you look at it; but having recognized the apprehension in my voice, he took it as it was meant.

"Oh, so ye're no particularly interested in the company of the fairer sex, is that it?" He glanced sideways at me, but for my part I remained silent. "Oh well then, I'll assume there's a verra good reason," he went on. "And anyway, I wouldnae want to seem to be intrudin'."

"Don't get any wrong ideas about me, Andrew," I said then. "But my wife and I divorced quite recently, since when—"

"Say no more." He nodded. "Ye're no ready tae start thinkin' that way again, I can understand that. But in any case, my Jennie's gone off tae Exeter: a day out with a few friends. So ye'll no be bumpin' intae her accidentally-like. And anyway, what do ye take me for: some sort of auld matchmaker? Well, let me assure ye, I'm no. As for my Jennie, ye can take it frae me: she's no the kind of lassie ye'd find amenable to that sort of interference in the first place. So now ye ken."

"I meant no offence," I told him.

"No, of course ye didn't." He chuckled. "Aye, and if ye'd seen my Jennie, ye'd ken she doesnae need a matchmaker! Pretty as a picture, that daughter of mine. Man, ye couldnae paint a prettier one, I guarantee it!"

Along the usual route back to the car, I couldn't resist the occasional troubled glance in the direction of Tumble Tor. Andrew Quarry must have noticed, for he nodded and said, "That auld tor: it's given ye nothin' but a load of grief, is it no so?"

"Grief?" I cast him a sharp look.

"With yer art and what all, ye're paintin'. It's proved a poor subject."

A sentiment I agreed with more than Quarry could possibly know. "Yes," I answered him in his own words, "a whole load of grief." And then, perhaps a little angrily, revealing my frustration: "But I'm not done with that rock just yet. No, not by a long shot!"

Leaving the car on the road outside Quarry's place, we walked and talked. Or rather *he* talked, simultaneously and unselfconsciously displaying his expertise with regard to the incredible variety of Dartmoor's botanical species. And despite my current personal concerns—about my well-being, both physical and mental, following the latest unpleasant episode at Tumble Tor—

I soon found myself genuinely fascinated by his monologue. But if Quarry had shown something of his specialized knowledge on our first meeting, now he excelled himself. So much so that later that day I could only remember a fraction of it.

Along the bank of the stream, he pointed out stag's horn and hair mosses; and when we passed a stand of birch trees just fifty yards beyond his house, he identified several lichens and a clump of birch-bracket fungi. Within a mile and a half, never straying from the path beside the stream, we passed oak, holly, hazel, and sycamore, their leaves displaying the colours of the season and those colours alone enabling Quarry's instant recognition. On one occasion, where the way was fenced, he climbed a stile, crossed a field into a copse of oaks and dense conifers, and in less than five minutes filled a large white handkerchief with spongy, golden mushrooms which he called Goat's Lip. When I asked him about that, he said:

"Aye, that's what the locals call 'em. But listen tae me: 'locals,' indeed! Man, I'm a local myself after all this time! Anyway, these beauties are commonly called downy boletus—or if ye're really, *really* interested *Xerocomus subtomentosus.* So I think ye'll agree, Paul, *Goat's* Lip falls a whole lot easier frae a *man's* lip, does it no?" At which I had to smile.

"And you'll eat them?" I may have seemed doubtful.

"Oh, be sure I will!" he answered. "My Jennie'll cook 'em up intae a fine soup, or maybe use 'em as stuffin' in a roasted chicken . . ."

And so it went, all along the way.

But in no time at all, or so it seemed, we'd covered more than two miles of country pathway and it was time to turn back. "Now see," Quarry commented, as we reversed our route, "there's a wee bit more colour in yer cheeks; it's the fresh air ye've been breathin' deep intae yer lungs, and the blood yer legs hae been pumpin' up through yer body. The walkin' is good for a man. Aye, and likewise the talkin' and the companionship. I'd be verra surprised if ye dinnae sleep well the nicht."

So that was it. Not so much the companionship and talking, but the fact that he'd been concerned for me. So of course when he invited me in I entered the old house with him, and shortly we were seated under a low, oak-beamed ceiling in a farmhouse-style kitchen, drinking freshly ground coffee.

"The coffee's good," I told him.

"Aye," he answered. "None of yer instant rubbish for my Jennie. If it's no frae the best beans it's rubbish . . . that's Jennie's opinion, and I go along with it. It's one of the good things she brought back frae America."

We finished our coffee.

"And now a wee dram," he said, as he guided me through the house to his spacious, comfortable livingroom. "But just a wee one, for I ken ye'll need to be drivin' home."

Seated, and with a shot glass of good whisky in my hand, I looked across the room to a wall of pictures, paintings, framed photographs, diplomas, and such. And the first thing to catch my eye was a painting I at once recognized. A seascape, it was one of my mother's canvases, and one of her best at that; my sketch of Tumble Tor—behind non-reflective glass in a frame that was far too good for it—occupied a space alongside.

I stood up, crossed to the wall to take a closer look, and said, "You were as good as your word. I'm glad my effort wasn't wasted."

"And yer Ma's picture, too," he nodded, coming to stand beside me. "The pencils and the paint: I think they make a fine contrast."

I found myself frowning—or more properly scowling—at my drawing, and said, "Andrew, just you wait! I'm not done with painting on the moor just yet. I promise you this: I'll soon be giving you a far better picture of that damned rock . . . even if it kills me!"

He seemed startled, taken aback. "Aye, so ye've said," he answered, "—that ye're set on it, I mean. And I sense a struggle brewin' between the pair of ye—yersel' and the auld tor. But I would much prefer ye as a livin' breathin' friend than a dead benefactor!"

At which I breathed deeply, relaxed a little, laughed and said, "Just a figure of speech, of course. But I really do have to get to grips with that boulder. In fact I don't believe I'll be able to work on anything else until I'm done with it. But as for right now—" I half-turned from the wall, "I *am* quite done with it. Time we changed the subject, I think, and talked about other things."

My words acted like an invocation, for before turning more fully from the wall my gaze lighted on something else: a framed colour photograph hung in a prominent position, where the stone wall had been buttressed to enclose the grate and blackened flu of an open fireplace. An immaculate studio photograph, it portrayed a young woman's face in profile.

"Your wife?" I approached the picture.

"My Jennie," Quarry replied. "I keep my wife's photographs in my study, where I can speak tae her any time I like. And she sometimes answers me, or so I like tae think. As for my Jennie: well now ye've seen her, ye've seen her Ma. Like peas in a pod. Aye, but it's fairly obvious she doesnae take after me!"

I knew what he meant. Jennie was an extraordinarily beautiful woman. Her lush hair was black as a raven's wing, so black it was almost blue, and her eyes were as big and as blue as the sky. She had a full mouth, high cheeks and forehead, a straight nose and small, delicate ears. Despite that Jennie's photograph was in profile, still she seemed to look at the camera from the corner of her eye, and wore a half-smile for the man taking her picture.

"And she's in Exeter, with her boyfriend?"

Quarry shook his head. "No boyfriend, just friends. She's no been home long enough tae develop any romantic interests. Ye should let me introduce ye some time. She was verra much taken with yer drawing. Ye hae that in common at least—designs, I mean. For it's all art when ye break it down."

After that, in a little while, I took my leave of him . . .

Driving home, for some reason known only to my troubled subconscious mind, I took the long route across the moor and drove by Tumble Tor; or I would have driven by, except Old Joe was there where I'd last seen him. In fact, I *didn't* see him until almost the last moment, when he suddenly appeared through the break in the hedge, stepping out from the roadside track.

He looked at me—or more properly at my car—as it sped toward him, and for a moment he teetered there on the verge and appeared of two minds about crossing the road directly in front of me! If he'd done so I would have had a very hard time avoiding him. It would have meant applying my brakes full on, swinging my steering wheel hard over, and in all likelihood skidding sideways across the narrow road. And there on the opposite side was this outcrop, a boulder jutting six feet out of the ground, which would surely have brought me to a violent halt; but such a halt as might easily have killed me!

As it was I had seen the old tramp in sufficient time—but only *just* in time—to apply my brakes safely and come to a halt alongside him.

Out of my window I said, "Old Joe, what on earth were you thinking about just then? I mean, I could so easily—"

"Yes," he cut me off, "and so could I. Oh so very easily!" And he stood there trembling, quivering, with his eyes sunk so deep that I could scarcely see them.

Then I noticed the mist. It was just as Andrew Quarry had stated—a freak of synchronicity, sprung into being almost in a single moment—as if the earth had suddenly breathed it out; this ground mist, swirling and eddying about Old Joe's feet and all across the low-lying ground beyond the narrow grass verge.

Distracted, alienated, and somehow feeling the dampness of that mist deep in my bones, I turned again to the old man, who was still babbling on. "But I couldn't do it," he said, "and I shall *never* do it! I'll simply wait—forever, if needs be!"

As he began to back unsteadily away from the car, I said, "Old Joe, are you ill? What's the trouble? Can I help you? Can I offer you a lift, take you somewhere?"

"A lift?" he answered. "No, no. This is my waiting place. It's where I must wait. And I'm sorry—so very sorry—that I almost forgot myself."

"What?" I said, frowning and perplexed. "What do you mean? How did you forget yourself? What are you talking about?"

"It's here," he replied. "Here's where I must wait for it to happen . . . again! But I can't—I mustn't, and won't ever—try to *make* it happen! No, for I'm not like that one . . ."

Old Joe gave a nod and his gaze shifted; he looked beyond me, beyond the car, out across the moors at Tumble Tor. And of course, as cold as I suddenly felt, I turned my head to follow his lead. All I saw was naked stone, and without quite knowing why I breathed a sigh of relief.

Then, turning back to the old tramp, I said, "But there's no one there, Joe!" And again, in a whisper: "Old Joe? . . ." For he wasn't there either—just a curl of mist in the hedgerow, where he might have passed through.

And a few minutes later, by the time I had driven no more than a mile farther along the road toward Torquay, already the mist had given way to a wan, inadequate sun that was doing its best to shine . . .

I had been right to worry about my state of mind. Or at least, that was how I felt at the time: that my depression under this atmosphere of impending doom which I felt hovering over me was some kind of mild mental disorder. (For after all, that's what depression is, isn't it?) Even now, as I look back on it in the light of new understanding, perhaps it really was some sort of psychosis—but nothing that I'd brought on myself. I realize that now because at the time I *acknowledged* the problem, while psychiatry insists that the psychotic isn't aware of his condition.

In any case, I *had* been right to worry about it. For despite Andrew Quarry's insistence that I'd sleep well that night, my dreams were as bad and even worse than before. The mist, the semi-opaque silhouette of monolithic Tumble Tor, and those eyes—those crimson-burning eyes—drawing closer, closer, and ever closer. Half a dozen times I woke up in a cold sweat . . . little wonder I was feeling so drained . . .

In the morning I drove into town to see my doctor. He gave me a check-up and heard me out; not the entire story, only what I felt obliged to tell him about my "insomnia." He prescribed a course of sleeping pills and I set off home . . . such was my intention.

But almost before I knew it I was out on the country roads again. Taken in thrall by some morbid fascination or obsession, I was once more heading for Tumble Tor!

My tank was almost empty . . . I stopped at a garage, filled her up . . . the forecourt attendant was concerned, asked me if I was feeling okay . . . which really should have told me that something was very wrong, but it didn't stop me.

Oh, I agreed with him that I didn't feel well: I was dizzy, confused, distracted, but none of these symptoms served to stop me. And through all of this I could feel the lure, the inexplicable attraction of the moors, to which I must succumb!

And I did succumb, driving all the way to Tumble Tor where I parked in my usual spot and levered myself out of my car. Old Joe was there, waving his arms and silently gibbering . . . warning me about something which I couldn't take in . . . my mind was clogged with cotton-wool mist . . . everything seemed to be happening in slow-motion . . . those eyes, those blazing *evil* eyes!

I felt a *whoosh* of wind, heard a vehicle's tyres screaming on the road's rough surface, saw through the billowing mist the blurred motion of something passing close—much too close—in front of me.

This combination of sensations got through to me—almost. I was aware of a red-faced, angry man in a denim jacket leaning out of his truck's window, yelling, "You *bloody* idiot! What the bloody hell . . . are you drunk? Staggering about in the road like that!" Then his tyres screeched again, spinning and smoking, as he rammed his vehicle into gear and pulled away.

But the mist was still swirling, my head still reeling—*and Old Joe was having a silent, gesticulating argument with a stick-thin, red-eyed man!*

Then the silence was broken as the old man looked my way, sobbing. "That wouldn't have been my fault! Not this time, and not ever. It would have been yours . . . or *his!* But it wouldn't have done him any good, and God knows I didn't want it!" As he spoke the word "his," he'd flung out an arm to point at the thin man who was now floating toward me, his eyes like warning signal lamps as his shape took on form and emerged more surely from the mist.

And that was when I "woke up" to the danger. For yes, it was like coming out of a nightmare—indeed it could only have been a nightmare—but I came out of it so slowly that even as the mist cleared and the old man and the red-eyed phantom thinned to figures as insubstantial as the mist itself, still something of it lingered over: Old Joe's voice.

As I staggered there on the road, blinking and shaking my head to clear it, trying to focus on reality and forcing myself to stop shuddering, so that old man's voice—as thin as a cry from the dark side of the moon—got through to me:

"Get out of here!" he cried. "Go, hurry! He knows you now, and he won't wait. He'll follow you—in your head and in your dreams—until it's done!"

"Until what's done?" I managed to croak my question. But I was talking to nobody, to thin air.

Following which I almost fell into my car, reversed dangerously onto the crossover track and clipped the hedge, and drove away in a sweat as cold and damp as that nonexistent mist. And all the way home I could feel those eyes burning on my neck; so much so that on more than one occasion I caught myself glancing in my rearview mirror, making sure there was no one in the back seat.

But for all that I saw no one there, still I wasn't absolutely sure . . .

Taking sleeping pills that night wasn't a good idea. But I felt I had to. If I suffered another disturbed night, goodness knows what I would feel like—what my overburdened mind would conjure into being—the next day. But of course, the trouble with sleeping pills is they not only send you to sleep, they'll *keep* you that way! And when once again I was visited by evil dreams, struggle against them as I might and as I did, still I couldn't wake up!

It started with Old Joe again, the old tramp, a gentleman of the road. Speaking oh-so-earnestly, he made a sort of sense at first, which as quickly lapsed into the usual nonsense.

"Now listen to me," he said, just a voice in the darkness of my dream, the silence of the night. "I risked everything to leave my waiting place and come here with you. And I may never return, find my way back again, *except* with you. So it's a big chance I'm taking, but I had to. It's my redemption for what I have thought to do—and what I have almost done—more times than I care to admit. And so, because of what *he* is and what I know *he* will do, I've come to warn you this one last time. Now you must guard yourself against him, for you can expect him at any moment."

"Him?" I said, speaking to the unseen owner of the voice, which I knew as well as I knew my own. "The man on the tor?"

While I waited for an answer, a mist crept into being and the darkness turned grey. In the mist I saw Old Joe's outline: a crumpled shape under a floppy hat. "It's his waiting place," he at last replied. "Either there or close by. But he's grown tired of waiting and now takes it upon himself. He risks hell, but since he's already halfway there, it's a risk he'll take. If he wins it's the future—whatever that may be—and if he fails then it's the flames. He knows that, and of course he'll try to win . . . which would mean that you lose!"

"I don't understand," I answered, dimly aware that it was only a dream and I was lying in my bed as still and heavy as a statue. "What does he want with me? How can he harm me?"

And then the rambling:

"But you've *seen* him!" Old Joe barked. "You looked beyond, looked where you shouldn't and too hard. You saw me, so I knew you must see him, too. Indeed he *wanted* you to see him! Oh, you weren't looking for him but someone else—a loved one, who has long moved on—but you did it in *his place of waiting!* And as surely as your searching brought me up, it brought him up, too. Ah, but where I only wait, *he* is active! He'll wait no longer!"

Suddenly I knew that this was the very crux of everything that was happening to me, and so I asked: "But what is it that you're waiting for? And where is this . . . this waiting place?"

"But you've *seen* him!" the old tramp cried again. "How is it you see so much yet understand so little? I may not explain. It's a thing beyond your time and place. But just as there were times before, so there are times after. Men wait to be born and then— without ever seeming to realize it—they wait again, to die. But it's when and it's how! And after that, what then? The waiting, that's what."

"Gibberish!" I answered, shaking my head; and I managed an uncertain laugh, if only at myself.

"No, don't!" The other's alarm was clear in his voice. "If you deny me I can't stay. If you refute me, then I must go. Now listen: you know me—you've seen me—so continue to see me, but *only* me."

"You're a dream, a nightmare," I told him. "You're nothing but a phantom, come to ruin my sleep."

"No, no, *no!*" But his voice was fading, along with Old Joe himself.

But if only he hadn't sounded so desperate, so fearful, as he dwindled away: fearful for me! And if only the echoes of his cries hadn't lasted so long . . .

Old Joe was gone, but the mist stayed. And taking shape in its writhing tendrils I saw a very different presence—one that I knew as surely as I had known the old tramp. It was the watcher on the tor.

Thin as a rake, eyes burning like coals in a fire, he came closer and said, "My friend, you really shouldn't concern yourself with that old fool." His voice was the gurgle and slurp of gas bubbles bursting on a swamp, and a morbid smell—the smell of death—attended him. The way his black jacket hung loose on sloping shoulders, it could well have been that there were only bones beneath the cloth. And yet there was this strength in him, this feverish, hypnotic fascination.

"I . . . I don't want to know you," I told him then. "I want nothing to do with you."

"But you have everything to do with me," he answered, and his eyes glowed redder yet. "The old fool told you to avoid me, didn't he?"

"He said you were waiting for something," I answered. "For me, I suppose. But he didn't say why, or to what end."

"Then let me tell you." He drifted closer, his lank black hair floating on his shoulders, his thin face invisible behind the flaring of his eyes, those burning eyes that were fixed on mine. "I have a mystery to unfold, a story to tell, and I can't rest until I've told it. You are sympathetic, receptive, aware. And you came to my place of waiting. I didn't seek you out; you sought me. Or at least, you *found* me. And I think you will like my story."

"Then tell it and leave me be," I replied.

"You find me offensive," he said, his voice deeper and yet more dark, but at the same time sibilant as a snake's hiss. "So did she. But what she did, that was *truly* offensive! Yessss."

"You're making as much sense as Old Joe!" I told him. "But at least he kept his distance, and didn't smell of . . . of—"

"—Of the damp, the mould, and the rot?"

"Go away!" I shuddered, and felt that I was shrinking down smaller in my bed.

"Not until you've heard my story, and then I'll be glad to leave you . . . in peace?" With which he laughed an ugly laugh at the undefined question in his words.

"So get on with it," I answered. "Tell me your story and be done with it. For if that's all it takes to get rid of you, I'll gladly hear you out."

"Good!" he said, and moved closer yet. "Very good. But not here. I can't reveal it here. I want to show you how it wasssss, where it wasssss, and what happened there. I want you to see why I am what I am, why I did what I did, and why I'll do what I've yet to do. But not here."

"Where then?" I asked, but I'd already guessed the answer. "At your waiting place? Your place on the moor, the old tor?"

"In my place of waiting, yesss," he answered. "Not the old tor, but close, close." And then, changing the subject (perhaps because he thought he'd said too much?) "What is your name?"

I wanted to refuse, defy him, but his ghastly eyes dragged it out of me. "I'm Paul," I replied. "Paul Stanard." And then—as if this were some casual meeting of strangers in a street!—"And you?"

"Simon Carlisle," he answered at once, and continued: "But it's so very, *very* good to meet you, Mr Stanard." And again, as if savouring my name, drawing it out: "Paul Stanaaard, yessss!"

From somewhere in the back of my sub-subconscious mind, I remembered something. Something Old Joe had said to me: "If you deny me I can't stay. If you refute me, I must go." Would it be the same with Simon Carlisle, I wondered? And so:

"You are only a dream, a nightmare," I said. "You're nothing but a phantom, come to ruin my sleep."

But it didn't work! He moved closer—so close I felt the heat of his blazing eyes—and his jaw fell open in a gurgling, phlegmy laugh.

Abruptly then he stopped laughing, and his breath was foul in my face. "You would work your wiles on me? On that old fool, perhapssss. But on me? Old Joe came with goodness in his heart, yessss. Ah, but which is the stronger: compassion, or ambition?

The old tramp is content to wait, and so may be put aside—but not me! I shall wait no longer. You came to my place, and now I have come to yours. But I can't tell my story here, for I want you to see, and to know, and . . . and to feel."

"I won't come!" I shrank deeper into my bed and closed my eyes, which were already closed.

"You will!" *His* eyes floated down on me, into me. "Say it. Say that you will come to my place of waiting."

"I . . . I won't."

His eyes burned on mine, then passed through them, to burn inside my head. "Say you'll come."

I could resist him no longer. "I'll come," I mumbled.

"Say you *will* come. Say it again, and again, and again."

"I *will* come," I said. "I will come . . . I'll come . . . I'll come, come, come, come, come!" Until:

"Yessss," he sighed at last. "I know you will."

"I *will* come," I was still mumbling, when my bedside telephone woke me up. "I will most definitely . . . what?"

Then, like a run-down automaton, blinking and fumbling, I reached for the phone and held it to my ear. "Yes?"

It was Andrew Quarry. "I just thought I'd give ye a call," he said. "See how ye slept, and ask if ye'd be out at the auld tor again. But . . . did I wake ye or somethin'?"

"Wake me? Yes, you woke me. Tumble Tor? Oh, yes—I *will* come—come, come, come."

And after a pause: "Paul, are ye all right? Ye sound verra odd, as if ye're only half there."

God help me, I *was* only half there! And the half that was there was in pretty bad shape. "Old Joe warned me off," I mumbled then. "But he's just an old tramp, an old fool. And anyway, Simon wants to tell me his story and show me something."

"Simon?" Quarry's voice was full of anxiety now. "And did I hear ye say Old Joe? But . . . Old Joe the tramp?"

"Old Joe," I nodded, at no one in particular. "And anyway, he says that I'm to take him back to his place of waiting. He's really not a bad old chap, so I don't want to let him down. And Andrew, I'm . . . I'm not at all well."

Another pause, longer, and when Quarry finally spoke again there was something more than concern in his voice. "Paul, will ye tell me where and when ye spoke to Old Joe? I mean, he's not there with ye this verra minute, is he?"

"He was last night." I nodded again. "And now I must go."

"Ontae the moor?"

"I *will* come," I said, putting the phone down and getting out of bed.

There was a mist in the house, in the car, on the roads, and in my mind. Not a really heavy mist, just some kind of atmospheric— and mental?—fogginess that had me squinting and blinking, but without completely obscuring my vision, during my drive out to Tumble Tor.

I had to go, of course, and all the way I kept telling myself: "I *will* come. I will, I will, I will . . ." While yet I knew that I didn't want to.

Old Joe went with me; he kept silent, but I knew he was in the car, relieved to be returning to his place of waiting. Perhaps he was reluctant to speak in the presence of my other less welcome passenger: the one with his cold fingers in my head. As for that one . . . it wasn't just that I could sense the corruption in him, I could smell it!

And in as little time as it takes to tell, or so it seemed to me, there we were where the dirt track crossed the road; and Tumble

Tor standing off with its base wreathed in mist, and the knoll far-ther yet, a gaunt grey hump in the autumnal haze.

I, or rather we, got out of the car, and as Simon Carlisle led me unerringly out across the moor toward Tumble Tor, I knew that Old Joe fretted for me where we left him by the gap in the hedge. Knowing I was too far gone, beyond any sort of help that he could offer, the old tramp said nothing. For after all, what could he do to break this spell? He'd already done his best, to no avail. Half turning to look back, I thought I saw him by the white-painted marker stone which he'd used as a seat that time. Like a figure carved from smoke, he stood wringing his hands as he watched me go.

But Simon Carlisle said, "Pay him no heed. This is none of his businessss. His situation—in a waiting place such as his—was al-ways better than mine. He has had a great many chances, yessss. How long he is willing to wait is for him to determine. Myself, I am done with waiting."

"Where are you taking me?" I asked him.

"To the tor," he answered. "Where else? I want to see just one more time. I want to fuel my passion, as once before it was fu-elled. And I want *you* to see and understand. Do you have your glasssses?"

I did. Like him, I wore my binoculars round my neck. And I knew why. "We're going to climb?"

He nodded and said, "Oh yessss! For as you'll soon see for yourself, this vast misshapen rock makes a superb vantage point. It is the tower from which I spied on *them!*"

My soul trembled, but my feet didn't stop. They were numb; I couldn't feel them; it was as if I floated through the swirling ground mist impelled by some energy other than my own. But all I could think of was this: "I . . . I'm not a good climber."

"Oh?" he said without looking back, his clothing flapping like a scarecrow's in the wind, while his magnetism drew me on. "Well I am. So don't worry, Paul Stanaaard, for I won't let you fall. The old tor is a place, yessss, but it isn't the place of waiting. That comes later . . ."

We drifted across the moorland, and despite the shadows in my mind, and the mist on the earth, I found myself scanning ahead for rushes and sphagnum mosses, evidence of boggy ground. Why I worried about that when there was so much more to concern me, I didn't rightly know. But in any case I saw nothing, and soon we approached the foot of the tor.

Simon Carlisle knew exactly where he was going and what he was doing, and all I could do was follow in his footsteps . . . if he had had any. But we continued to float, and it was only when we began to climb that gravity returned and our progress slowed a little.

We climbed the knoll side of Tumble Tor, where I had first witnessed Carlisle scanning the land beyond. And as we ascended above the misty moor, so he instructed me to place my feet just so, making opportune use of this or that toehold, or to secure myself by gripping this or the other jutting knob of stone, and so on; and even a blind man could have seen that he knew Tumble Tor intimately and had gone this route many times before.

We passed carefully along narrow ledges with rounded rims, through stepped, vertical slots or chimneys where the going was easier, from level to striated level, always ascending from one fearful vertiginous position to the next. But Carlisle's advice—his sibilant instructions—were so clear, timely, and faultlessly delivered that I never once slipped or faltered. And at last we came to that high ledge behind its shoulder of rounded stone, where I'd seen and even tried to photograph Carlisle as he scoured the moorland around through his binoculars.

"Now then," he said, and his voice had changed; no longer sibilant, it grated as if uttered through clenched teeth. "Now we shall see what we shall see. Look over there, a quarter mile or so, that hollow in the ground where it rises like the first in a series of small waves; that very private place surrounded by gorse and ferns. Do you see?"

At first I saw nothing, despite that the mist appeared to have lifted. But then, as if Carlisle had willed it into being, the tableau took shape, becoming clearer by the moment. In the spot he had described, I saw a couple . . . and indeed they were coupling! Their clothing was their bed where they lay together in each other's arms, naked. Their movements, at first languid, rapidly became more frenzied. I thought I heard their panting, but it wasn't them—it was Carlisle!

And then the climax—their shuddering bodies, the falling apart, gentle caresses, kisses, and whispered conversation—the passion quenched, for the moment at least. *Their* passion, yes . . . but not Carlisle's. His panting was that of a beast!

Finally he grew calm, and his voice was as before. "If we were to stay, to continue watching, you'd see them do it again and again, yessss. But my heart was herssss! And as for him . . . I thought he was my friend! I was betrayed, not once but often, frequently. She gave me back the ring which was my promise and told me her love could not be, not with me. Ah, but it *could* be with him! And as you've seen, it wassss!"

I didn't understand, not entirely. "She was your wife? But you said—"

"—I said she gave me back my ring—the *engagement* ring I bought for her. She broke her promissse!"

"She found someone she loved better or more than you."

"What?" He turned to me in a rage. "No, she was a slut and would have had anyone before me! She betrayed me—deserted

me—gave him what she could never give me. She sent me my ring in a letter, said that she was sssorry! Well, I made them *sssorry!* Or so I thought. But now, in their place of waiting, still they have each other while I have nothing. And if they must wait forever what does it matter to them? They don't wait in misery and solitude like meeeee! Even now they make love, and I am the one who sufferssss!"

"*Blind hatred! Insane jealousy!*" Now, I can't be sure that I said those words; it could be that I merely thought them. But in any case he "heard" my accusation. And:

"Be very careful, Mr. Stanaaard!" Carlisle snarled. "What, do you think to test me? In a place such as this? In this dangerous place?" His red lamp eyes drew me from the stone shoulder until I leaned out over a gulf of air. For a moment I was sure I would fall, until he said, "But no. Though I would doubtless take great pleasure in it, that would be a dreadful waste. For this is not my waiting place, and there's that which you still must see. So come." As easily as that, he drew me back . . .

We descended from Tumble Tor, but so terribly *quickly* that it was almost as if we slid or slithered down from the heights. As before I was guided by Carlisle's evil voice, until at last I stood on what should have been solid ground—except it felt as if I was still afloat, towed along in the wake of my dreadful host to the far side of the outcrop. But I made no inquiry with regard to our destination. This time I knew where we were going.

And off across the moor he strode or floated, myself close behind, moving in tandem, as if invisibly attached to him. Part of my mind acknowledged and accepted the ancient, mist-wreathed landscape: a real yet unreal place, as in a dream; that was the part in the grip of Simon Carlisle's influence. But the rest of me knew I should be fighting this thing, struggling against the mental miasma. Also, for the first time, I felt I knew for sure the evil I'd come up against, even though I couldn't yet fathom its interest in me.

"Ghosts," I heard myself say. "You're not real. Or you are—or you were—when you lived!"

Half turning, he looked back at me. "So finally you know," he said. "And I ask myself: how is it possible that such a mind—as dull and unimaginative as yours—lives on corporeal and quick when one as sharp and as clear as mine is trapped in this place?"

"This place? Your place of waiting?"

"No, Mr. Stanaaard." He pointed ahead. "Theirs! Mine lies on the other side of the tor, halfway to the bald knoll where first I saw you and you saw me. You'll know it when you see it: the mossesss, reedsss, and rushesss. But this place here: it's theirsss! It's where I killed them—where I've killed them a hundred times; ah, if only they could *feel* it! But no, they're satisfied with their lot and no longer fear me. We are on different levels, you see. Me riding my loathing, and them lost in their lust."

"Their love," I contradicted him.

He turned on me and a knife was in his hand; its blade was long and glittering sharp. "That word is *poison* to meeee! Maybe I should have let you fall. How I wish I could have!"

Logic, so long absent from my mind, my being, returned however briefly. "You can't hurt me. Not with a ghost knife."

"Fool!" He answered. "The knife is not for you. And as for your invulnerability: we shall see. But look, we are there."

Before us the place I had seen from Tumble Tor, the secret love nest surrounded by gorse and tall ferns; the lovers joined on their bed of layered clothing; Carlisle leaping ahead of me, his coat flapping, knife raised on high. The young man's broad back was his target; the young woman's half-shuttered eyes saw the madman as he fell upon them; the young man turned his head to look at his attacker—and amazingly, *he only smiled!*

The knife struck home, again and again. No blood, nothing. And Carlisle's crazed howling like a distant storm in my ears. Done with his rival, he turned his knife on the girl. Deep into her right eye went the blade, into her left eye, her throat, and bare breasts. But she only shook her head and sadly smiled. And her eyes and throat and breasts were mist; likewise her lover's naked unmarked body: a drift of mist on the coarse empty grass.

"Ghosts!" I said again. "And this is their waiting place."

Carlisle's howling faded away, and panting like a mad dog he drifted to his feet and turned to me. "Did you see? And am I to be pitied? They pity me—for what they have and I haven't! And I can't *stand* to be here any longer. And you, Mr. Stanaaard—you are my elevation, and perhaps my salvation. For whatever place it is that lies beyond, it *must* be better than this place. Now come, and I shall show you *my* place of waiting."

Danger! That part of me which knew how wrong this was also recognized the danger. Oh, I had known the precariousness of my position all along, but now the terror was tangible: this awful sensation of my soul shrinking inside me. I felt that I was now beyond hope. But before my fear could completely unman me, make me incapable of speech, there was something I must know. And so I asked the ghost, ghoul, creature who was leading me on, "What is . . . what *is* a place of waiting?"

"Ah, but that's a secret!" he answered, as we drew closer to Tumble Tor. "Secret from the living, that is, but something that is known to all the dead. They wouldn't tell you, not one of them, but since you will soon *be* one of them . . ."

"You intend to kill me?"

"Mr. Stanaaard, you are as good as dead! And then I shall move on."

It began to make sense. "You . . . you're stuck in your so-called waiting place until someone else dies there."

"Ah, and so you're awake at last! The waiting places are the places where we died. And there we must wait until someone else dies in the same place, *in the same way!* To that treacherous dog and his bitch back there, it makes no difference. They have all they want. But to me . . . I was only able to do what I do, to watch as I did in life, to hate with a hatred that will never die, and to *wait*, of course. Then you came along, trying to look beyond life, searching for someone who had moved on—and finding me."

"I called you up," I said, faintly.

"And I was waiting, and I was ready. Yessss!"

"But how shall you kill me? I won't die of fright, not now that I know."

"Oh, you won't die by my insubstantial hand. But you will die of my doing, most definitely. Do you know that old saying, that you can lead a horse to water—"

"But you can't make him drink?"

"That's the one. Ah, but water is water and mire is mire."

"I don't understand," I said, though I was beginning to.

"You *will* understand," he promised me. "Ah, you will . . ."

Passing Tumble Tor, we started out across the low-lying ground toward the knoll. And in that region of my conscious mind which knew what was happening (while yet lacking even a small measure of control) I remembered something that Carlisle had said about his place of waiting:

"You'll know it when you see it: the mossesss, reedsss and rushesss."

"We're very nearly there, aren't we?" I said, more a statement of fact than a question. "The sphagnums and the rushes—"

"—And the mire, yessss!" he answered.

"The quagmire where you killed yourself, putting an end to your miserable life: that's your place of waiting."

"Killed myself?" He paused for a moment, stared at me with his blazing eyes. "Suicide? No, no—not I! Never! But after I killed *them* I was seen on the moor; a chance encounter, damn it to hell! And so I fled. I admit it: I fled the scene in a blind panic. But a mist came up—the selfsame mist you see now—and as surely as Satan had guided me to my deed, my revenge, so God or Fate led me astray, brought me shivering and stumbling here. Here where I sank in the mire and died, and here where I've had to wait . . . but no longer."

We were halfway to the knoll and the mist was waist deep. But still I knew the place. Andrew Quarry had pointed it out on the occasion of our first meeting: the sphagnums and the reeds, pointers to mud that would suck my shoes off. But it now seemed he'd been wrong about that last. Right to avoid it but wrong in his estimation, for it was much deeper than that and would do a lot more than just suck my shoes off.

And it was there, lured on in the ghostly wake of Carlisle—as I stumbled and flailed my arms in a futile attempt to keep my balance, managing one more floundering step forward and wondering why I was in trouble while he drifted upright and secure—it was there that what little remained of my logical, sensible self took flight, leaving me wholly mazed and mired in the misted, sucking quag.

Carlisle, this powerful ghost of a man, as solid to me now as any man of flesh and blood, stood and watched as it began to happen. His gaunt jaws agape, and his eyes burning red as coals in the heart of a fire, he laughed like a hound of hell. And as I threw myself flat on the mud to slow my sinking: "Murder!" he said, his voice as glutinous as the muck that quaked and sucked beneath me. "But what is that to me? You are my third, yes, but they can only hang a man once—and they can't hang me at all! So down you go, Paul Stanaaard, into the damp and the dark.

And with your passing I, too, shall pass into whatever waits beyond . . . while you lie here."

It appeared I had retained at least a semblance of common sense. Drawing my legs up and together against the downward tug of viscous filth, I threw my arms wide and my head back, making a crucifix of my body and limbs in order to further increase my buoyancy. Even so, the quag was already lapping the lobes of my ears, surging cold and slimy against my Adam's apple, and smelling in my nostrils of drowned creatures and rotting foliage; in which position desperation loaned voice to what little of logic remained:

"But where are you bound?" I asked him, aware of the creeping mud. "Do you know? Do any of you know? What if your waiting places are a test? What if someone—God, if you like—what if *He* is also waiting, to see what you'll do, or won't do? What if this was your last chance to redeem yourself, and you're throwing it away?"

"Do you think I haven't—we haven't—asked ourselves the very same questionsss?" he answered. "I have, a thousand times. But think on thisss: if the next place doesn't suit me, I shall move on again by whatever means available. And again, and again . . . alwaysss."

"Not if the next place is hell!" I told him. "Which I very much hope it is!"

"Wrong!" he said, and burst out laughing. "For my hell was here. And now it's yoursss!"

I strained against the suction of the mud. I tried to will myself to stay afloat, but the filthy stuff was lapping my chin and surging in my ears, and I could feel my feet sinking, going down slowly but surely into the mire. Weeds tangled my hair and slime crept at the corners of my mouth; immobilized by mud, all I could do was gaze petrified at Carlisle where he stood like a demon god on the surface of the quag, howling his crazed laughter from jaws that gaped in a red-glowing Hallowe'en skull, his lank limbs wreathed in mist and rotten cloth.

Muddy water was in my nostrils, trickling into my mouth. I felt the hideous suction and was unable to fight it. I was done for and I knew it. But I also knew of another world, more real than Simon Carlisle's place of waiting. The world of the quick, of the living, of hope that springs eternal. And at the last—even as I gagged at the ooze that was slopping into my mouth—I called for help, cried out until all I could do was choke and splutter.

And my cries were answered!

"Paul!" came a shout, a familiar voice, which in my terror I barely recognized. "Paul Stanard, is that ye down there? Man, what in the name of all that's—?"

"Help! Help!" I coughed and gurgled.

And Carlisle cried, "No! No! I won't be cheated! It can't end like this. Drink, drown, die, you bloody obstinate man! You are my one, my last chance. So die, *die!*"

He drifted toward me, got down beside me, tried to push at my face and drive my head into the mud. But his hands were mist, his furious, burning face, too, and his cries were fading as he himself melted away, his fury turning to terror. "No, no, *noooo!*" And he was gone.

Gone, too, the mist, and where Carlisle's claw-like hands had sloughed into nothingness, stronger hands were reaching to fasten on my jacket, to lift my face from the slop, to draw my head and shoulders to safety out of—

—Out of just six inches of muddy water!

And Andrew Quarry was standing ankle deep in it, standing there with his Jennie, her raven hair shining in the corona of the sun that silhouetted her head. And nothing of that phantom mist to be seen, no sign of Carlisle, and no bog but this shallow pond of muddied rain-water lying on mainly solid ground . . .

"Did you . . . did you see him, or it?" I gasped, putting a shaking hand down into the water to push myself up and take the strain off Quarry's arms. But the bottom just there was soft as muck; my hand skidded, and again I floundered.

"Him? It?" Quarry shook his head, his eyes like saucers in his weathered face. "We saw nothin'. But what the hell *happened* to ye, man?" And again he tugged at me, holding me steady.

Still trembling, cold and soaking wet—scarcely daring to believe I had lived through it—I said, "It was him, Carlisle. He tried to kill me." As I spoke, so my fumbling hand found and grasped something solid in the muddy shallows: a rounded stone, it could only be.

But my thumb sank into a hole, and as I got to my knees I brought the "stone" with me. Stone? No, *a grinning skull*, and I knew it was him! All that it lacked was his maniac laughter and a red-burning glare in its empty black socket eyes . . .

At Quarry's place, while Jennie telephoned the police—to tell them of my "discovery" on Dartmoor—her father sat outside the bathroom door while I showered. By then the fog had lifted from my mind and I was as nearly normal as I had felt in what seemed like several ages. Normal in my mind, but tired, indeed exhausted in my body.

Andrew Quarry knew that, also knew why and what my problem had been. But he'd already cautioned me against saying too much in front of Jennie. "She would'nae understand, and I cannae say I'm that sure myself. But when ye told me ye'd been warned off, and by Old Joe . . ."

"Yes, I know." Nodding to myself, I turned off the shower,

stepped out and began to towel myself dry. "But he's not real—I mean, no longer real—is he?"

"But he was until four years ago." Quarry's voice was full of awe. "He used tae call in here on his rounds—just the once a year—for a drink and a bite. And he would tell me where he had been, up and down the country. I liked him. But just there, where ye parked yer car, that was where Old Joe's number came up. He must hae been like a wee rabbit, trapped in the beam of the headlights, in the frozen moments before that other car hit him. A tragic accident, aye." Then his voice darkened. "Ah, but as for that *other* . . ."

"Simon Carlisle?" Warm and almost dry, still I shivered.

"That one, aye," Quarry growled, from behind the bathroom door, which stood ajar. "I recognized his name as soon as ye mentioned it. It was eighteen years ago and all the newspapers were full of it. It was thought Carlisle had fled the country, for he was the chief suspect in a double moors murder. And—"

"I know all about it," I cut him off. "Carlisle, he . . . he told me, even *showed* me! And if you hadn't come along—if you hadn't been curious about my . . . my condition, my state of mind after what I'd said to you on the phone—he would have killed me, too. The only thing I don't, can't understand: how could he have drowned in just six inches of water?"

"Oh, I can tell ye that!" Quarry answered at once. "Eighteen years ago was a verra bad winter, followed by a bad spring. Folks had seen nothin' like it. Dartmoor was a swamp in parts, and *that* part was one of them. The rain, it was like a monsoon, erodin' many of the small hillocks intae landslides. Did ye no notice the steepness of that wee knoll, where all the soil had been washed down intae the depression? Six inches, ye say? Why, that low-lyin' ground was a veritable lake of mud . . . a marsh, a quag!"

Dressed in some of Quarry's old clothes, nodding my under-standing, I went out and faced him. "So that's how it was."

"That's right. But what *I* dinnae understand: why would the damned creature—that dreadful man, ghost, thing—why would it want tae kill ye? What, even now? Still murderous, even as a revenant? But how could he hope tae benefit frae such a thing?"

At that, I very nearly told him a secret known only to the dead . . . and now to me. But, since we weren't supposed to know, I simply shook my head and said nothing . . .

As for those pictures I'd snapped, of Simon Carlisle on Tumble Tor: when the film was developed there was only the bare rock, out of focus and all lopsided. None of which came as any great surprise to me.

And as for my lovely Jennie: well, I've never told her the whole thing. Andrew asked me not to, said there was a danger in people knowing such things. He's probably right. We should re-member our departed loved ones, of course we should, but how-ever painful the parting we should also let them go. That is, if and when they *can* go, and if they're in the right place of waiting.

Myself: well, I don't go out on the moor any more, because for one thing I know Old Joe is out there patiently waiting for an ac-cident to set him free. That old tramp, yes, and Lord only knows how many others, waiting in the hedgerows at misted crossroads on dark nights, and in remote, derelict houses where they died in their beds before there were telephones, ambulances and hospitals . . .

So then, now I sit in my garden, and as the setting sun begins to turn a few drifting clouds red, I rotate these things in my mind while watching the last handful of seagulls heading south for Brixham harbour. And I think at them: *Ah, but you've missed out on a grand fish supper, you somewhat less than early birds. Your friends set out well over an hour ago!*

Then I smile to myself as I think: *Well, maybe they heard me. Who knows, maybe that flying-ant telepathy of theirs works just as well with people!*

And I watch a jet airplane making clouds as it loses altitude, heading for Exeter Airport. Those ruler-straight trails, sometimes disappearing and sometimes blossoming, fluffing themselves out or pulling themselves apart, drifting on the aerial tides . . . and waiting?

Small fluffs of cloud: revenant vapour trails waiting for the next jet airplane, perhaps, so that they too can evaporate? I no longer rule out anything.

But I'm very glad my mother died in hospital, not at home. And I *will* have the pool filled in. Either that or we're moving to a house without a pool, and one that's located a lot closer to the hospital.

And when I think of disasters like Pompeii, or the Titanic—

—Ah, but I mustn't, I simply mustn't . . .

Hamlet's Father

ORSON SCOTT CARD, author of *Ender's Game* and its many sequels, as well as what I consider one of the finest horror stories of the past fifty years, "Eumenides in the Fourth Floor Lavatory," is the winner of the prestigious genre awards, the Hugo and the Nebula, being the only author, as of 2007, to win science fantasy's top prizes in consecutive years.

I've had the serendipitous pleasure to discover quite a few theatre scholars who, like me, have sought careers in less direct manners than our hearts might have dictated: Ray Russell, certainly, and Tanith Lee, and lately I've learned that Scott (as he likes to be called by friends) is an active theatre person, adapting works of The Bard for modern school audiences. His ghost story, "Hamlet's Father," richly mines his awareness and (very personal) opinions of Shakespeare's arguably most famous tragedy, *Hamlet.*

by ORSON SCOTT CARD

Hamlet's father sent him to the university at Heidelberg as soon as he turned fourteen. Even though he had to leave all his friends behind, Hamlet was glad to go.

It wasn't Denmark he wanted to leave. It was the castle at Elsinore; it was the throne that he would probably never occupy; it was Mother's endless sadness and infinite distance from him.

It was Father.

To be son of a King—it must sound so wonderful to boys with ordinary, nonregal fathers. The reality was far different.

Father was once as powerful as God, or so it seemed to Hamlet. Indeed, when the Bishop discussed God, Hamlet couldn't see how there was any difference between God and Father. They were both all-knowing, all-powerful.

But gradually it became clear to Hamlet that Father, with his infinite knowledge and wisdom, had judged his only son and found him permanently wanting. It began when Hamlet was six, playing with his Companions—the sons of nobles or wealthy commoners, brought to the castle to study Latin with him and to learn the arts of war. Hamlet could hear Father preparing for the hunt with a visiting lord from Jutland and his retinue. How Hamlet begged to be taken along on such expeditions! The hounds were barking, the horses stamping and whinnying, and servants were shouting orders to each other. All the boys stopped in their game to listen, to yearn.

Then came Polonius, Father's lord chamberlain and the father of Laertes, one of Hamlet's favorites among the Companions. Hamlet felt a thrill of anticipation: Father had sent for his son to accompany him!

Instead, Polonius called out to another of the Companions, Horatio, and beckoned to him.

There was no explanation. Horatio left. Soon after, the horses and hounds went away, and there was silence from the courtyard. In the garden where Hamlet played with his remaining friends, there was nothing but somberness, and games ended without ending, petering out for lack of interest.

Finally Hamlet ended up where he always went when he wanted to be alone—the graveyard behind the chapel. Hamlet had no fear of the dead—weren't they all his family and their faithful servants, or Kings and Queens from ancient lines that had withered away?—but the other boys were leery of the place, and Hamlet had long since reassured them that their duty to stay with him "at all times" did not include his graveyard visits. They were still officially "with him" if they remained in the garden. "All I do is rest and think," he said.

But that was not entirely true. Sometimes he dreamed. Sometimes he prayed. Sometimes he cried.

He was still in the graveyard when he heard the hunt return. He did not rush to join his Companions in greeting Father and the Earl of Jutland and his retinue. But he could not lie peacefully upon any of the graves now. He got up and began to pace. Then he climbed the apple tree nearest the ancient tomb of another family that once ruled in Elsinore but had been replaced by Grandfather, and tested himself to see if he was tall enough now to cling to a branch and swing himself onto the roof of the tomb. He quickly discovered that while he was definitely taller, he was also heavier, and bowed the branch lower, so he could only kick the wall of the tomb, not swing his legs up on top.

By the time he was big enough, he had become too big.

Angry, he let himself drop to the ground.

"The fruit has grown large and ugly this year," said a familiar voice—Yorick, the old jester.

"It's too early for apples."

"Then what kind of weather is it that drops ugly boys out of the sky?"

"I'm not ugly. Mother says I'm a very pretty little boy."

"Better to be ugly," said Yorick, and there was sadness in his voice.

"Why is that?" said Hamlet. "Pretty is always better."

"When you're older, if you're still pretty, then when you marry a woman you won't know whether she is marrying you for your pretty looks or because you're a prince."

"Why not both?"

"Why not neither?"

"I don't want to marry anybody," said Hamlet.

"But you will," said Yorick, "and you must be sure that she never knows you're pretty. Marry someone who lives far away. Let her think you're ugly as a toad. Then you'll be sure she's marrying you because of your royal blood."

"Why would I want that?"

"If she marries you because you're pretty, then when you get old like me she'll love some other young man. But if she marries you because you're a prince, then when you're old you'll still be prince—or King. So she'll keep on loving you."

"It's a good thing you're a fool," said Hamlet, "or I might believe you."

"It's always good not to believe me," said Yorick. "Ask your mother."

"Ask her what?"

"If she married your father because he's pretty." Then Yorick turned serious. "I'm sent to call you in. Your father doesn't know yet that you left your Companions, but he'd be angry if he knew. Don't get your friends in trouble."

"I didn't tell them to leave the garden," said Hamlet. "They could have stayed."

"They all thought you would go to meet the hunt as well. And they can't go back and do what they should have done—they're in the castle now, and people are starting to ask where you are. Your mother sent me for you."

If he had said Polonius sent for him, Hamlet would not have gone—not till they sent soldiers for him, or Mother herself. But since it was Mother doing the sending, Hamlet went.

"And you're filthy," said Yorick. "Covered with the dust of the dead. Go wash your face or people will think you're a ghost."

"I will if there's warm water."

"If you need warm water to wash in, you'll never be man enough to be king."

"Cold water makes a King?" asked Hamlet scornfully.

"Cold water makes a King wise," said Yorick, "and in Denmark, only a wise man is clever enough to persuade the lords to make him King."

"Then why don't Kings swim in the cold cold sea every day of the year?"

"Because," said Yorick, "only a fool would do that." Then he laughed and cackled and cavorted till Hamlet was laughing, too, and followed him toward the castle.

He stopped and washed at the same fountain that the soldiers used—it was an excuse to be near the foul-speaking men who smelled of horses and dogs and sweat and farts and ale; Hamlet adored them, and they liked him, too. But there were none about right now, for Father had invited all the hunt to his supper, where they would share the hog that had been roasting all the long morning.

Yet Hamlet thought he heard someone speaking, and not inside the stables, where grooms would be caring for the horses, and not in the kennels, either, where the barksome dogs were being fed and petted. The voice came from around the corner of the great keep, and when Hamlet went toward the sound he realized it wasn't speech; it was someone crying.

It was Horatio. Hamlet knew his voice.

Hamlet made a noise, so Horatio would know someone was coming. Thus when Hamlet came around the corner, Horatio was not crying at all, though his eyes were red and his nose was red and a little snotty, as was his sleeve.

"How was the hunt?" asked Hamlet.

Horatio tried a little smile. "I'm sorry to go, when I know you wanted to."

"I don't mind," said Hamlet, though of course that was a complete lie.

"I asked your father why he didn't take you, but he only said, 'I take the one who's ready for the hunt.' I said, 'The Prince is ready,' but he had them hoist me up on his horse in front of him."

My place. He took my place.

"That's your place," said Horatio. "I'm sorry."

"How was the hunt?" asked Hamlet again. It wasn't Horatio's fault, he knew, so he didn't need apologies. But he still had to know what they actually *did* on this day's hunt. So he could think about it. Lying on a grave, he could remember a day that he didn't actually have, the day with Father on the hunt.

Horatio told about it, but he never got excited. And when it came to the kill, he couldn't say anything at all. "I saw a hart and two hinds astraddle the horses on the way home," he said. "And the Earl of Jutland killed them all, so he was very proud and also grateful to your father for letting him take three from his deer-park."

"Father didn't kill any of them?" asked Hamlet.

"We got lost," said Horatio. "We didn't rejoin the hunt until on the way home. The Earl of Jutland wasn't going to take a deer without the King, but old Bearhand told him that the King wanted him to take three—one for himself, one for the King's house, and one to be cut up and shared with the poor."

"That was done like a Christian," said Hamlet.

"That's what they all said," said Horatio.

"You must have been sorry, though, to miss the kill."

Horatio almost sobbed again. "I was very sorry to miss it," he said, as soon as he had control of his emotions again.

"I hope next time I can go," said Hamlet.

But Horatio said nothing at all. Hamlet took him by the shoulder and got him to wash his face, and by the time they got into the castle no one could tell that Horatio had been crying.

If it had been only the once, Hamlet might have forgiven his father the shame of taking someone else before him. But as the months and years went by, and all the other boys were taken on hunts and other expeditions, and Hamlet never, it became more than a mere disappointment, more than a shame. It was Father's way of repudiating him; Hamlet could see that. Whatever it is that Father valued in a boy, Hamlet did not have it.

Not that Hamlet thought for a moment that the other boys were actually better. Hamlet always took pride in never allowing them to allow him to win at any of their contests. When he lost, he took it without shame or anger, and no one reported on the outcome to Father or Polonius, lest they interfere and punish someone for outdoing the Prince. Thus, whenever Hamlet won, he knew that his victory was real. He was the fastest runner, save Laertes; he was the best at Latin, save Rosencrantz; he was the strongest at wrestling, save Guildenstern, and then only on some days could the older boy throw him down.

At one thing, though, Hamlet was the best save *nobody,* and that was the sword. It was a natural gift—the armsmaster said so. Right from the start, Hamlet had a way of sensing just where his opponent's sword was going to be. With training, he began to understand this gift and refine it; by the time he was twelve he could watch a match with the swordmaster of Elsinore and name for him all the moves and tell what the losing swordsman should have done. It was all clear to him, all parts of swordsmanship— the stance, the flow, the point, the shaft, the heft, the guards, the parries, the slashes, the lunges. Left hand or right, taller opponent or heavier or shorter or lither, it didn't matter, Hamlet could see what they were doing just a split second before they did it, and even if he spent half a match dancing away from a longer-armed opponent, no one ever laid point or blade on Hamlet's body.

Whether he had a gift for it or not, however, Hamlet took every activity seriously. Even when Mother brought the boys in and began their training as pages, teaching them orders of precedence and heraldry, and the meaning of various dishes and how each day's dinner was the product of months of planning in garden, field, orchard, sty, pen, coop, and, above all, larder. How do you know when you need to hunt? How long must meat age? What spices preserve a sausage, and which merely make it palatable? What should be smoked and what should be salted down for winter? How many calves, lambs, and goslings should be allowed to live, and how long?

Why should I know this, Mother?

"Because you are Prince, my darling boy, and you have to know at a glance if your people are rich or poor, if they need relief or help from you, or if they are prosperous enough to be well and deeply taxed. You need to know if you have food enough for the men you keep around you, and you need to know how to order them—and the lords as well—so that quarreling is kept down and merit is always named and known."

So Hamlet set out to become the best at this as well, so that by the age of thirteen he was able to greet every visitor graciously by name and inquire after his family, and address all men by their right titles and afford them their right recognition.

The more he learned, though, the more Hamlet realized that his father was not, in fact, very good at any of it. He treated powerful men of ancient family as if they mattered little, and then inadvertently showed too much favor to one who had not earned it and had no right to it.

Like the way Father treated his brother, Uncle Claudius, as if he were the royal fool instead of old Yorick. Holding him up to ridicule in front of visitors. Yet Claudius bore it with dignity, showing neither rancor nor eagerness to please. He bore it as if he had been afforded great honor, as he deserved, being also a prince and son of one King and brother of another.

It had seemed natural and funny, back when Hamlet was little and Prince Claudius was still not yet fully a man. Beardless, too thin, gawky—of course Father teased him.

But by the time Hamlet began to get his growth at age thirteen, Claudius was as strong and sturdy a man, as fine-looking, as sharp-minded as any lord. As the King himself. Or perhaps stronger, sturdier, finer-looking, and sharper-minded than the

King. To Hamlet, long used to his father's public disdain of him, Uncle Claudius seemed more kingly than the King. And yet still Father publicly shamed him.

Didn't Father see that it made himself, not Claudius, look ridiculous? Oh, people laughed, because it was plain the King wanted them to. But Hamlet saw that when the japery was over, people cast looks of pity at Uncle Claudius. And more than that—more than once Hamlet saw lords and great men of the realm conferring quietly with Uncle Claudius, and with great solemnity, as if they discussed matters grave and stately. This they would not do if they thought Uncle Claudius a fool.

Hamlet even said so once, when he and Laertes were alone on the riverbank after a long swim. The other Companions were still in the water, and could not hear them.

"I wish Uncle Claudius were my father," said Hamlet.

Laertes turned on him savagely—angrily, even. "Do you wish your mother were an adulteress then? Or do you wish *her* not to be your mother, either?"

"I was just . . . wishing," said Hamlet. "Father hates me, so I might as well not be his son."

Laertes looked out across the water, his face dark with— what, anger? "There is no boy happier than the King's own son," he said.

"Then all the boys in the world must be sad all the time," said Hamlet, "because I am. No matter how hard I work to become the prince he wants me to be—"

"And Prince Claudius admires you? Is that it? Instead of becoming what your father wants you to be, you'd rather have a father who is satisfied with what you already are? What kind of King will you be, then? The kind who surrounds himself with toadies who always tell him that he's wonderful and brilliant? Or the kind of King who surrounds himself with men who are wiser and stronger than he is, so he can use their wisdom and strength for the good of the Kingdom?"

Hamlet always hated it when Laertes got into a mood to preach sermons. It was a trait he shared with his father; Polonius was so full of platitudes they slopped out of him like milk from a swinging bucket.

"If the King surrounds himself with men who are wiser and stronger," said Hamlet, "then why is he King, and not those men?"

"Be careful," said Laertes. "There's only so much treason I can listen to without having to behead myself."

"I'm not talking about my lord Father anymore," said Hamlet. "I'm speaking of myself. I know our history. Many a son has been passed over when he wasn't worthy to be King. If my father shows such disrespect for me, then why would the earls look for virtues that my father didn't find in me?"

"And if he kept you with him as his constant companion," said Laertes, "then you'd learn only the way to be a King like him, instead of a better one."

"Do you really think he shuns me so I'll be a better King?"

In answer, Laertes got up and plashed out into the water.

Hamlet watched him, thinking two things:

Why is there no one I can talk to about the things that matter most to me?

How beautiful he is.

They are all beautiful, Hamlet thought, looking at his Companions as they swam and splashed and dived. Strong and vigorous, lovely of face. As if my father chose them for me to make sure I never thought of myself as strongest, most vigorous, or handsomest. As if he wanted to make sure my opinion of myself stayed forever as low as his opinion of me.

What kind of scrawny, weepy, screaming, drooling, pissing,

puking, shitting, flatulent wretch was I as a baby, that he hated me from the moment I was born?

"No more or less of those things than any other baby," Yorick told him, on the day Hamlet dared to ask him the question. "And you still do all those things, just like everybody else. All that's changed is that you now know when and where to do them."

"All I have of my father is his name," said Hamlet.

"What if his greatest gift," said Yorick, "is to give you no gift?"

"Which is the greater fool," answer Hamlet, "the fool who thinks he's wise, or the fool who knows he's a fool and plays the part?"

"The fool who knows he's a fool is wise, and therefore no fool," said Yorick. "But the greater fool is the wise man who does not know he is wise, for then he follows not his own counsel."

"Where did you learn *that* bit of wisdom?"

"From Polonius."

"I thought so."

"It's one of my duties in the castle of Elsinore," said Yorick. "To clean up after my betters. I mop up the excess wisdom that drops upon the floor, stew it into a soup, soup it into a stew, and then serve it back to my betters as a fine feast of foolery."

"Better to steep it into soap," said Hamlet, "so we could wash with it."

"How can wisdom go into soap, since soap is full of lyes?"

"Sometimes to lie is wise."

"And sometimes to ask why is a lie," said Yorick. "So lies are wise and whys are lies."

"You pile so many meanings together that none of it means anything," said Hamlet.

"Which is why I'm still employed here at Elsinore. If anyone ever found a meaning in what I said, I'd soon be dead."

An observation that pretended to be mere jest, but which Hamlet knew to be true. Yorick might be a fool by trade, but even he could see that Father was not much of a King.

Hamlet was at sword practice, the last time he saw his father alive. He no longer practiced with his Companions, for he had long since proven himself their master and had nothing to learn from them, even with old Bernardo, the Italian swordmaster watching to criticize. These days his arms were long enough to practice with men—with strong soldiers who had wielded sabers, cutlasses, and great two-handed swords in battle, and with lordlings who had dueled with rapiers and remained alive to tell of it.

They practiced with nocked and dull-edged blades, their bodies covered with heavy padding—except that Hamlet wore almost none, because it hindered him. So when Father came out to watch, Hamlet was afraid he'd rail at Bernardo for risking royal blood by letting him duel without enough protection.

But that was Mother who worried about him; Father gave no sign that he cared one way or another.

When the practice was done, and Bernardo had his man gather the practice swords into the wheelbarrow, Father did the thing he never did. He called his son by name.

"Hamlet!"

It made him tremble inwardly, to hear his name in that voice. At once he turned and trotted to his father; he would have run full out, except the distance was so short.

"My lord Father," said Hamlet, falling to one knee.

"Oh get up," said Father. "Why should a servant waste time washing those leggings because you had to kneel in the mud?"

So there was no honor intended when Father called him.

"Your mother's been pestering me for months that we've run out of useful teachers for you. So we're sending you to the university in Heidelberg. Try not to turn yourself into something useless—clerks make poor Kings."

As if Father knew what a good King was. "Which of my Companions may I take with me?"

"I'm dissolving your Companions and bringing them all directly into my service," said Father. "You'll take none of them—only enough servants and men-at-arms that you don't embarrass Denmark by appearing paltry compared to the German princes who attend there."

"As my lord Father wishes," said Hamlet. "When is my journey to begin?"

"Tomorrow," said Father. "As I told your mother, once I agree to let you go, what's the point of keeping you here?"

Hamlet bowed. It was bitter, to hear how Father still despised him; but he couldn't help but be glad that there would be no waiting. It would be hard to leave home—to leave his Companions, especially Laertes and Horatio, and, too, he would miss Mother. And Yorick. But it would be good to go somewhere else, to see something of the world. To be away from the darkness of Father's disregard for him.

None of the Companions were with him at supper, and Hamlet realized that Father was punishing him. Even though Hamlet hadn't asked to go anywhere, Father had apparently disapproved of his going, and so he would be barred from saying good-bye to his friends.

Then, after supper, he walked on the battlements of the castle to take his last look at the lingering sunset of early summer. The sun spread its pink light along a row of clouds on the western horizon, over the low hills of Zealand. On the eastern side, darkness gathered on the Swedish side of the Oresund, as if night had to work up a great deal more strength before it could leap the straits and land in Denmark.

Someone was walking on the battlements. But staying in the shadows.

For one moment Hamlet felt a thrill of fear as he thought: This is how an assassin might come.

But in a moment his stealthy visitor came out into the open, and it was Laertes, not a murderer. Hamlet had to laugh at his own fear. "I thought for a moment you were someone who had come to kill me," he said. "The way you stayed in the shadows." As if anyone would find Hamlet worth killing.

"I hid because your father forbade any of the Companions to speak with you."

"Of course he did," said Hamlet. "For fear you'd make me feel as though I might be missed."

"You will be," said Laertes. "More than you know."

"Father's taking you into his own service. Men now, not Companions to a boy prince."

"It's an honor I did not want."

"Nor did I want to be a prince and get sent off to Heidelberg," said Hamlet. "Sometimes we just have to be patient with inconvenient honors."

Hamlet's tone had been jesting, but the darkness that came upon Laertes's face was almost painful.

"What is it?"

"Hamlet, I beg you, before you go, ask your father to send me away. To France. My mother's brother is there, lord of a small holding on the border between Normandy and the Ile-de-France. Father will never ask—he's too much the courtier. But if you ask—"

"Laertes, when did you ever see my father listen to me and do something that I asked him?"

Laertes turned away, his face a mask of despair. "I know," he said.

"Besides," said Hamlet, "how can you go, when your sister Ophelia is beginning to need the protection of a good sword?"

"Ophelia's in no danger from any man in Elsinore," said Laertes.

"If you want a favor from my father, perhaps you ought to enlist the help of the person who was able to persuade him to send me away."

"And who was that?"

"The Queen my mother," said Hamlet.

"Queen Gertrude doesn't even know my name," said Laertes.

"Then let's go to her, and I'll introduce you."

It took some persuasion, but Laertes was so desperate to leave Elsinore that at last he trailed along behind Hamlet through the halls of the castle. Finally they came to the Queen's chambers, which were on the south side of the castle, overlooking the practice grounds. How often, wondered Hamlet, has she watched from here as I bested every opponent with my sword? If she ever did, he had not heard of it.

But Mother, at least, knew he was alive. She had taught him much, and thought enough of him to think he might benefit from more education. She cared enough to persuade Father of it. That was more than the nothing he got from Father.

Hamlet knelt before her and she took his hands in hers, then glanced up at Laertes, who waited just inside the door of her rooms.

"Father isn't coming here, is he?" asked Hamlet.

"Small chance of that," said Mother cheerfully. "Why have you brought me Polonius's boy?"

"To ask your help for him," said Hamlet. "He wants to go live with a cousin in France, but his father won't plead for him to be released from the King's service in order to do it."

"The King's service?" asked Mother.

So she hadn't known that his Companions were being taken directly into the King's own guard. And when he explained it, she frowned and reached out a hand to Laertes. "One would have thought," she said to the boy, "that you served him well enough already."

She stood, and saw that Laertes was already as tall as she was, and laughed. "Well, it seems you're determined to be taller than your father."

"I should be," said Laertes. "My mother was."

"I think that if you bide only a little while, my dear husband will have no further use of you."

Laertes looked away. "If I live so long."

"Live," said Mother. "I command it."

"Then I'll obey," said Laertes, but it didn't sound like playful banter; he sounded sad.

"I'll speak to the King about releasing all the Companions. I think that all your fathers would be glad to have you back, since you are no longer with the Prince. You are all the sons of barons, and can't be commanded like the sons of commoners."

Laertes gave one short bark of a laugh.

"Your service," said Mother, "is not the King's to take, but rather your father's to offer."

"Do you doubt that my father would offer me?" said Laertes.

"I doubt he would offer you willingly," said Mother. "But no, I do not doubt that he'd give you over to the King's service. So I will frame it to my dear husband in such a way as to keep him from holding on to you just because your father dares not stand up to him. But when it happens, then get yourself to France as quickly as you can, and stay out of sight, because my dear husband will be in a snappish mood for some months to come, if I know him at all."

"I thank you with all my heart, my lady Queen," said Laertes. "Know that I am forever in *your* service, if you ever have need of me."

"I take that pledge of honor most seriously, Laertes," said the Queen. "Now leave me with my son. I *will* say good-bye to him, as my dear husband knew perfectly well I would do, even though he commanded me not to and I promised faithfully to obey him."

Hamlet had no idea what it meant, for her to claim on the one hand that Laertes's word of honor was worthy of respect, and on the other hand that she had given her own oath to Father with the full intent of breaking it. Women were not to be understood; it was as simple as that.

As soon as Laertes had slipped out and closed the door, Mother rose to her feet and embraced Hamlet. "You're a better son than your father and I had any right to hope for," she said.

"It's a well-kept secret from my father."

"You do not know what you do not know," said Mother. "Your father has loved you better than you think."

Then she turned away and said, "Come out and bid your nephew Godspeed."

To Hamlet's surprise, Uncle Claudius emerged from behind a tapestry. "Your uncle and I were conferring about a matter of some estates in Holstein," Mother explained. "But since my dear husband has forbidden him to take an interest in the royal lands, I can only get his advice by stealth. When you knocked on the door, I commanded him to hide."

Claudius stepped forward and held out his hand. "I'm sorry you'll be leaving us," he said. "I've taken much pleasure in watching you play with your opponents on the practice field."

So *someone*, at least, had been watching. "Thank you, my lord," said Hamlet.

"He called me 'my lord,'" said Claudius to Mother with a smile. "Even though he's one of the three in this land who don't owe me any honorifics. You've raised him to be gracious."

"No one raised him," said Mother. "He is what he is because of the nature God gave him, and nothing he got from parents or teachers."

"I learned everything from you, Mother," said Hamlet, "except war."

"Ah," she said. "But war is the all in all, isn't it? That's what separates princes from other folks—the power to lead great numbers of men out to kill people, without fear of reprisals from God."

"No man is above the judgment of God," said Hamlet. "Not even Kings—you taught me so yourself."

"You have me confused with the archbishop," said Mother. "I don't teach anybody about God. He and I are little acquainted of late, and I wouldn't presume to speak for him."

"Whom are you little acquainted with?" asked Claudius. "You are unclear. The archbishop or his master?"

"I referred to neither," said Mother, smiling. "I spoke of God."

Claudius laughed lightly and moved away toward the window.

So Mother thought the archbishop's "master" was not God. Then who did she think owned the man? Father? Or the devil?

"There's so much you never taught me," said Hamlet.

"Or me, for that matter," said Claudius confidingly, as if he and Hamlet were brothers in an old conspiracy. "Ever since your father became King, the only teacher I've had is your mother. But she holds back the juiciest bits of information for herself. She's afraid we'll become too powerful, if we know what she knows."

"*I* don't even know what I know," said Mother. "I don't dare ask myself a single question for fear I'll tell me an answer that I can't afford to hear."

Claudius laughed again, but Hamlet didn't understand the jest, if it *was* a jest.

"God be with you, Mother," said Hamlet. "I'll try to make you proud of me by all I do in Heidelberg."

"I'm glad of that," said Mother. "I'll be waiting for you when you come back. I'm proud of you. I'm proud of the man I see you ready to become."

"And the King," said Claudius.

"What about him?" asked Mother.

"The King that your son is nearly ready to become," said Claudius. "I spoke of that."

"My father your brother is still a young man," said Hamlet. "It will be a long while before Denmark needs another King."

Claudius seemed about to say something else, a bitter remark that twisted his mouth a little; but Mother held up her hand and he did not say it. But Hamlet knew what would have been said—that Denmark *needs* another King right now, but isn't likely to get one. It bothered him that Claudius and Mother seemed to speak freely between themselves about Father's shortcomings as King. There was much to be said on that score, of course, but it was unseemly for the King's wife and brother to scorn him, even privately.

Hamlet put it out of his mind. Claudius and Mother had both praised him, and Hamlet held his uncle in such high esteem that he knew that *his* respect should be enough.

But it wasn't.

He bade them good-bye and returned to his chamber, where his clothing for the next day's journey was already laid out, and all his other clothing packed away in trunks and bags that littered the floor of the room. He expected to lie awake, dreaming or fretting about Heidelberg, or mourning for the childhood that had just ended so abruptly. But he fell asleep instead, and if he dreamed, he remembered nothing of it in the morning. By noon he was aboard a ship, with the oarsmen pulling strongly into the currents of the strait, heading northward to round the coasts of Jutland and bring him, eventually, up the Rhine to the Neckar, where Heidelberg awaited him.

What is there to say of Heidelberg? It was the happiest time of Hamlet's life. Though at first he was homesick—how could he help but be, so far from the sea, so far from the friends he had known from childhood on, so far from his mother? But he soon found new friends, and of a different sort than he had ever known before.

There were few lordlings in Heidelberg, save of course the local dignitaries. He paid his visits and gave them their due, but made it clear he was at Heidelberg to be an honest student, and would have little time for hunting or dancing or the other pastimes of the nobility.

And he made good on his word. He found himself far behind many others in Latin and Greek, for his fellow students were no hand-picked firstborn sons of nobles; they were the second, third, and later sons of barons and knights, who had no prospects of inheriting their family lands and therefore had nowhere to turn but to the church; as well as the promising children of tradesmen looking to raise their families' stations through a lofty church appointment.

There were few who had any interest in swordplay or other games of war; they pounded their heads against their books and conversed continually in Latin, arguing theology from Augustine and Aquinas, as well as philosophy from the Greeks, while reciting poetry from Homer to Virgil, with many a stop at Ovid and other racier poets along the way.

At first, feeling uncomfortably ill-prepared, Hamlet made a show of carrying his sword with him wherever he went, and he managed to take offense in several of the pubs frequented by students. But he so quickly disarmed his few opponents that there was no sport in it; nor was anyone impressed, at least not among the students of the sort he wanted to befriend. Within a few months, he hung the sword on a peg on the wall of his rooms and carried books like everyone else.

He soon found that the road to acquaintanceship was to spend his money, not on fine foods, but on precious books. He found out from the best professors what books they most coveted, and then endowed the appropriate monasteries with funds enough to procure copies at the earliest date. It took a few months for the first of these books to arrive, but when they did, he made a point of forbidding the professors to tell how they had obtained them. As he well knew, this absolutely guaranteed that his generosity would be celebrated throughout the university, along with a reputation for modesty.

Meanwhile, he paid poorer students to tutor him and practiced his Latin as once he had practiced with the sword. Soon enough, though he never lost his Danish accent, he was fluent enough not only to be understood when he spoke and to make sense of most of what he read, but also to be able to overhear others' conversations, without knowing the topic, and understand them. He was, in a word, fluent, and it felt to him as if the whole world had opened its gates to him. He made friends, not only with young men of the armiger class, but also with the sons of tradespeople, a sort of person he would never have known in Denmark, except to order their obedience. And by the second year he found that some of his best friends were men long dead, whose books spoke to his heart with such brilliance and power that he revered them more than any living men he had ever known.

For four years he studied, and if he had not been the heir to the throne of Denmark, so that he could not take holy orders, he would have been offered many a prestigious post; even with his high birth, he was invited to come to Rome to study there, and gave it serious consideration for a while, though eventually he decided it would not be wise to be seen in Denmark as a tool of the Pope, which would imply too close a connection to the Holy Roman Empire, which always loomed on the southern borders of Denmark, despite its ups and downs. The Danish earls would need to be assured of his loyalty to Denmark and his fealty to no one but God and the Danish people.

Out of his father's shadow, he was happy. There were people who loved and admired him, not for his birth or his beauty (though neither was ignored), but for his mind and his wit and his loyalty and his kindness. He liked being loved, and he looked forward to the day when he would govern Denmark with generosity and rectitude. "Even as ye have done it unto the least of these, ye have done it unto me": He intended this to be the guiding principle of his reign, and aspired that someday he might be remembered, not as King Hamlet the Great, but rather as Hamlet the Good or Hamlet the Just. He would not go a-conquering; he would labor to keep the peace and help his Kingdom prosper, unburdened by a luxurious court or excessive military adventures.

Then came the messenger with a letter from Elsinore that could not await the normal post. He had hastened from Denmark on horseback, with a military escort as befitted the message.

"Hamlet, my son, your father has died, and you are needed at home. I send with this letter money enough for you to settle your debts if they are not unreasonable. Please come home at once." It was from his mother, who continued to style herself Queen

Gertrude, though, of course, she would only bear that title until Hamlet married.

"Does this mean you're King now?" asked one of his professors, when he stopped to tell the news before he left.

"Not in Denmark," said Hamlet. "Though I'm the likeliest heir, the earls can choose from any of the lords. I must win their hearts to be considered. They hardly know me now. The last they saw of me I was a boy."

"So your Kings are elected, like the Holy Roman Emperor?"

"Yes—but then we have more power, once we're chosen."

"More power than the Emperor?"

"Our country is smaller, of course, but our freedom to choose is greater, so that we can make decisions with less need to look over our shoulders."

"I know of no man readier to be a King," said the professor. "Plato once longed for a King like you, who was a philosopher first. We are Christians; we want our Kings to be philosophers *and* saints."

"I'm no saint," said Hamlet. "But I hope I will disappoint my people in neither wisdom nor virtue—nor strength and courage in battle."

"I know nothing of you as a soldier," said the professor. "But I know you to be fierce in argument."

"Here I've been gentle with my hands and fierce with my speech," said Hamlet. "At home I'll need to reverse that, for we Danes are still a violent people, when the need arises. And it arises too often for our own good."

"Then take that sword of yours off the peg on your wall. I hope you haven't lost any of your ability."

Hamlet laughed. "Who remembers now that I ever thought myself a swordsman?"

"We all remember, Prince Hamlet, though we don't speak of

it. You bested the finest swordsmen in Heidelberg, who made a point of provoking you in the public houses."

Hamlet was surprised. "I thought it was I who was too quick to take offense, and that my opponents were all unskilled, so that it did me no honor to fight them."

The professor only laughed again. "There was even talk of the wealthier students paying for a mercenary to come and teach you manners. But then you put your sword away, and they ceased to fear for their lives. It was widely rumored that you had killed half of Denmark, and that's why you were sent here."

"I've never killed a man, sir," said Hamlet.

"And never will, God willing," said the professor.

Hamlet gave the messenger and his men a day to rest, while he settled all of his accounts; there were few debts to pay, since he had lived simply, having sent home all but one of his servants after the first year. His amusements had not been of the expensive kind, and the books he bought and gave away were paid for in advance.

It was an uneventful journey, and more than once he wished he could have gone by sea, which could scarcely have been slower, since it would have been a voyage down, not up, the Rhine, and then over sea. But the ship that came for him would not have made such good time with the news of his father's death; haste in the sending had been chosen over haste in the return. And so he rode, using the evenings and mornings to exercise and bring himself back into fighting trim. By the time they neared the borders of Denmark, he felt like he was nearly back to being himself with the sword, and he had made friends of all the soldiers in his guard. He even wondered, though he said nothing of it, whether some of these men might not be worthy of elevation to the King's Guard, should he be chosen King.

Then came word from another messenger, sent to intercept

him on the way, that even though Hamlet's father had not yet been buried—they awaited Hamlet's arrival to seal the body in its tomb—the earls had met and, without awaiting Hamlet's return, had chosen the new King.

Claudius. Uncle Claudius was King now.

It was the worst possible news. Hamlet had assumed that if the earls chose someone else, it would be an old man, who would function more as regent until Hamlet came fully of age, ready in the eyes of all to assume the throne. But Claudius was not that much older than Hamlet himself, and if he lived his three score and ten, Hamlet would be sixty years old before the throne would be available, and by then Claudius would surely have children of his own.

The blow was devastating, but not for the reason that others might have supposed. Indeed, it surprised Hamlet himself how very little he cared about the fact that he would not be King. Though he had spent his life preparing for the crown, he realized that in Heidelberg he had gained something that he loved more than the honor or power of rule. If Claudius wore the crown, then perhaps he would allow Hamlet to remain at court to advise him; or perhaps he would send Hamlet abroad as ambassador; or perhaps he would gift him with lands of his own. With any of these Hamlet would be content. But another possibility entered his mind: If he were neither King nor heir, perhaps he *could* take holy orders and live his life among books and professors. So even though it was wrenching to turn his mind to many possible futures once unthought-of, it did not bring him any unhappiness, not really.

No, what devastated him was the other news: that even as the funeral preparations were under way, Claudius had asked his brother's widow, Hamlet's mother, to marry him.

It had not crossed his mind that his mother would wish to

remarry. But now he had to think of who she really was: a young woman, not yet thirty-five years of age, young enough to bear children. Claudius was younger than she was by eight years at least, but what of that? He was King. What woman wouldn't want to be married to the King?

But *Mother?* Hamlet had never thought of her as ambitious. She had endured Father's slighting treatment of her for all of Hamlet's life. He always thought that it was for his sake that she lived; it had never occurred to him that she might have loved being Queen so much that she cared little who sat on the throne, as long as she sat beside him.

Unworthy thoughts—he tried to drive them from his mind. And to the men who were with him, he betrayed no doubt or disappointment. Indeed, he knew they would remark upon it to all, that when he heard of Uncle Claudius's elevation to the throne, Prince Hamlet's response was immediately to smile and say, "He's the best man in Denmark; the earls have chosen well." None would hear him utter a word of complaint. And if some thought that his cheerfulness was hiding the bitterness of broken hopes, let them.

There was another part of him, though, something deep inside that had a different reason for concealing his thoughts from all men. It was a recognition that he did not know Claudius all that well—hadn't he learned from his studies that only God could truly know the hearts of men? What if Claudius thought that Hamlet was, not his beloved nephew, but a bitter rival? Wouldn't Hamlet then have reason to fear his uncle? And wouldn't a pretense of loyalty and happiness be his best protection? For if he showed even the slightest trace of sullenness, if he even allowed himself to seem ill . . .

In the few days of riding after they crossed the borders into Denmark, though, Hamlet learned that feigning cheerfulness was a hard duty to perform. It wore him down. It wore him out. And besides, the men knew him too well: They had seen him quiet, thoughtful, even stern of face as he thought his thoughts. Now to have him full of nothing but smiles would look so false and unconvincing that King Claudius, hearing report of it, would quickly decide that it was insincere, meant to conceal something dark and bitter.

No, the protective mask Hamlet wore would need to be something closer to his natural disposition: solitary, thoughtful, even brooding. He had been sharp of wit at school, a good comrade, but he had also been earnest and serious, and often quiet, seeking the company of books or his own thoughts. Like when he was a child and lingered in the graveyard, seeking to be alone for hours at a time. His own natural temper would be his best disguise.

"I can't pretend," he said to the men around him. "I've tried this whole journey to show my faith in God, not to grieve for my father's passing. A good Christian must be cheerful in the face of death, having a certainty of a glorious resurrection for himself and all those he loves best. But I can't lie to God, so why should I lie to you? My faith is too weak. I grieve for my father's death, and I won't pretend otherwise."

The men listened, nodding, sympathetic. The messenger even dared to commiserate. "May not a good Christian mourn for the loss of company, even if the dead have gone to heaven?"

"He may," Hamlet answered solemnly, and took the conversation no farther. For he had no wish to lie to these men any more than he had to. He did not love his father. Hamlet's only grief was that now he would never have a chance to earn his father's love and respect. And since it was unlikely he would ever have achieved such an apotheosis, it wasn't cause for that much grieving. Denmark was better off without Father as King. And better off, no doubt, without his brooding, scholarly son as King after him. God had ordained that Claudius be King; Mother that Claudius be her new husband; Hamlet would be content with all, so long as he could be allowed to return to his books and his philosophy as soon as possible after the funeral and the wedding.

He would not even begrudge Mother and Uncle Claudius their happiness. There was no blood relation between Claudius and Mother, after all. And didn't the Bible command that a man take his brother's widow to wife, to raise up progeny to his brother? Of course, that was only if the dead brother had no sons.

It was not a matter of legalisms. God had taken Father away from Denmark, away from Mother, away from them all. Whatever dark and brooding spirit had kept Father from showing genuine love to him or Mother, he was gone now, and with him the shadows he had cast in their lives. They were all free, and Hamlet most of all, for instead of having to bear the royal burden Father had borne so badly for all these years, he could live his life as he saw fit.

Of all Hamlet's companions, only Horatio sought him out when he returned. This was hardly surprising—while Hamlet was in Heidelberg, Guildenstern had inherited his father's estates, and Rosencrantz had gone to live with him and help spend his money while waiting for his own father to die. Laertes was in France; he had been sent for, but not with the same urgency as Hamlet, since the dead King had not been his father. The others were sons of lesser barons, whose fathers could not afford to keep them at court once the King stopped paying for their upkeep as Companions.

But if Horatio was his only friend left in Elsinore, he was enough, at least for now. In some ways Horatio was still a boy, for to Hamlet all the practicing for war and death was a child's game, now that he had become a man of thoughts and words. In other ways, though, Hamlet was in awe of him, for Horatio had grown to be a strong man, looking older than his nineteen years, with an easy manner and a confidence born of strength—Horatio had nothing to fear.

It was Horatio who told him that the kingdom was secretly arming for war. In Norway, Fortinbras had recently succeeded to his father's throne, and anyone who was not a fool knew that he would, at the first opportunity, attempt to avenge his father's defeat at Denmark's hands fifteen years ago. There were lost lands that Fortinbras would want to reclaim, and the death of his old enemy, Hamlet's father, would be taken as an opportunity.

"So that's why the barons gave the throne to my uncle so quickly," said Hamlet.

"We're bound to have war this summer," said Horatio, "though no one speaks of it openly. In case Fortinbras wavers, there's no reason to provoke him by making known our own preparations for war. Better to keep the peace for another season."

"But we *do* prepare."

"Well, we do *now.* Your late father, God rest his soul, insisted that he had nothing to fear from Norway. 'I beat the father; the son won't dare attack while I'm alive.'" His imitation of Hamlet's father was nearly perfect—Horatio had the deep voice to bring it off.

"And now he's not alive," said Hamlet.

"He may have thought that he could easily defeat an untried boy who studied with the clerics in Heidelberg," said Horatio, winking. "You and I know that you're as skilled at the arts of war as any man, but Fortinbras had no idea."

"A war is not a duel," said Hamlet. "The barons were right to give the throne to my uncle, at a time like this."

"I'll not quarrel with their choice of a King," said Horatio. "Nor even with their haste in choosing. But you would have been a fine King, up to the challenge, and you may be yet."

"No talk of that," said Hamlet. "Even between the two of us, my friend. I have no ambition that should make my uncle mistrust me, but any speculation about my future will make him find disloyalty where there is none."

"You don't fear good Uncle Claudius, do you?" asked Horatio.

"The throne changes a man. I haven't seen him privately since I came back, and only twice at public ceremonies. He's busy—I attribute his ignoring me to that. But it might as easily be a dread of what he'll find in me. I'm the son of his new wife— that makes me the most dangerous man in the kingdom, if I choose to be, because it would be all the harder to strike me down if I undertook some sort of treason. No, Horatio, the best place for me is far from Denmark, and in circumstances where I'm not seen as a threat. I think there's a monastery in my future." And then he added, for no particular reason, "Perhaps in Rome."

"I don't see you becoming a priest," said Horatio.

"Not a *good* one," said Hamlet. "Taking orders and being a good father confessor are two different matters. A son of a King can hardly be a parish priest. But there might be a bishopric for me somewhere."

"And someday a red cap," said Horatio. "And someday pope!"

"There's no place for ambition in the Church," said Hamlet.

"Oh ho," said Horatio, "so you *are* still a child."

"*I* have no ambition, anyway," said Hamlet. "I love my books as I once loved the sword."

"Have you slain any opponents in bookish duels?"

"I've slain no one with the sword, either, so both scores are even, at zero."

"When scholars duel, do they pitch the books like stones? Or bring them down on their opponent's head like a battleaxe?"

"Neither," said Hamlet, laughing. "We drive them into the other man's ear like a dagger, piercing his brain, which must find an argument to thrust it out again, before he bleeds to death."

"So books draw blood?"

"Scholars don't have blood flowing in their veins," said Hamlet. "When they're wounded, they bleed logic, and when all of it is gone, their brains die, and they become . . . soldiers."

Horatio pantomimed being pierced by an arrow through the heart. "Look! I'm pierced through, but I have no logic to bleed with!"

The joke had gone far enough, though, and Hamlet spoke earnestly: "You've always been my wisest friend."

"A deadly insult to Laertes, then. He was always proud of being the smartest one."

"No one is prouder of his wisdom than a fool," said Hamlet, holding up one finger in a parody of Polonius reciting a maxim.

"Are you quoting someone? Is that a translation from Latin?"

"I was imitating Laertes's father," said Hamlet.

"I'm glad you told me," said Horatio. "Because otherwise I wouldn't have known it."

"Speaking of Laertes . . ."

"Ophelia is still unmarried. Waiting for you, they say."

"Waiting for me to what?"

"To pay attention to her. To court her. Hamlet, don't tell me you didn't know how Polonius always hoped she'd marry you when you came of age."

"That was back when I had a crown in my future," said Hamlet.

"That might change the father's mind, but the daughter looks with different eyes."

Hamlet shook his head. "Having a wife is often taken by the Church as a discouragement to ordination."

"Do you really mean to live a life of celibacy?"

"I have all the ordinary lusts of the flesh," said Hamlet. "But to me, a woman is much like a pudding: when you're hungry, of all things the most beautiful; but when you've had your fill, the dregs are disgusting to look at, and you can't wait for someone to take the dish away."

"You're describing a whore, when a man's had too much to drink. Not a lady like Ophelia."

"You might be right," said Hamlet. "I haven't seen her since I came home."

"Hardly seen your uncle, little conversation with your mother, haven't seen Ophelia—they all live here, you know. Do you walk around blindfolded?"

"I haven't sought company," said Hamlet.

"Except the company of books."

"I'm glad you sought me out," said Hamlet. "I didn't know how much I missed you till we talked again."

"And that's how it'll be with Ophelia, I promise you. Whatever love you had for her four years ago will be rekindled when you see her—I promise you, a single look will fan every spark of love into a fire."

"Then why haven't *you* courted her, if the sight of her fans every spark?" asked Hamlet.

Horatio laughed. "Why do you think I'm still in service here, Hamlet? My father's lands won't support my father's family, let alone a son like me at court. I have nothing to offer a lady like Ophelia. I'm the poorest of your Companions."

"The poorest? The best."

"Laertes is and always was the best," said Horatio. "And in case you've forgotten, the best-loved by you."

"Was he?" said Hamlet. "I don't remember."

"It seems to me that memory must have leaked out of your brain to make room for all that logic."

"I never had a favorite," said Hamlet.

"You never showed favor to one over another," said Horatio. "That was the good prince in you. But Laertes could challenge you like no other, and you bore it without anger."

"But I would have borne it from any of you," said Hamlet. "If Laertes was the only one who dared, then that's about him, not me."

"Laertes was the angriest," said Horatio. "I suppose that's all."

"Angriest?" said Hamlet. "What do you mean? At me?"

Horatio blushed. "I meant nothing. He was choleric, that's all. Quick to anger."

But Hamlet knew it was *not* what Horatio meant. There was some grievance, and Horatio meant not to speak of it.

Well, Hamlet wouldn't force the issue. Those days with his Companions were done with now.

They soon made their way out to the practice grounds and Hamlet drew his sword for the first time in years, not because he cared whether he was still good at the art of swordplay, but for old times' sake.

"You have to *try*," said Horatio. "It's no fun to best you when you aren't even trying."

"I *am* trying," said Hamlet. "You're a soldier now, and I'm a scholar."

"Yes, which has nothing to do with how you fight, only with how much or little you care about fighting."

"I'm not angry with you," said Hamlet. "Nor do I mind being defeated by you. I'm duelling for company."

Horatio laughed. "You've become a lunatic! Imagine—a man so lonely that the only way he can have any companionship is to challenge someone to a duel!"

Hamlet laughed with him. "That would be a miserable life! You'd make a friend and have him only long enough to kill him."

But in the next bout, Hamlet began to concentrate on what he was doing, instead of playing around. Only now, when he was actually trying to fight well, remembering some of his old moves, did he begin to see how much better Horatio was than he used to be. Tricks that would have disarmed Horatio back in the old days were now parried skillfully, and Horatio soon pressed on him in a way that Hamlet had never seen from him.

"Now we're playing well together," said Horatio. "Like musicians in tune."

"You've learned a few things," said Hamlet.

"And you've forgotten a few," said Horatio. "But not as many as you think."

Then Horatio made a brute-force move to disarm him, and Hamlet, alert now, sidestepped and spun the sword out of Horatio's hand, all in one quick, dancing move. Horatio's own momentum sent him sprawling into the dirt. He got up laughing. "I should have known!" he said. "You were toying with me!"

"Hardly," said Hamlet. "I'd never seen that move before—no one was strong enough to try anything like that."

"I thought it *might* work."

"It almost did," said Hamlet. "My heart's beating as if I had just swum from Sweden. You gave me a scare!"

"Well, that's something," said Horatio. "But don't give me

any more nonsense about how you've forgotten all your skills with the sword."

"Be honest, Horatio. Beating you never took *all* my skills."

"With a *sword,* maybe," said Horatio, smiling with mock malice. "If we stood at either end of a stone wall, pitching heavy rocks as we walked toward each other, I bet I'd win."

"Unless you got confused and threw your head at me."

Whereupon they began a wrestling match, which ended as such matches always did, with Hamlet flat on his back, fully pinned, and Horatio nonchalantly pretending not to see the prince wriggling under him to get free.

At supper they were boisterous enough to draw the attention of King Claudius, but it was a smile he gave them, not a frown. "I'm glad to see your grief at your father's death has eased enough to give you room to laugh," he said.

Grief at Father's death? But Hamlet could hardly say, in front of the whole court, that he barely remembered that he'd *had* a father, and it was only his native soberness of mind and carefulness that kept him so quiet up to now. "For a moment with an old friend I forgot my grief, sir," said Hamlet. "But at your reminder, the shadow of mourning is reawakened, and I regret it if I seemed to show disrespect to my father's memory."

"I meant no rebuke to you, Prince Hamlet," said Claudius.

"And I did not take it that way," said Hamlet. "I rebuke myself, and thank you for helping me remember my duty to my father."

Hamlet had meant it to be a conciliatory statement, but Mother frowned a little, and the way Claudius turned away to converse with someone on the other side of the table left Hamlet wondering what he had done wrong. The currents in this court were too tricky for him; Aquinas was plain and simple compared to the moods of Kings and Queens.

Hamlet found himself wishing he could go home. Even though he *was* home, supposedly.

It was the middle of the night two days later when Hamlet awoke from a dream of being awakened in a monastic cell to join his holy brothers for prayers. It was no monk shaking him, though— it was Horatio.

"Hamlet," he said. "Quietly, quietly . . . nothing's wrong, except I need you to come with me."

"It's full dark outside," said Hamlet.

"Last night I thought maybe it was too much wine at dinner," said Horatio, "but then in the morning I had no headache, and I realized that I had drunk only a little."

"What are we talking about?" said Hamlet as he dressed.

"I think I saw your father last night."

Hamlet looked at him sharply. "Didn't you hear? He died. Or are you saying that the whole kingdom is deceived and he's only pretending to be dead?"

"Dead," said Horatio. "I saw him dead, but walking the battlements of the castle."

"A ghost," said Hamlet, not even trying to conceal his skepticism.

"He looked right at me," said Horatio, "but with such contempt that . . . I don't think I'm the one he wanted to see."

"Spirits are either in heaven or hell," said Hamlet. "They don't walk the earth."

"Excellent," said Horatio. "I'm glad to hear it. In fact, I told the ghost so myself, but he ignored me and continued to exist. Perhaps tonight, if you tell him, he'll go."

Horatio's words were light and bantering, but his voice trembled a little, so Hamlet knew he was frightened. And nothing frightened Horatio.

"Has he been seen tonight?" asked Hamlet as they left his room.

"He came last night in the hour just before dawn, and left when the light came. Marcellus and Bernardo saw him first, and then brought me. Every night he comes."

"And the word of this hasn't already flown through the castle?"

"They're afraid of being thought lunatics," said Horatio.

"But you have no such fear?"

"I don't fear the opinions of fools," said Horatio.

"So you fear only the ghost itself?"

"No," said Horatio. "A spirit is airy; it's nothing, not even a fog. I could see through it, the walls behind it. When it passed between me and Marcellus, I could see Marcellus plainly. What is there to fear from something insubstantial?"

"And yet you're afraid," said Hamlet.

Horatio was silent until they came to the stair leading up to the battlement. "I'm afraid," said Horatio, "because of what the thing might say."

"Its body isn't real," said Hamlet, "but its words might be?"

"Words can be as sharp as swords, and stab as deep. I fear that what this ghost might have to say will leave this castle draped with corpses."

"Or perhaps he'll have words to save us," said Hamlet. "Perhaps he knows something of the plans of Fortinbras."

"Why should hell care what befalls kingdoms here above?"

"Hell?" asked Hamlet.

"Or heaven," added Horatio.

"You're sure my father must be in hell?"

Again Horatio kept his silence.

Marcellus and Bernardo waited, sitting and leaning in a corner. "If I didn't know better," said Hamlet, by way of greeting, "I'd say that you were drunk."

"I wish we were, Your Highness," said Bernardo.

"Fellow soldiers now," said Hamlet. "On guard against the world invisible."

"I wish it *were* invisible," said Marcellus.

"We'll be glad of it someday," said Horatio with bravado. "To tell our grandchildren that we saw the ghost of the old King on the battlements in the days before he was buried."

"No doubt that's why he appears to you," said Hamlet. "Because his body has been so long kept out of the tomb."

"Then in God's holy name," whispered Bernardo, "let's bury him."

"Deep," said Marcellus.

"When should we expect him?"

"Soon," said Horatio. "The same time every night—he walks for half an hour, and leaves at the first light in the east."

"Nonsense," said Hamlet, trying to lighten the mood. "My father would never flee from anything he saw coming from Sweden."

They didn't laugh. Instead, Marcellus turned his face away and pointed at something behind Hamlet.

Hamlet turned, and there he was, staring coldly at him: his father, just as he was in life, except insubstantial, like a few wisps of fog so clearly defined that Hamlet could see his features, the expression on his face, and above all, his eyes, which shone as if black fire burned within them.

"Father," he whispered.

The ghost said nothing, but looked at Hamlet and did not move.

"Have you come to give us warning?" asked Hamlet. "To protect the kingdom?"

"He never speaks," whispered Bernardo. "We've asked him all these questions."

"I'm not the King, Father," said Hamlet. "Should I bring your brother Claudius here to confer with you?"

The ghost's face shivered and contorted as if a hot wind had come to melt it or blow it away.

"No," it said.

Bernardo cried out in alarm, and Marcellus whimpered. Hamlet did not blame them. It was not a human voice; it seemed not to fall upon his ears, but struck in his heart, shaking his heart like the tones of a deep bell rung loud and close.

"Are you my father?" asked Hamlet. "Or some demon in disguise?"

"If he means to deceive you," murmured Horatio, "then he'll give the same answer as any honest spirit."

Still the ghost did not take his gaze from Hamlet. "He wants to talk to me," said Hamlet. "Now that we know he's capable of speech, leave us alone so I can hear his message."

"I won't leave you," said Horatio. "What if it means to harm you?"

"Why would my father want to hurt me?" asked Hamlet. Though he recognized the question as soon as he asked it—it was the very one he had asked inside his heart through all the years of growing up without ever having his father's high regard or company.

"A ghost may not be able to strike you," said Horatio, "but what if he entices you off the battlements, to fall to your death?"

"Then either I'll be deceived, and die, or not, and live," said Hamlet. "But you can see this spirit is not to be denied. Let me speak alone with him, or he'll be back again and again."

"I don't want to leave you," said Horatio. "This is our watch of the night."

"You would stand with me before any mortal foe," said Hamlet. "No one doubts your courage or your loyalty. Nor would you abandon your post. But this is a spirit, and no man has any strength against it. As Prince I order you to go, then, and leave me to hear his message."

It took no more words, but several minutes yet for Horatio to get Bernardo onto his feet and Marcellus with him, and shepherd them down from the battlements.

"Why have you come here, Father?" asked Hamlet.

The lips did not move, and yet it spoke. "Avenge me," he said.

More than the sight of the ghost itself, more than the way its words shook his body, the idea that his father had been murdered struck him hard and deep. For he knew at once that there was only one man who might have done it—the man who now wore the crown in Father's place.

The brother whom Father had mistreated from childhood; the brother who had won the respect of the barons; the brother that all were glad to follow, now that Fortinbras of Norway was threatening war.

The uncle Hamlet loved more than he ever loved his father.

"So you came with no message to benefit the kingdom?" asked Hamlet.

Rage came to his father's face then, and he loomed closer. And yet the closer he came, the more transparent he was to Hamlet's eyes, so he could barely see his father's spirit.

The words, though, rung more harshly with the ghost almost on top of him. "Murder and usurpation, treason and adultery," said the ghost. "I live now in hell. Will you have all Denmark join me there? Avenge me, and purify this kingdom."

"Who killed you, Father?"

"You know already," said the ghost. It backed away.

"How was it done?" asked Hamlet.

"Do you doubt me?"

"Will I kill my uncle on the word of one witness?" asked Hamlet.

"No one but the murderer saw the crime!"

"How will it benefit Denmark for me to kill my uncle now, with Fortinbras preparing his long ships against us?"

"I speak of blood and horror in your own family, and you answer me with fleets and armies."

"What duty do I owe to you?" asked Hamlet.

"Then you consent to my death, and God will damn you as a patricide."

"Why should I listen now, who never heard your voice when you were still alive?"

"I was a better father to you than you know," said the ghost.

Hamlet said nothing, trying to think how his father could have been worse.

"I never laid a hand on you," the ghost said.

"Not your hand, not your heart, barely your eyes if you could keep from seeing me."

"My beautiful son," said the ghost.

"Too late," said Hamlet.

"My sweet, pure-hearted, golden-haired, lovely, strong, and clever son. How often I stood at the window and watched you practice with the sword, the grace of God upon you, the sun shining in your hair. You were the only joy in my life."

Hamlet gasped and sank to his knees. To hear these words now . . .

"The only good gift your mother gave me. My only hope for the future. All lost. All stolen from me just when I was ready to take you into my confidence and set you on the throne beside me."

Is this what Uncle Claudius stole from me? The hope of having, at last, my father's love? "Why did you wait?" whispered Hamlet. "Why did you keep me at such a distance?"

"I would have coddled you. Spoiled you. I needed you to be a man of firm resolve. Strong, cold-blooded as a King must be, and yet I knew I injured you. Even that was a gift to my people: Out of your anguish would come your compassion. A just and merciful judge you would have been, but now you are supplanted, as I was supplanted."

"I'm a scholar now."

"You are the healer of the kingdom's wounds," said the ghost.

"When we have the victory over Fortinbras," said Hamlet.

"There will be no victory," said the ghost. "Not with Denmark led by a murderer and adulterer."

"My mother was hasty to marry your brother," said Hamlet, "but you were dead, and it was not adultery."

"Better my death would have been, if I had left a faithful widow behind me."

"Do you say my mother sinned with him while you were still alive, Father?"

"I knew it in my heart for many years," said the ghost. "Our bed turned cold when you were still a baby. I was content to think we had this one perfect son, and no other to rival him. But your mother is young. She means to bear more sons. She means to kill me again as my brother slew me first, for he killed my body, but she will kill all my seed. You are doomed, if you do not strike first."

"To avenge a crime I might strike," said Hamlet. "But not to win a throne. I'll take holy orders and go abroad."

"Why do you think that you were born?" demanded the ghost. "To whimper in some monastery? To scratch on parchment all your life? No! To sit on the throne and wear the crown and rule this kingdom after me! Avenge me!"

"There was no mark on your body."

"I lay asleep in the garden," said the ghost. "He crept near enough to pour a savage poison into my ear. It burned through into my brain so quickly that I was dead before I could rise up. The heart stopped in my chest so quickly that I never bled. If any other had approached me, I would have woken up, but his footstep had been part of my life since he was born, and in my sleep I felt no fear of him. This is why treason is of all crimes the most detested by heaven. It is an act made possible by love and trust. Nature shudders when such deeds are done. Didn't you feel the earth shake, even there in Heidelberg?"

"I felt nothing," said Hamlet.

"And feel nothing even now," said the ghost contemptuously.

"I feel too much."

"If you love me, avenge me."

"How could I love you? What did you ever give me to love?"

"I gave you life. What more does a father need to give? You were born with the duty of reverence to me. Nothing I did or didn't do absolves you of that duty."

"And you had no duty to me?"

"I fulfilled my duty to you, better than you know."

The second time he'd made that claim. "Tell me now," said Hamlet, "and then it *won't* be better than I know."

"Are you my true son?" asked the ghost. "Your deeds will show."

"I will serve justice," said Hamlet.

"Then you will serve me, for my cause is just."

"I never saw a murderous nature in my Uncle Claudius."

"Do you argue with a spirit bound in hell? Stay your hand, then. I will walk the earth in agony until my murder is avenged and justice served, but what is that to you? Young as you are, you're content to let the earth fill up with suffering souls, so long as you're not inconvenienced."

"Why should I hurry you on to eternal torment?"

"The torment is here upon the earth," said the ghost. "The torment is knowing that I was murdered, and no one lives who will avenge me. Must I choose another to be my son? Must I lay this charge on one of your Companions? Then they are my sons in truth."

"I am your son!" cried Hamlet.

"Then swear to me that you will do what sons do: Avenge me!"

"I swear it," said Hamlet.

"And will you keep your word?"

"I swear by God. I swear in the name of Christ. May my own heart be torn out if I do not serve justice in this matter."

"Do it, and we will not meet again until you die."

"You will be at rest soon enough, then, Father," said Hamlet.

But even before he finished the sentence, the ghost was gone. Hamlet looked only at the stones of the battlement.

I have sworn to kill my father's murderer. To do justice. But how can I be sure that justice would be served by killing Claudius? He is my mother's husband now, which should be a cause of mercy, unless he and she were adulterers together before my father's death. And I always loved him better than my own father—should I kill him now, for causing a death I did not grieve for?

Yes, if he killed my father. But that's the question, isn't it? As the ghost said, Only the murderer was witness to the deed. Not my father—he was asleep. Are ghosts so quickly made, that they can see, in the moment of the body's dying, how it died, and at whose hand?

He called me beautiful. He watched me from the window as I practiced with my sword. He wanted me to have his throne.

Or does he only know that these are the words to make me serve him as his slave? Am I his puppet, killing where he wants murder done? He says he's already tied to hell. What more can he suffer, then, for the sin of lying to me? What if he only wants to bring down his brother?

What kind of man *was* my father? For that's the kind of man he must be now. Souls don't change their nature, merely because the body's set aside. If he had a lying nature then, he'll lie now, too. If he was spiteful then, he'll claim vengeance where none is owed him.

This much is sure: The spirits of the righteous do not walk the earth. They are caught up into heaven, and look no more upon this poor land of shadows, having beheld the light that can be seen only by the pure in heart. My father is here because he was a wicked man. Now he is an angry spirit, and mine are the hands that he has chosen to act out his rage.

And yet by justice and ancient law, my hands *do* belong to him, until his murder be avenged.

Horatio and the others were waiting at the bottom of the stair.

"Go up," said Hamlet. "Resume your watch. He'll never come again, or if he does, it's just to speak to me, and all you need to do is fetch me here at once. But swear to me now that you won't speak of this to anyone."

"I swore as much before you asked," said Bernardo. "Do you think I want my friends to think I'm a superstitious fool? But I swear again, a solemn oath."

"I swear it, too," said Marcellus. "No man will know of any spirits walking here, tonight or any other night."

"And you, Horatio?" said Hamlet.

"Do you need any more oath," he said, "than my vow of loyalty and obedience from when we both were lads? Then you have my oath all over again. No one will learn from me of anything you tell me to keep to myself."

"You have always been worthy of my trust," said Hamlet. "I know you still are. So you, Marcellus, Bernardo, is it still your watch?"

"Till dawn," said Marcellus.

"Then go up and keep watch. Fortinbras might come at any time."

"We will, sir," said Marcellus.

At once they jogged up the stairs, leaving Hamlet and Horatio by themselves.

"What did he want to say?" asked Horatio.

"Good-bye," said Hamlet.

"Where are you going?"

"He wanted to tell his son good-bye," said Hamlet. "I'm not going anywhere."

Horatio laughed nervously.

"What passed between my father and me is for us alone," said Hamlet. "For him to say, and for me to remember."

"I'll never ask again, my Prince," said Horatio.

"Even if I choose not to tell," said Hamlet, "I'll never be offended by the asking."

"Then I'll ask this: Was he murdered? Did he ask you to avenge him?"

"Do *you* believe that someone murdered him?" asked Hamlet.

"It would take a fool not to wonder," said Horatio. "Too many people stood to benefit from his death. It might have been some spy from Fortinbras. It might have been an agent of some baron."

"But there was no mark on the body," said Hamlet.

Horatio laughed. "I'm only a soldier," he said. "But I always thought assassins must know ways to kill a man that leave no marks upon the body."

"I want to hear more of your suspicions, Horatio," said Hamlet. "Who you think did the deed, and how."

"You've already heard it all, my Prince," said Horatio. "I only wondered if your father's death might have been unnatural. But I couldn't bring myself to suspect those who benefitted most, since one is King, and the other is the mother of my dearest friend."

"You think this is a benefit for her, then?"

"Isn't a younger husband always better for a woman?"

"Faithful love of your husband, that's what's better," said Hamlet. "And I'll kill any man who says my mother wronged my father before he died."

"No one says she did," said Horatio. "But it's hard for some to believe she would have wed so quickly if she hadn't already felt some swelling of affection for your uncle."

"Then I hope such people keep their opinions to themselves, so my sword can stay unstained with such unworthy blood."

Horatio put a hand on Hamlet's shoulder. "I don't believe any story that would have your mother *or* your uncle doing wrong by your father. I believe them both to be honorable. And their quick marriage was, I think, to ensure your place. Doesn't your uncle mean to adopt you as his heir?"

"I haven't spoken to him alone since I got home," said Hamlet. "He seems shy to speak to me."

"For fear you believe the rumors, I'd bet," said Horatio.

"No one has anything to fear of me," said Hamlet. "And yet they all walk around me as carefully as if I were a skittish horse, ready to kick at the first shadow."

"What *did* the ghost say to you? I heard you say, 'I swear.'"

"Then you were listening closer than a loyal friend should have."

"You shouted it, Hamlet. How could I help but hear the words and wonder what great oath you had taken with a ghost?"

"An oath of filial duty," said Hamlet. "Beyond that I'm sworn not to say, and I'd count it as a kindness if you *didn't* ask, after all. Now walk with me to the garden where my father died. I want to see the place."

"Garden?" asked Horatio.

"He told me he lay sleeping in the garden."

"I didn't know that," said Horatio. "I thought they found him in his bed."

"He said the garden," said Hamlet.

"Then let's go look at it."

It was a private garden, walled off from the rest of the grounds of the castle. From the outside, it looked cold and stony; once Hamlet passed through the doorway, though, he could see why Father had come to the place, had considered it a refuge. The walls were not visible, completely hidden behind greenery. The stones were covered with ivy, and the ivy was hidden behind shrubbery, much of it evergreen. A few stately shade trees offered respite from a summer sun; tall firs blocked the northwest, shielding from the blasts of winter; and yet the garden was large enough for flowerbeds to flourish in full sunlight.

It was among the flowers that two stone benches were arranged so that two might sit on each bench, across from each other in earnest conversation; or one might lie down on a single bench. A tall man, like Father, could not lie on his back without his legs dangling; but he could curl up on his side, his knees bent, his head pillowed on one arm, and nap in the sunlight on a day in spring.

And someone could creep up behind him and pour cold poison into his ear, first to chill his skin and then to burn its way into his brain.

Did he waken at the cold touch of the poison? Waken, and try to rise? What if the killer held him down? Covered his mouth until the poison had done its work? Hamlet tried to picture what the murderer had seen. He must have been fearful of being discovered. He must have planned what to do or say if Father was awake. He must have had a legitimate errand. Yet it could not have been a decision of the moment—the murderer had to be hoping the King would be asleep, and brought the poison in the expectation of using it.

Hamlet turned and looked upward toward the battlements of the castle itself. It loomed to the northeast of the garden, where it would never cast shade.

But between the castle and the garden a row of pines had been planted. All year they would thickly block any view of what took place in the garden, except at the northwest and southeast corners. The garden was a place for privacy. Once inside these walls, a man could do what he wanted without fear of being seen, unless he was careless.

"What are you looking at?" asked Horatio.

"There's no view of this place from the battlements."

"He didn't come here for company," said Horatio.

"And yet he *had* company," said Hamlet.

"Once too often, I suppose, if this is where it was done."

"If it was done," said Hamlet.

"Do you doubt his word?"

"I haven't told you what his words were," said Hamlet. "Nor shall I. So I can hardly tell you my doubts, or if I have any."

"Then you have no need of me here," said Horatio.

"More need than you know," said Hamlet. "Because you knew him."

"Who?"

"My father. Who else?"

"I feared that you thought I knew his murderer."

"If you did, you would have told it," said Hamlet. "You knew my father, as I could not."

"If anyone knew him," said Horatio.

"Everyone knew him better than I did," said Hamlet. "Why would a man come to a garden to sleep on a hard bench, when he has a dozen soft beds he could sleep in, if he chose?"

"A King is a warrior. Perhaps he hardened himself for war."

"The way a monk punishes himself, to get ready for the fires of hell?"

"I thought they did it to avoid those fires," said Horatio, chuckling.

"It depends on the monk," said Hamlet.

"I think it likely," said Horatio, "that your father slept in the garden when he wearied himself with working here."

"Working?"

Horatio looked embarrassed. "Working here," he said. "Gardening."

"My father? Gardening?"

"He pruned and planted here. It was spring. My guess is that he lay down in the warm sun after planting those flowers that are already blooming now."

"My father, with his own hands?"

"He kept a pair of shears, a hook, a knife, a saw, and several spades. I thought you knew. This garden was only worked by him, except for carrying away the winterfallen twigs and dead plants. What had died was not for him, but what was alive, that he loved and cared for."

It struck Hamlet with new bitterness. He had more love for plants than for his son.

"This wasn't a secret, surely," said Hamlet.

"Everybody knew. It was how he stilled his mind. After councils, after judgment, he'd come out here. No one disturbed him."

"Yet no one told me," said Hamlet.

"Perhaps," said Horatio, "it did not occur to anyone that you might not know."

"Then someone would have said in passing, Oh, Prince Hamlet, when your father comes in from the garden, or Oh, Prince Hamlet, have you seen the fine work your father has done with that old hedge?"

Horatio looked away.

"Everyone knew that I was not to be spoken to about my father."

"It seemed to cause you pain," said Horatio. "No one wanted to hurt you."

Hamlet sighed. "I wish I were back in Heidelberg."

"You've spoken to your father now," said Horatio. "He came to talk to you, even after death. Hell could not stop him."

"Nor heaven," said Hamlet.

"I imagine God *could* have stopped him, but chose not to."

"A spirit comes to me," said Hamlet. "Does that mean it has God's consent to come? Are its words therefore the words that God intends for me to hear?"

"Did the spirit of Samuel come to Saul through the witch of Endor by God's consent?" asked Horatio. "Or does hell send its angels to further the cause of evil in the world?"

"So you've studied the Old Testament," said Hamlet. "And philosophy."

"I was tutored by a priest who loved to terrify us with ghost stories."

"Spirits of the dead with messages for the living. Do they ever come with good news?"

"Did this one?" asked Horatio.

"No," said Hamlet.

"I wonder," said Horatio, "on which of these benches your father lay when he was slain."

"I wonder," said Hamlet, "who was the slayer?"

Horatio looked up at him with heavy-lidded eyes. "*Do* you wonder, my Prince?" he asked.

Hamlet shook his head. "No," he said. "My father told me who it was."

"And you don't believe him?"

Hamlet didn't know how to answer. He believed—of course he did. And yet, despite his oath, he felt a terrible dread at the thought of acting on that belief. "I believe and don't believe," he said.

"Why? Do spirits lie?" asked Horatio.

"Spirits from hell might deceive," said Hamlet.

"Then spirits from hell will *say* they came from heaven," said Horatio, "so how can we know which ones to trust?"

Father did not pretend to come from heaven. "Spirits from hell might sometimes lie and sometimes not."

"What will you do, if you become certain?" asked Horatio.

Hamlet looked away at the flowers. Bees alit and rose again from the blooms, yellowed with pollen. How quickly the flowers must have bloomed, if Father only recently planted them. If you asked me, from the evidence of my eyes, how long these plants had been in place, I would have said a month at least. Yet I believe Horatio because he's a truthful friend, and because he has no reason to lie. Was that faith? Knowledge? Probability? Mere desire to believe?

"Certainty is a hard thing to achieve," said Horatio.

"If to know a thing is to feel certain of it, then most people achieve it all the time, especially about the things they think about least. But if to know a thing is to be certain *and* be right, and *know* that you're right, then that's another matter."

"Certainty is about how you feel," said Horatio, nodding. "But being right is about what truly happened in the past. What you feel means nothing."

"That's a good thing," said Hamlet, "since I feel no certainty."

"And yet you swore an oath."

"I can be certain of what *I* will do, even when I'm not certain of what others have done."

Horatio smiled grimly. "But can you be certain of the rightness of the act?"

"Some acts are always right," said Hamlet. "And some are always wrong."

"You learned more in Heidelberg than I thought was possible," said Horatio. "If they told you which was which."

"I'm not sure where I learned it, except that I know it's true."

"In other words," said Horatio, "you *feel* certain that it's true."

"Something has to be sure in this world," said Hamlet.

"Why?" asked Horatio.

"Because if we could never be sure, we'd never be able to act. No man would ever marry a woman, no soldier would ever fight for his King and his country, no tailor would ever cut his cloth, and no man of trade would ever trust the value of the money he was paid."

"As long as we're talking philosophy," said Horatio, "then just because people have to believe in something enough to act on it doesn't mean that they're right, not ever."

"Then we live like animals in this world, not knowing right from wrong."

"Muddling through," said Horatio.

"And God judges us for *that?*" asked Hamlet.

"Let God judge as he judges. Let *us* remember that we don't have God's knowledge."

"Amen," said Hamlet.

Horatio rose to his feet, agitated. He moved away from Hamlet, then came back. "I don't believe you believe what you said, my Prince. That some things are always right or always wrong."

"I do believe it," said Hamlet.

"What if one of Herod's men, hearing the command to slay all the innocent babes of Bethlehem, had decided instead that he would strike down the giver of that command rather than obey it? It's always wrong to kill innocent babies, isn't it? Even if your King commands? And it's always wrong to kill the King, isn't it? Even if he means to do something evil?"

"Are you sure you didn't sneak off to some university yourself?" said Hamlet.

"You don't need a professor to wrestle with the hard questions," said Horatio. "And you wrote me letters."

"Not about this."

"You told me what the great questions were. And your father let me read his books."

"Father read books?" asked Hamlet.

"The testaments only," said Horatio. "But I have Latin enough for that."

"So all your philosophy comes from scripture."

"You didn't answer me about Herod's good soldier."

"Why must he choose between murderous treason and murderous obedience? Why not run away?"

"Like Jonah?" said Horatio. "If you know that King Herod's vile order will be obeyed by someone, and you run away when you could have prevented the slaughter of the innocents, then how are you any less guilty than the ones who wield the swords?"

"But if you kill Herod, you'll die. They'll torture you to death as a traitor."

"There are worse things than death, my Prince."

"Are there?" asked Hamlet.

"Of all men, you should be most certain of that," said Horatio.

"Why?"

"Other men fear death because they don't know if the soul survives. But you've spoken to your father. You know the ghost was real because I and two other witnesses also saw him. Why would *you* fear death now? Or me? Knowing that life continues."

"It's the continuation of life," said Hamlet, "that might be the most fearful thing. Maybe death would hold less fear if we knew it *was* the end of all."

"Is this what you pondered all those times you went to the graveyard alone?" asked Horatio.

"What this garden was to my father," said Hamlet, "the cemetery was to me."

"A place to nap?"

"A place to listen to my own soul."

"My Prince," said Horatio, "you know that whatever you decide is right, I will be your true friend and loyal servant."

"You're not my Companion any more, my friend, and your duty is to your King, not to a prince who will never ascend a throne."

"You don't know you'll have no throne," said Horatio.

"I would refuse it if it was offered me. That's how I know. But it will never be offered."

"Then your resolve will die untested," said Horatio.

Hamlet laughed. "My whole life is one long round of preparing for a test I'll never face. To be King, but now I'll be no King.

To be a good son to my father, but while he lived he never gave me the chance to try. As a child I dreamed of greatness. I practiced for war. I practiced for government. At the university I even practiced for holy orders. But I'll never govern, never go to war, and never take orders, either."

"You might," said Horatio.

Hamlet did not say, they rarely ordain a man during the few hours between murdering a King and being drawn and quartered for the crime. He merely looked away.

"God doesn't judge us by whether men think we're great or not," said Horatio.

"No, his standard is even harsher. It's easier to be great than to be good, and easier to be good than to do right."

"There's a distinction there too fine for me to see."

"A good man does what he believes is right. He might be wrong about what's right, but because he intended to do good, he's a good man."

Horatio nodded gravely. "Whatever you swore to your father, Hamlet, don't be afraid to do it."

Am I afraid? "I'm not."

"Don't hesitate," said Horatio.

Trust a man who never trusted me. Strike down an uncle I have always loved, for the sake of a father who never loved me. Why would I hesitate to do that? "I won't," said Hamlet.

"And yet you stay your hand."

If I strode into King Claudius's court with drawn sword, I would be dead before I got near enough to strike. "God has not yet put the opportunity before me," said Hamlet. Some secrets are too heavy for a man to want to burden his friends.

Besides, Horatio had already made his point, with that story of Herod: If he knew that Hamlet meant to kill the King, Horatio would have no choice but to kill Hamlet first. You do wrong to prevent a greater wrong; thus wrong becomes right.

Did Marcellus and Bernardo keep their word, and tell no one of the ghost? Hamlet couldn't help but wonder; wherever he went in the castle, on the grounds, in the stables, anywhere at all, he could feel all eyes upon him. They may not know the charge that his father had placed upon him by oath, but they seemed to have heard that a ghost had visited him; they looked at him as one with a fey upon him, a mixture of dread and pity.

And if word had spread of a ghost, then surely they had guessed whose ghost it was; and if they knew who it was, then it took no scholar to guess what the ghost had sworn Hamlet to do.

If King Claudius was, indeed, a bloody-handed fratricide, then what would stop him from killing the nephew as easily as he had killed the brother? Then what would come of Hamlet's vengeance, if he himself were dead?

If they look at me as a fey spirit, then let them see what they look for. Let it not be vengeance they see in my eyes, but madness. Let them see an orphan who grieves too much, not a son who calculates revenge. Let me stay alive until I have a chance to get Uncle Claudius alone.

He began his masquerade when by chance he heard laughter up a stair. He thought he knew the voice, and when he bounded up the long flight of steps he soon learned that he was right. It was Ophelia, laughing with one of her maids. Ophelia, who was Laertes's sister and Polonius's daughter, had been only thirteen when Hamlet left for Heidelberg. Even then, he had felt her eyes upon him and had known that, quite apart from any wish of her father that his daughter be allied with the royal house, she herself had thoughts of, if not feelings for, the crown prince of Denmark.

Not any more, thought Hamlet. No crown prince now, and so no dynastic alliance and no yearnings.

. But he could make use of her all the same.

He paused for only a moment in the corridor, to half undress himself, as if he had been in the midst of putting on his clothes, but got distracted. Carrying his shoes and doublet, he strode into her room. At once the maid fell silent in the midst of some tale, and Ophelia leapt to her feet, her sewing dropping from its place on her lap to the floor. "Your Highness," she said. "What brings you to my room?"

Hamlet fixed his gaze on her and never let it wander as he walked closer and took her by the hand. She smiled tentatively. He did not smile back; he only stared into her eyes.

"Will Your Highness take refreshment?" she asked.

He said nothing.

"How can I serve you, my Lord?" she asked.

Hamlet reached his hand to his forehead and bent over her, almost as if to kiss her. He could hear her breathing more heavily, and saw her close her eyes. For a moment he thought that he had frightened her, that she was about to faint. But then he realized that her lips were parted. She was waiting for a kiss.

That was not what he had intended. She was not supposed to want him now. She had been a sweet girl, when he knew her years ago; she was a pretty woman now, and though he had no particular desire for any of her tribe, he knew it was wrong to trifle with her. She thought he meant something by coming here.

And yet her misunderstanding would do as well as any other purpose. Let them think he was pining for love of her.

But he could not kiss her. That would be a kind of promise, and knowing that soon enough he would be a murderer and traitor, doomed to die, how could he encourage her to love him?

He sighed at his own foolishness. Then sighed again, this

time as if in pain. He screwed up his face as if in agony, then fled the room and ran pell-mell along the corridor and down the stairs.

After that he shunned everyone's company for the rest of the day, refusing to let the servants open his door. Whenever he heard footsteps approach, he groaned as piteously as he could. When someone called through the door, "Your Highness, are you well? Are you ill? May I bring you something?" he answered with a muttered "Leave me alone" or "Why are you cursing me like this?" or "What harm have I done you?"

Meanwhile, he lay on his bed and read *The Confessions of St. Augustine*. Here was a miracle and also madness, that the words of a man who lived in Africa before the heathen Arabs stole the land from Christ could speak so powerfully to him now; a man of the south, teaching a man of the north; a priest full of power comforting a prince full of death.

He knew enough of court and courtiers that his absence from dinner would be noticed by everyone; that Ophelia would have gone to her father and her father to the King and Queen; that they would be guessing about what was going on in Hamlet's mind. If they knew about the ghost, they might think the spirit had driven him mad. If they suspected him of harboring ill will because his uncle had the throne *and* his mother, then they would see him, not as a resolved and dangerous enemy, but as a pouting boy. If they thought he yearned for the love of Ophelia, then perhaps they would be contemplating some kind of wedding. If they thought he was transported by grief for his father's death, they would be thinking of amusements to distract him.

Just so they didn't think to take away his sword, or keep him from the presence of the King. He could seem mad, but not so mad that they would find a need to shut him up behind a locked door, where only the ghost of his father could visit him, to condemn him for having failed so thoroughly.

If they saw him sane, they would be wary of him; if too mad, they would be afraid for another reason; he must hew to the middle ground, so they would leave him to wander about as he wanted, ignoring him or coddling him.

And so it was the next day. It began when he found Rosencrantz and Guildenstern outside his door, waiting on two chairs that hadn't been there earlier. They pretended they had only happened to be there, but were delighted to see him.

It was a simple matter to call them by the wrong names, and then speak of Father as if he were still alive. "Did you mean to join my father on the hunt today?" he asked. "My father goes a-hunting—don't you hear the horns?"

Rosencrantz shied away at this, but Guildenstern only smiled. "The pleasures of the hunt are not done, just because your father is no longer here to enjoy them."

"I hunt like a fisherman," said Hamlet. "I sit in my boat, pull up the net, and see what has come to me."

"Then you'll catch no deer, not in any woods I know of," said Rosencrantz.

"I'll have the eight-pronged buck," Hamlet retorted. "I'll have him through and through with a syllogism—old stags aren't much for logic, it stuns them and they stand there waiting for the dogs."

"What are you talking about, Your Highness?" asked Guildenstern.

"Into your ears, but above your head."

"Let us go with you," said Rosencrantz. "Where are you going?"

"Only a few steps," said Hamlet. "All the way to hell. No, stay here, there's not room for you yet, I have to sweep out the room where Judas used to dwell. Stay. I don't need you with me right now."

They didn't know what to make of his reference to Judas Iscariot's room in hell. They would wonder if he was accusing them of disloyalty. Which, of course, he was, since they had obviously been brought to court to try to bring him to his senses.

It was almost fun, and certainly exhilarating, to feign a bit of madness and watch them all hop. Hamlet hadn't realized before how much of his life had been devoted to doing what they all expected of him, acting out the role of prince. Now he had no role, and was improvising a new one that made no one comfortable—except himself. Madness kept them all at a greater distance than his rank had ever done.

Hamlet came into the court with a book in front of his nose; he held it too close to read the letters. Everyone fell silent—Uncle Claudius was hearing someone's petition. Mother rose to her feet as if to go to Hamlet, but Polonius waved her off with a small gesture and took Hamlet by his arm, leading him back out of the room.

"What are you reading?" Polonius asked.

"Words, words, words," said Hamlet.

"And what's the subject?"

"Lesser than the King, but still not nothing."

It took Polonius a moment to realize he had answered another meaning of "subject." "I mean what do you read about?"

"All in a line, back and forth," said Hamlet. "I go from left to right with my mind full, and then must drop it there and head back empty-headed to the left side again, and take up another load to carry forward. It's a most tedious job, and when I'm done, there are all the letters where I found them, unchanged despite my having carried them all into my head."

Polonius laughed, as if he hoped that Hamlet was joking. "As fine a description of reading as I ever heard. But what does the book *say?*"

Hamlet looked at him with pity. "It says that old men grow confused, and ask young men for wisdom. You could listen at this book all day and night and hear nothing, but if you threw it at my head, I'd learn much and you'd hear more."

Polonius looked at him quizzically. "I think you mean something by this."

"More than you think, and less than I know," said Hamlet. "You have a daughter, sir?"

"I have." Polonius's eyes lit up at that. It made Hamlet sad that even a madman would be regarded as an interesting match for his daughter, even if he could only sire mad children on her.

"Be sure to keep her out of the sun," said Hamlet. "Bright sunlight can breed maggots in a dead dog; who knows what it can do to daughters, sir."

"I thank you for your counsel," said Polonius.

"I'm sure it's worth as much as the counsel you gave my mother, sir," said Hamlet. He turned to leave.

"What do you mean by that?" demanded Polonius, following him.

"By what?"

"The counsel I gave your mother. What counsel was that?"

"How should I know what counsel you gave her? I only hoped that mine was as valuable."

"But when?" asked Polonius.

"When you were counseling with her. Must I tell you *all* your business?" Then Hamlet took off at a run.

He felt giddy as he fairly flew down the corridors, watching servants and courtiers shy out of his way. It was a foolish kind of bravery, though, to lie so much that he could then tell the truth and pretend it was also a lie. But dangerous also, for Polonius kept trying to make sense of what he was saying, and there was sense to be made of it, if he only kept at it.

Thus passed the next few days, with Hamlet making forays out of his room, stirring up trouble while seeming innocent.

What he could not determine to his own satisfaction was what he was actually trying to do. Was he really trying to protect himself from suspicion? Or to keep Claudius from fearing him as a rival? Was he biding his time, as he told himself, until he could get his uncle alone and kill him without interference? Or was he doing all this mummery to fill the time and make more and more delay because he hadn't the heart or stomach for murder, after all?

More likely he was doing this, he realized, to protect himself. I will do foul treason, but men will not call me a traitor if they think me mad. I will still be slain, but not seen with horror. It will be pity that fills men's hearts when they see my grave or hear my name. Is that what this sham is for, to make my name a sad one instead of an evil one, after I'm dead?

What does it matter? Why should I care?

I'm a coward, that's what my madness is about, to delay the day of action, and then delay some more.

And yet he could not let go of it. They brought Ophelia to him, and now he saw that she was indeed sincere; she spoke to him of how she had thought of him often when he was in Heidelberg, and waited eagerly for his return, and missed him even more than she missed her brother, who was off in France. It broke his heart, and he regretted his foolish play on the first day of his mad charade. He should not have gone to her.

He could correct it now, though. He could, in the midst of his madness, make sure she understood that she shouldn't look for anything from him. Not love—there was no room for love in a heart that he was trying to steel for murder.

He could have loved her, though, he saw that. If he had come home from Heidelberg without his father dead, without his mother married to his uncle, without a ghost demanding vengeance, then he might have seen this girl and wanted her. He might have courted her with poetry, with pleasantries, with flowers and little gifts, with kisses that were freely given, but pretended to be stolen.

He might have married her, and lain with her, and fathered sons and daughters, not just one as his mother had, but many, and watched Ophelia grow fat with babies and then sat with her to see the children playing in the garden or the fields. They would have taken them out to sea, plying the coasts of Denmark in the long ships that once struck terror throughout the world, but now were meant for wealthy families on pleasure cruises.

It made him angry, to think of what had been taken from him. His father had stolen his childhood, and now was stealing his future as well.

What right do you have, Father? Stay dead. Don't walk the earth swearing your son to loyalty you never showed him when you were alive.

I refuse to kill for you. Does that make me an oathbreaker? To slay a King must be at least as great a sin as breaking an oath. But what about killing a King who is also a murderer himself? Then again, what about breaking an oath to a man who never acted the father to me, yet now expects me to be a true son to him? Where is the justice in any of this? Why does my duty demand that I do the worst thing, or be condemned? To save myself from condemnation, will I damn myself? Am I merely choosing between two different rooms in hell?

He was summoned on an afternoon when court was finished, and brought without his sword before King Claudius. The soldier—there was only one, a man he did not know—made no special point of coming without a sword. He found Hamlet reading, and urged him to come quickly, so there was no time to arm himself or even dress properly for an audience.

Mother was there, and smiling at him, so it would not be something harsh. Polonius beamed at him also—prospective father-in-law to a madman—but King Claudius looked serious.

"I knew you all your life as my nephew and my prince," said Claudius. "Now, married to your mother, I hope I may also view you as my son. Certainly you are my heir."

"The barons name the King, Your Majesty," said Hamlet. "But I am grateful for your trust in me."

"Here is how far my trust goes. The Orkney Islands have forgotten their duty, or else some terrible storm has destroyed their crop or sunk their fleet. I must send a man I trust, and one whose presence will prove to them my great concern. That man is you, if you will go in my name."

"Like any other Dane, Your Majesty, I will serve you where you ask, honored to be remembered."

"And so that you will not have to do this work unsupported, take Rosencrantz and Guildenstern with you."

So he was *not* trusted. "I'll be grateful for their company," he said.

"Then that's done," said King Claudius.

"Will you have me go at once? Or may I stay until my father's body is laid inside the tomb?"

Uncle Claudius frowned. "Your father's body lies in state; we have not dishonored his memory."

"And yet his burial is delayed. Who knows what unrest this might cause his spirit?" asked Hamlet.

Mother reached over and touched her new husband on the arm.

He did not look at her, but he nodded. "We wait for Polonius's son, Laertes. You know that your father and he were close."

"Closer than he ever was with me," said Hamlet. But it was I, not Laertes, that he charged to avenge him. "What will you do, then, Your Majesty? Send away the old King's son before the funeral, and yet await the son of your chancellor?"

Claudius looked stung. "I meant no such insult to my brother's honor or to his son. Of course you can wait to leave for the Orkneys until Laertes comes."

"He's looked for every day," said Mother.

"So I also will look for him." Hamlet knelt a second time before King Claudius. "Your Majesty, may I ask to see my father's body?"

"No," said Claudius.

"May a son not bid good-bye to his father?"

"We keep the corpse on ice," said Claudius. "The days grow warm. We'll keep the icehouse tightly closed until the funeral day."

"The nights are still cool enough. I'll go to him at night."

"And take a lantern's heat into the room? No."

"A single candle," said Hamlet. "Not even that, if you prefer. I can find my father in the dark. I'm not afraid of him." Though of course he was.

"Is this another part of your madness?" asked Claudius sharply.

"What madness, Your Majesty?" asked Hamlet.

"The way you spoke to my daughter," said Polonius. "And to Rosencrantz and Guildenstern. And to me!"

"If I said something I should not have said, then I'm ashamed, and heartily beg your pardon."

"The icehouse will not be opened," said Claudius.

"Then open the ancestral tomb and let me in," said Hamlet, "so I can see where my father's body will lie."

"Hamlet," said Mother, "that's morbid."

"No, Mother," said Hamlet. "It's lunatic. I mean to play at juggling with my ancestors' skulls."

She looked as if he had slapped her.

"Do my mother and my uncle mean to keep me from anything that has to do with my father? I last saw him alive four years ago. I look around this court, searching for some sign of grief for him, and I see none."

"There was much grieving before you came home," said King Claudius.

"I came home quickly, and yet the grief was so far done with that I found my widowed mother already married, and a new King on a throne whose previous occupant was still unburied."

"We did as the barons wanted," said Claudius. "Fortinbras is coming."

"I do not argue with the barons' choice," said Hamlet. "I was not ready to lead Denmark's ships and soldiers, and they must be led. You know you have my love and loyalty in all things, Your Majesty. But I am also a son, not only a loyal prince, and I owe a duty to my father. Will you shame me by forbidding me to have any access to the poor remnant his spirit left behind him when he died, or even to the stone house where it will dessicate?"

"The tomb will be unlocked for you," said King Claudius.

"Pardon me, but I would rather have the key, so I can come and go as I wish."

"Then have it," said Claudius. He waved a hand at Polonius. "See to it."

"I thank Your Majesty with all my heart," said Hamlet.

"Please," said Mother. "Come and see me today. You've been home for more than a week, and you haven't come to see me."

"I was not invited until now," said Hamlet. "Of course I'll come. Give me an hour in my father's tomb."

*   *   *

It took more than a little argument to get Rosencrantz and Guildenstern to let him visit the tomb alone. It was obvious they had been assigned to stay with him whenever he ventured out of the walls of the castle. But they had been his Companions, and they knew that when he entered the graveyard he must be alone.

The tomb's lock was ancient but well oiled; it opened readily. The door also opened silently. The house of the royal dead was well tended.

Not so their bodies. The moist sea air could not be kept out, however tightly sealed the tomb might be. The place was damp inside, and the bodies that still had flesh on them sagged onto their stone beds, their fine robes sliding into ragged patches. It looked as if this were some great oven, and the corpses all were melting like butter. The freshest body here was Father's mother, whom Hamlet had known when he was little; she was a nightmare of decay, if Hamlet had not already seen the spirit of her son. Corpses that had no power of speech, that could not lay dire oaths upon him, could not frighten him. What children imagined, terrifying themselves in the dark of night, Hamlet had seen with his own eyes, and lived.

There was no place prepared for Father. No new bed of stone. Did they plan to toss his body on the floor?

Or did they have some plan to bury him at sea, on a flaming ship, like the Viking Kings of an earlier time?

It was not about keeping the body cold. It was not about waiting for Laertes. King Claudius did not want his brother's body seen.

There must be some mark on the corpse, after all. Some proof that he was murdered. There could be no other explanation for this. He would never lie here in the tomb. Whatever Claudius and Mother might have planned, it did not include putting Father's body on public display.

Hamlet came forth out of the tomb and locked it behind him. The dead were safe enough from his intrusions now; would that he had been kept safe from theirs.

The graveyard itself was familiar ground. What was not familiar was Horatio, perched like a gargoyle atop a simple headstone belonging to some loyal family servant.

"They sent you?" asked Hamlet.

"You're a lunatic, and must be closely watched," said Horatio.

"Better you than Rosencrantz and Guildenstern. They're not the friends that I remember."

"Things changed in the four years you were gone. When the Companions were dissolved at your parting, they decided not to dissolve themselves. Living four years together on Guildenstern's estates has made them as fusty and peculiar as an old married couple. I pity the woman who tries to wed her way into that house."

"They're not my friends at all, I think," said Hamlet.

"They serve the King."

"Don't we all."

A new-dug grave lay open only a few steps away from the stone where Horatio perched. "Who's to be buried here?"

"A cousin of the royal house," said Horatio. "The body will arrive in a day or two. They've already had the funeral; it's just a matter of laying it in the ground."

"I wonder if it's someone that I knew."

"It's your family's graveyard," said Horatio. "You knew them all."

Only then did Hamlet look at the name on the stone where Horatio sat. "Yorick," he read aloud. "Yorick's dead!"

"You've been here this long and didn't notice he was gone?"

"But no one wrote to me," said Hamlet. "I assumed he was away. Or living privately, pensioned off. But dead!"

"Not long after you left," said Horatio. "Suddenly, in his sleep."

"He wasn't old enough to die."

"How old is *that?*" asked Horatio. "I think there are tiny graves enough to prove that death knows how to find us all, however old we might not be."

Hamlet laughed bitterly at that, ashamed of the tears that streamed down his cheeks. "I know you're right, Horatio. But Yorick—it's a terrible thing to say, but his death strikes me harder than my father's." And with that, he turned away and sank down to his knees, crossing himself in respect for the old fool. "He spoke the words I might have heard from my father, if I'd *had* a father," he said.

"Oh, you had father enough, I think," said Horatio.

"One father too many, I sometimes thought," said Hamlet, "and yet one too few. I hated you, every one of you, when he took you with him, spent hours with you, and yet never had time for me."

"It was never by our choice," said Horatio.

"I know it," said Hamlet. "But I've always been a lunatic."

"Playing among the graves? No doubt of it—we all knew it. But what's your game now? Sometimes mad and sometimes lucid."

"It's a lunar lunacy. It rises and sets, waxes and wanes."

"And brings the tides along, no doubt."

"Don't blame the tides on me."

"I blame you for nothing," said Horatio. "I'm only sorry for how things turned out for you. Who would have guessed that your father's death would not mean your accession to the throne? Your mother dotes on you—I would have thought she'd rather die than marry the uncle who took your rightful place."

Hamlet knew he should be angry, to hear Horatio criticizing Mother. But it was the simple truth, and no man should be punished for saying it aloud. At least in private. To a friend.

"Everyone finds his own way in the world," said Hamlet. "And does what seems right. Or at least most useful. Or most desirable."

"Most desirable," said Horatio. "They only do what's right if they desire what's right. Or most useful if they desire to be useful. Always it comes down to desire."

"Then all men are equal, the good and the bad," said Hamlet, "since they do no more than follow their desires."

"But wouldn't you rather live in a country governed by those who desire to do good?" said Horatio.

"And haven't you always preferred to be friends with women who desire to do bad?" said Hamlet.

"I want them to do bad, but do it well."

"Where I try to do good, but do it badly."

"Tell me the burden the ghost laid upon you, Hamlet. Let me counsel with you. How can you be bound by an oath to the dead? Think about it—the most solemn of oaths—holy orders, matrimony—those sacraments dissolve at death. All sacraments do, all oaths, death's the end of them. So how can you even call an oath binding when you make it with one who is already dead? It was dissolved before you swore."

Hamlet shook his head. "I've chopped logic with better hypocrites than you," he said. "Your oath as a Companion is dissolved, and yet you still honor it."

Horatio laughed, but Hamlet had hit him square, and he made no more argument.

"I have to see my mother," said Hamlet.

"And I have to look for the mother of my children," said Horatio.

"Do you have someone in mind?"

"As always, I ask for volunteers, and then choose the best."

"Princes aren't so free."

"Princes are as free as they want to be," said Horatio. "Virtue—which *you* desire—is what keeps you chaste."

"I wish that women were as good company as my Companions were," said Hamlet. "Women seem to want so much. The ones I've met—as a man, that is—they're all enticement, but when you let yourself be lured a little closer, you find out that they have all their plans laid out, and want only a fly to wander into the web. The fly is never consulted about how the strands of the web should go, or where it should be placed."

"There'd be a world of hungry spiders if that were how it worked."

"And far too many flies," said Hamlet. "The analogy breaks down. The parable is false. Aesop's animals are not at risk from any fable of mine." He arose from the ground. "I sat upon old Yorick's grave, and felt the grass of it in my hands. That's more funeral than I'll ever get for my father."

"I thought they waited for Laertes."

"They wait forever. I'll never see my father's body."

"You've seen his spirit," said Horatio. "Isn't that more? You've had the walnut; why would you need the shell?"

"I couldn't weep over the ghost—it wouldn't stop talking long enough."

"Will you weep over the body, then?"

"Yes."

"But you often said that you hardly knew him."

"That's what I'll weep for." He threw his arms around Horatio and held him close. "I'll weep for the boys we were, and for the man I'll never be."

Horatio followed him as he walked away. "What's that supposed to mean? The man you'll never be?"

Hamlet had no intention of telling him how soon he expected to die. "I think I would have been a better man if I'd had a father," he said.

"And what if I say not? Did knowing your father make better men of *us?*"

"It might have," said Hamlet. "But you had your own fathers, all of you—I had none."

"You had Yorick. You had your uncle Claudius."

"Horatio, all I meant was, I'll never know what I would have become, if my father had been a father to me. Now leave me, my friend, unless you intend to greet my mother with me."

Horatio laughed then, and let him go.

On his way to his mother's chamber, Hamlet passed the chapel. He heard a voice inside—a priest at prayer, no doubt. And yet he knew the voice, and stopped, and stepped inside.

It was King Claudius who knelt at the altar before a statue of bloody-handed Jesus. Hamlet could not hear his words.

Here he is, alone, with no one to see or hear. I have no sword, but I have my dagger. This is the moment I've been waiting for.

But his hand would not move toward the hilt.

If I kill him at his prayers, his shriven soul will go to heaven, he thought.

And mine will not.

Nothing I do will let my soul go to heaven. Let him live and I'm damned. Kill him and I'm damned.

I can't do it secretly. The way he killed my father—I won't do that. When I slay him it will be in the open for all to see, for everyone to hear me tell them why. He killed my father with stealth, so he could steal all that my father had; I want nothing that he has, and so I do not have to hide my deed.

That's my reason for staying my hand.

And the fact that it is not my desire to kill him, or any man.

And rank fear.

Cowards strike from hiding; but I strike not at all. What does that make me? More fearful than a coward.

He moved silently out of the chapel and moved on, threading his way to his mother's room.

Mother was not alone. The door to her chamber opened as Hamlet approached, and there stood Laertes.

Hamlet cried out his name, joyfully, and took a step toward him. But Laertes stepped back, and his manner was cold.

"I hear that you've been trifling with my sister," he said.

"I haven't," said Hamlet.

"She needs no lunatics," said Laertes.

"Then she'll have none," said Hamlet. "Laertes, is this our greeting after four years?"

Laertes bowed. "My Prince," he said. "You look well."

"And you do *not*," said Hamlet, trying to jolly him into a smile. "You're thin. Don't you eat? You look as if you've sharpened your face."

"I live by the blade now," said Laertes. "Haven't you heard? I'm quite the swordsman now."

"What, have you strewn the fields of France with the bodies of duelists?"

"I've watered them with their blood, though none have died," said Laertes. "So be warned. I'll brook no insult to my sister."

"Are you threatening me?"

"I'm telling you of the consequences. Good day, sir." Laertes pushed past him and was gone.

Hamlet looked after him for a moment, then turned and strode into his mother's chamber. "Why is Laertes so angry with me?"

"He's had a hard four years," said Mother. "But he's home now, and we'll get him right, soon enough."

"If he doesn't kill me first," said Hamlet. "What was my offense?"

"That mad display you put on for Ophelia," said Mother. "You have to tell me now, my son. Was that some attempt to show her how much you love her? Or something else? She's a sweet girl, and worthy of a prince, if you want her to wife; but too good to be trifled with, or teased, or mocked—there are girls in the kitchen who will play those games with you, if that's the sort of man you are."

"You know it's not."

"I know that I don't understand a thing you do or say since you returned."

"Which brings us to a balance, my lady mother."

"We've hardly seen each other," she said.

"I've seen enough of you to know what you've become."

"Have you forgotten the respect you owe me?"

"No more than you've forgotten it yourself," said Hamlet. "Did you have them put my father's corpse on ice so you'd be sure it was cold before you got into my uncle's bed?"

She flung out her hand to slap him, but he caught her by the wrist. "You won't strike me for saying the truth," he said.

"You don't know what's true," she said.

"I know my father hated me," said Hamlet, "and yet I seem to be the only one in Denmark who ever loved him."

"Don't judge what you don't understand."

"If there's something I don't understand, is that my fault? No one has told me anything my whole life. Did you hate my father? Is that why he hated me?"

"Your father never hated you," said Mother.

"Then why didn't he ever take me with him? I had no part of him."

"Because I forbade it," she said.

"You—why?"

"For good enough reason," she said. "And that's the end of it."

"That's not even the beginning," said Hamlet. "That was nothing—do you think you'll make me love my father better by making me hate you?"

"Your father's dead. It came in good time for Denmark—and for me."

Hamlet seized her by the shoulders and dragged her from her chair. "So you knew! You knew that Uncle Claudius murdered him!"

"Let go of me!"

He threw her down onto the ground. "You don't even deny it."

"Of course I deny it! Your uncle never raised a hand against your father!"

"Who did it, then? You? Poison is a woman's tool—I should have known."

"What are you talking about? No one murdered your father!"

"I know a lie when I hear one. All you're doing is convincing me that you're part of the conspiracy."

He drew his dagger. If Claudius was still in the chapel, he would kill him now, prayer or no prayer. After what he'd said to his mother, there would be no secret about who did it.

But when she saw the dagger, she mistook the prey he intended to kill with it.

"Help! No! Someone help me! He means to kill me!"

And then a second voice, behind a tapestry, crying out. "Stop! Help! To the Queen!"

Hamlet whirled to the curtain, saw the hands trying to brush it aside, saw the feet moving blindly forward, and in a moment he had his dagger through the cloth and into the man's chest, whoever it was.

For a moment the man hung heavily upon the blade, supported by the thickness of the tapestry.

The fabric was thick, and held; the blade was strong, and did not break. But the hangings of the tapestry were slender and too few, and they gave way. The tapestry came down, and the man pitched forward. Hamlet pulled his blade away, which turned the body from him; when it fell, he lay upon his back. It was Polonius.

"You killed him!" cried Mother.

"He was hiding in your chamber," said Hamlet. "What was he doing here? Concealed? I thought he was a murderer."

Two soldiers appeared in the doorway. One of them was Marcellus. "What happened here?"

"I saw a man was hiding behind the tapestry. Mother called for help. I slew him through the cloth. I didn't see his face until he fell."

He did not turn to look at Mother. Everything he said was true; it was up to her if she wanted to correct what he said and tell them that it was her son she feared, and not the hidden observer.

For that was what he surely was. Polonius must have been meeting with Mother and Laertes, and when Laertes left and spoke to Hamlet in the hallway, Polonius hid himself—with Mother's consent—so he could hear what was said.

She had consented to let this man spy on him. Their first

private meeting since he came home, and she had asked Polonius to stay and spy. What did she think that Hamlet would do?

I killed a man. A good and decent man, who served his King and Queen well.

No, *she* killed him. By ordering him to spy on her son, she killed him. By calling out for help that she didn't need, she killed him. Did she think he would *ever* raise his hand against her? Apparently she did. And now Polonius was dead because of it.

"Tell King Claudius," said Hamlet. "I will bear whatever penalty he sets for me. It was my hand killed him. A mistake— but the mistake was his, hiding behind a curtain in my mother's chamber. How could he imagine this would end?"

Hamlet turned to his mother, who still sat on the floor, her face stricken. "I know what you are; what you never understood was what *I* am."

"You know nothing," she said.

"If that's true," he said, "whose fault is that?"

He left the room, still holding his dagger. If he had passed King Claudius on the way, he would have put the blade in him on the spot. But Claudius was protected, for the moment, and Hamlet found his way out into the graveyard again, still holding the bloody dagger. Horatio was gone. He saw no one. He plunged the dagger into the grass and dirt of Yorick's grave, and washed it with the damp of the grass and wiped it on his own doublet.

He could hear the tumult in the castle. A woman screaming. Men shouting. But no soldiers came for him. Mother must be standing with the story of its being an accident. She was honest enough to know that the fault was hers, and would not accuse him of murder.

Too little honesty, too late. Poor Polonius. An old fool, dead for doing what Kings and Queens commanded.

And then a strange, exhilarating thought:

I've killed a man. It was easy. As natural as breathing. Now there's nothing stopping me from doing what must be done.

It was as if he heard his father's voice, that deep spectral sound that had shivered him to the soul that night on the battlements: Good, my son. Well done, my son. Hurry up and finish it, my son.

It came more quickly than he thought it would. By torchlight, in the great hall.

Hamlet was in the garden where his father had died. Horatio brought him his sword. "Laertes is looking for you," he said.

"I don't have time for Laertes. He must know I didn't mean to kill his father," said Hamlet.

"It's not his father," said Horatio. "It's his sister."

"Ophelia? I didn't touch her."

"She killed herself. Walked out into the sea, dressed in her heaviest gown. A funeral gown. Two soldiers went in after her, and a boat was launched, but when they brought her body back, she was dead."

"And for that he wants to kill me?"

"He blames you. Between killing her father and trifling with her affections—"

"I don't want to fight Laertes."

"Hamlet—he's been practicing for four years in order to fight you."

"What? We were friends! Until this afternoon I thought we still were!"

"It's not what you think. He meant to kill your father. But he believed that in order to kill him, he'd have to fight you first. He knew that nobody could beat you with a sword—but he was determined to try. Now your father is dead, but his rage isn't. If you leave, just stay away for a few days—take ship for the Orkneys, Hamlet, I beg you to do it. Laertes will be back in his right mind before you return."

"But I won't be," said Hamlet. "My father is unburied."

"He's also dead," said Horatio. "You aren't, and so far neither is Laertes."

"And neither is Claudius."

"Exactly. Leave bad enough alone, Hamlet."

But Hamlet had already strapped on his sword and was striding toward the castle.

"O God!" cried Horatio. "Stop him! Stop this all!"

The torches flickered and danced. Several courtiers were already there, as were the King and Queen. Laertes was pacing up and down in front of them, shouting, demanding justice, vengeance, satisfaction. "My sister's dead body is still drenched in seawater and I'll have the heart's blood of the rogue who drowned her!"

"No one drowned her but herself," said King Claudius.

It galled Hamlet to hear his uncle plead for him. "Enough talk!" he cried from the far end of the chamber. "Do you want my heart, Laertes? You had it all our lives; it still belongs to you. Take it now, if you can!"

Their swords drawn, they fairly flew at each other across the room, blades flashing. Everyone moved out of the way, behind the arches, trusting in the stone pillars that held up the ceiling to keep them safe.

How many times had they fought, as boys? Laertes had learned much since then. There was no playfulness about it now. Laertes's every blow and thrust was intended to kill or maim; he moved in a fury, taking no pause for breath.

Yet Hamlet saw very quickly that Laertes could not win unless he let him. It was not a lack of skill—Laertes was as good a swordsman as Hamlet had ever seen. Nor was it Laertes's rage: He fought with control, with a furious calm that made no mistakes.

He simply wasn't quick enough. All his practice and study with the sword in France had made him an interesting opponent, but not one that could defeat Hamlet, even with his lack of practice. Laertes had new and clever moves that Hamlet had not seen before; but he understood them at once and countered them and that was it.

"Laertes, stop this," Hamlet said. "You aren't good enough. You won't win."

"Then I'll die," said Laertes. "I have nothing left but this. You've taken it all from me."

"I've taken nothing from you. I grieve at your father's death. Your sister's suicide destroys me. I cared for her as much as I could for any woman, and I wished no harm on either of them. Nor do I wish to hurt you."

"Kill me or die," said Laertes.

"The only way I'll die is if you poisoned your blade and some of it spills on me," said Hamlet.

Laertes's answer was a furious onslaught. But he drew no blood. He didn't even nick the clothing Hamlet wore.

Hamlet maneuvered the fight so that his back was to his mother and King Claudius.

"I have only one enemy in this room," said Hamlet, "and it isn't you. It's the man who killed my father, married his widow, and stole the crown."

He could hear people gasping at his words. And Mother cried out, "He didn't! It's a lie! Who told you such a thing!"

Hamlet gave a twist and a spin and Laertes's sword flew up to the ceiling and then clattered back down a dozen yards away. With his opponent disarmed, Hamlet whirled on King Claudius.

"The ghost of my father told me!" cried Hamlet. "How you poured poison in his ear while he lay asleep in the garden! I swore an oath to avenge him, and this day I honor my father's command!"

Uncle Claudius was rising to his feet—to fight? to flee? it mattered not a whit. For Hamlet ran him through the heart and had the sword back out again in time to whirl and face Laertes, who was running at him from behind, his sword again in hand.

There was not time for finesse. With Claudius's blood still hot on the blade, it went through Laertes's heart as well.

"No!" cried Hamlet.

"O God!" cried Horatio. "O God, how could you punish them all for my sin!"

"Your sin?" said Hamlet.

"I killed your father!"

Hamlet stared at him dumbfounded. Horatio, unarmed, tore open his shirt. "Here's my heart! Kill me! I'm the one you vowed to murder to avenge your father! I'm the one who killed him!"

Hamlet staggered back, turned a little, touched his uncle, who lay sprawled across the table while Mother wept over him.

"But Father said—"

"He lied! The old bastard lied!" cried Horatio. "Why didn't you tell me what he said? I would have told you. I thought you knew the truth—I offered to let you kill me right there in the garden! I thought you understood!"

"Offered? But I never—why would *you* kill him?"

"Because he was evil. Because of what he did to us. All of us. The Companions. All the boys but you!"

Behind him, Hamlet heard his mother wail.

"What did he do?" asked Hamlet.

"He had us," said Horatio. "All of us, one by one, over and

over again. Told us how much we owed him. Our duty to the King. How to thank him."

"Thank him?"

"With our bodies! You've never heard of such a thing? You read the Greeks and Romans and you never heard of it?"

"But you never told me."

"He swore he'd kill us if we told."

"All of you?"

"It twisted us. I saw it in the others. Rosencrantz and Guildenstern, they could never look at women. Laertes—he told me, even before he left for France, that his stick was broken and would never grow again. And me—I thought I was all right. I thought . . ."

He broke down and wept.

Mother's voice came from behind him. "When I found what he was doing to the Companions, I almost killed him myself. I caught him fondling you when you were practically a baby, Hamlet. I held a knife at his throat and vowed that I'd have his blood if he ever touched you or was alone with you again. I'd tell the barons and they'd kill him themselves. He took a solemn oath never to touch you and he kept it. I didn't know what he did with the Companions until—until Laertes came to me and told. Then I made him dissolve the Companions and let them all go free. But it was too late."

"Too late," echoed Horatio. "A few months ago, a new page came to the castle. I taught him. He followed me everywhere like a dog. I delighted in his company. And then one day I found myself . . . I had him naked, I was telling him how a boy shows love to his friend and teacher . . . the words your father used, the very words. I was the worst of all of them! I was *like him!* I stopped myself. I told the boy to dress and never come near me again. That I was evil. A monster. And then I went out into the garden to kill your father. There he was, asleep. As if the devil had a right to rest in such a place! I took my dagger and poised it over him. Then with my other hand I clamped his mouth closed, holding his head in place, and then I pushed the dagger down into his ear and through his brain. He twitched, he pissed, he shat, he died. And that's where your mother and Claudius found me. I was working up the courage to put the knife into my own heart. They took it from me, and then your mother washed the blood as best she could and Claudius and I carried the body to the icehouse and wrapped it. Hamlet, it was me."

"He said it was poison in his ear."

"The blade must have felt cold at first, and then it burned going in," said Horatio. "He never turned his face. He never saw."

"But spirits . . . don't they *know?*"

"Maybe he did," said Horatio. "But he wanted Claudius dead because he was the *King* your father never knew how to become. He lied to you! He used you as surely as he used the rest of us!"

"What have I done?" whispered Hamlet.

"Your father's ghost appeared to you?" said Mother.

"He said that Claudius . . ."

"I know the things he'd say," she said. "Oh, the liar. The monster. I should have killed him when I could. Better to have my hands stained with a husband's blood than all the evil that has come from letting him survive!" She fumbled for something in the waistband of her dress. "It was my fault, all of it!" she said. "I should have denounced him to the barons!"

She found what she was looking for—a small phial. Before Hamlet could reach to stop her, she had it open and drank it down.

"I love you, Hamlet," she said. "I tried to protect you. Horatio did only what I should have done. What the law of God demanded." Then the poison struck and she cried out in agony. She threw herself upon the body of King Claudius, cried out his name, and died.

Hamlet turned to face Horatio, who was still standing there, bare-chested, head bowed, waiting for the blade.

"Keep your oath," said Horatio. "Kill the killer of your father."

"If you had told me," said Hamlet. "If I'd known, do you think I'd have shed a drop of blood to avenge him?"

Hamlet knelt beside Laertes. "What my father meant to do to me, he did to you instead, my friend. All my friends. And now how many suffered, and how many died, to protect me from the monster whose blood half-fills my veins?"

Then he staggered to his feet and went to his mother's body, which lay half overspreading Claudius's. "Mother, you did for me what you could; you thought it was enough; and it was. He never touched me. And you, Uncle Claudius, what a good King you were. You should have been King all along. I would to God you had been my father."

Hamlet was still holding the sword, but when he turned again to Horatio, he let it fall. "I forbid you to die," he said to Horatio. "You are the one good man still living. You did justice on a devil. You served me well, and the King, and the kingdom. I command you to live. When Fortinbras comes, hail him King of Denmark. Let the kingdoms be united. Tell him that he has the vengeance he long wanted, and now I charge him to be a good King to Norse and Danes alike."

"Tell him yourself."

"My father deserved to die," said Hamlet. "There was no sin in what you did. But how will the deaths of my mother and my uncle and good Laertes and Polonius and Ophelia be avenged? If only I had let Laertes kill me. But I didn't, and now his blood joins the others."

"You're innocent of any wrong," said Horatio.

"God gave me only one gift—to know how to handle a blade. Too bad it took me this long to learn where the point of it most needed to be put."

Then Hamlet drew his dagger and pushed it, smoothly, unhesitatingly, into his own chest, between the ribs, just beside the breastbone. It found his heart—he felt it as a searing agony. He heard it as a song.

As he fell to his knees, he could hear Horatio weeping. "Live," Hamlet whispered one last time.

"I will," said Horatio. "Ah, Hamlet, I love you!"

Then Hamlet's body slumped onto the floor.

But his spirit did not go where his body went. His spirit arose and looked around the hall. To where Laertes's spirit held his father's and his sister's hands; then they arose into heaven. To where his mother and Claudius, bright spirits both, embraced each other, and also rose into the air, toward the bright light awaiting them.

And finally to the dark shadowy corner where his father's spirit stood, laughing, laughing, laughing. "Welcome to hell, my beautiful son. At last we'll be together as I always longed for us to be."

The Haunted Single Malt

It's always embarrassing to write an introduction to one's own story, so I'll just say that I'm in this collection because Tanith Lee personally invited me to be one of the four, for which thanks, my dear transatlantic friend.

A native of Philadelphia, I began my writing career in the mystery genre, which, however, I never cared for as much as fantasy/science fiction. My fantasy/ghost novels include *A Cold Blue Light* (with Parke Godwin), *Ghosts of Night and Morning*, *Fantastique*, *The Possession of Immanuel Wolf* (with Brother Theodore) and *The Last Christmas of Ebenezer Scrooge*. I have edited many fantasy/ghost anthologies, most of them for the Science Fiction Book Club, and am editor of *H. P. Lovecraft's Magazine of Horror*.

a Spectral Symposium

by Marvin Kaye

– I –

Every first Monday of the month the back room of The Tron is given over to ghost stories, and anyone interested can ask the bartender to point them towards the Jamesians, a loose gaggle of folk, present company included, whose pretentious (I think) aggregate name is not reflective of the ambiguous Henry, and certainly not his brother Bill, but was chosen in honour of Montague Rhodes James and his proposition that benevolent, troubled spirits are but pale shades (sic) not worth reading or, as we see it, telling about. To hold our interest each month, spectres are expected to be baleful, inimical, vengeful, in a word, terrifying, which admittedly is no longer quite so easy to accomplish in this faith-twisted bloodthirsty age.

Now don't form the wrong impression. The Jamesians don't sit around reading supernatural stories, not that we don't like them, as witness the writer we're named after, but we're all much more interested in hearing about those paranormal occurrences that produce what the French call *un frisson,* and Yanks describe as goose-bumps. The experience must always be personal, or at least verifiable by its narrator, and we're very picky about the permissible degrees of separation. If it happened to a near relative or a close friend, it's allowed, but the raconteur who attempts to pass off a tale based on hearsay or urban legend is swiftly interrupted and spurned.

To be fair to those who get it wrong, it's no small condition to satisfy our criteria. Ghost stories are like folk songs: they fall into a handful of thematic patterns, and if you doubt this, read Louis C. Jones's fascinating sociological study, *Things That Go Bump in the Night.* It's not easy to come up with first-hand new tales of what I like to call "cold grue" month after month; as one may expect, there's a deal of fluctuation in membership, and only four Jamesians are really what you could call denizens. There are only so many ghost stories to be told . . . a pity, since our egocentric species never tires of them, for paradoxically, they're the very spirit of life . . .

(Now, that's not to be confused with *uisgebaugh,* the water of life, which any good Scot will tell you means a wee dram of single malt, though in winter, when the North Sea wind clashes with the cutting air that rips down off the Pentlands, I've been known to tolerate a bit o' blended, particularly when poured in equal portion with Crabbie's Green Ginger Wine. There are few mixed drinks you can work with scotch, but blended and Crabbie's are legitimate mates in these parts, probably because Crabbie's is headquartered in our maritime district, Leith; the mix is called Whisky Mac, and it makes a brisk palate-cleanser alongside a comforting platter o' haggis and tatties and neeps. But I've digressed. The thought of a wee dram has that effect. *Slainté!* That's Celtic for "Your health," or if you're a Yank, "Cheers").

So anyway, if you're in town the first Monday of the month, and you would like to sit with us and listen to our stories, you're more than welcome at our table, though do be aware that the management doesn't take kindly to teetotalers, and though the bartender's in the other room, he keeps an eye on us so we won't parch ourselves from too much dry talking.

My name is Wallace Kimble, D. O., retired psychiatrist, and before that I was a surgeon, but carpal tunnel syndrome dictated a change of specialty. I'm a native of Pitlochry, some fifty miles north of here, here being Edinburgh, capital of Scotland, and if you're a Yank, we're talking about a city roughly the size of Hartford. (Connecticut figures in the story I'm going to tell you, which is why it now comes to mind.)

Edinburgh is configured in three strips: to the north, New Town; south lies the Meadows district that rolls down into broad green countryside where stallions race the wind. The middle, oldest section of "Auld Reekie" (Edinburgh's nickname), is Old Town, where you'll find The Tron, not far from the site of the gallows that once stood at the western edge of St. Giles Cathedral a short distance down the Royal Mile. The "Mile," Old Town's main east-west street, begins at the upper part of a volcanic ridge with a castle dominating the skyline, then runs east past St. Giles and City Hall (both of them haunted), and ends at Holyrood Palace, where the queen puts up when she has a mind to visit, not that we give a damn.

The Tron's got two entries. If you come in off the Mile you'll be greeted by a wide-angle view of Edinburgh's kitschiest pub, for that entry point brings you onto an upper shelf with a couple of tables, a dumb waiter and a small service bar. But if you take a few steps to the right, you'll come to a steep flight of wooden steps leading down to the main bar, a space that looks like Aubrey Beardsley designed it either during a fey moment, or while having a monumental hangover. None of the five sofas match, the rickety tables are internationalists made of foreign woods not so much painted as attacked, and somewhere in the midst of this chromatic fantasia there's a ponderous wastebasket (seldom empty) that's fashioned from a rhino's foot (left rear, according to the old bartender Mike, though I never asked him how he knew).

The front room's funky chaos is dominated by a fifty-foot bar that for many years was ruled over by the dourest bartender you'd ever be likely to meet. Mike reminded me of Edward Woodward, the actor who played *Breaker Morant* in the movie. Laconic and contained, but tough. Once someone mentioned Sean Connery and Mike snorted. "Tam he was when he was a bouncer. He come in here, loud and lookin' for trouble, so I give it 'im. I bounced *'im* out on 'is arse."

By which you may conclude Mike had a bit of temper. Fortunately, he and I got along well. He called me Doc, most everybody does, and of course sometimes he'd lay it on about my being a retired shrink, for he'd remind me he didn't hold with "that crap," but still, I was on Mike's good side once he found out that besides medicine, ghost stories and single malt, my expertise includes Laurel and Hardy (I used to be Grand Sheik of the Edinburgh "tent" of The International Laurel and Hardy Society, Sons of the Desert).

"There were two fine, funny gents." Mike would smile, sipping his favourite single malt, Glen Turret. "Arthur Stanley Jefferson, that was Laurel's real name, y' know. More than once he came to play the Old Course at St. Andrews, but then he'd pop down to The Tron for nineteenth hole."

The bar itself was (still is) worthy of its monarch: there's fifty feet of prime *uisgebaugh*, which includes the usual wine, the house ale, export, bitters, and a few imports like Cafferty's and Guinness. Then there's the gins ("if 'y must," Mike would grumble, "stick with Bombay"), there's the vodkas, plus some fine Yankee single barrel bourbons and sour mash, as well as Irish from Eire *and* the northern counties (a topic of debate that occasionally grows feisty). Said potables were Mike's "accommodations" to those without an educated palate, for, as he frequently explained to tourists, "In the heart of Caledonia, for that's what Scotland was once called, single malt whisky is the only serious libation." (Mike conceded blended has its place. I asked him once what place that might be, and he replied, "An accommodation for the impecunious.")

Single malt, it's true, generally costs more than blended, which you may or may not be aware of, but if you don't know the lore and lure of the single malt, I'd best expand upon the theme. By all the dogs and peacocks of Abbottsford, I promise to tell you about the haunted single malt, but the tale hinges on the passion of the aficionado, so bear with me with the patience single malt imbues in one's spirit.

Blended scotch is made from the blending of different "singles"; some brands are quite respectable, with a spectrum of tastes and textures from the softness of a Cutty Sark to the peatier Johnnie Walker in its various chromatic guises. (Don't get me started on the stratospheric cost of Johnnie Walker Blue, a blended with delusions of adequacy.) A decent blended scotch like Ballantine's or Famous Grouse makes a respectable accompaniment to the aforesaid Green Ginger Wine, and when the Tron serves haggis, you may be sure the chef employs a blended to lace the grain, for to use a single malt would be, as Mike once put it, "a crime to any true Scot."

Personally, I drink blended for its effect and single malt for its taste. Some enthusiasts call that an overstatement, but it's *my* overstatement; I stand by it. At any rate, I've only mentioned blended as a point of reference. Single malt is what I ask you to focus upon. Though after you've absorbed my exegesis, if you still find yourself perplexed, hie thee to a pub and study the subject first-hand.

A single malt is the distillation of one and only one Highland, Speyside, or Islay whisky, or wherever it's made, provided it's Scotland. (We knew better than to joke with Mike about Suntory "scotch" from Japan; the only laugh we would have fetched would have been in appreciation of the arabesque our prat described as it hit the sidewalk.)

True single malts are matured and bottled at one distillery apiece; each uses local spring water, or a similar source, and peat that's dug up close by gently smokes the grain. There are literally hundreds of "singles" in varying ages of maturation. Every one of them owes its character to the water and peat of their district, plus the distiller's carefully-guarded methods: shape, size, and constituency of the kilns; even the prior use of the barrels the liquor ages in has its impact. Some brands mature eight or ten years, some are defined in terms of decades, but no matter how, where and when the charactery, most are worth sampling for their subtle and sometimes bold variations in the nose, foretaste, body, texture, depth, character, and aftertaste. Wine may have its place, and beer is liquid bread, but without a wee dram of fruity Bruichladdich, stern Cragganmore, gentle Dalwhinnie, amiable Edradour, idyllic Glenkinchie, friendly Glenmorangie, robust Lagavulin, chocolate-hued Loch Dhu, mystical Oban, explosive Talisker, or rough and ready Laphroaig, and the list could go on for pages, there is neither respite, nepenthe, nor balm in Gilead. (Look it up; it's in Poe.)

I only recollect one single malt Mike would not stock, Blair Athol, and that was a pity, for it's a decent scotch made a block away from where I used to live in Pitlochry. No use pointing out to Mike that he didn't consider politics reason for not stocking Bushmills. "Ireland doesn't count," he growled. "They never had a king. *We* did, Doc, and that's why I won't buy Blair Athol, it's part of the Thatcher combine!" Margaret was long gone as the

Brits' P. M., but Mike had a long memory. Quite long, it turned out.

– II –

Now let's come back to the ghost-loving Jamesians.

We're not an organized club with officers, minutes and dues. We never had many regular members, and what began as a chance discussion between affable strangers The Tron parlayed into tradition. Four of us you could call denizens. Besides me, there's wee Harry Glamis, a cheerfully loquacious fellow who always wears some combination of purple and gold garments, for those are the colours he sported when he was quite the successful jockey. He's retired now and lives with his missus in New Town near the Royal Scots Club, his home away from home.

In contrast, Ian Napier plays Mutt to Harry's Jeff, and if you don't get the reference, you're much younger than me. Ian's a lanky chap who wears muted greys and blacks. You might mistake him for a mortician, and he's got the voice to match, but he's a damn fine shoemaker. (He prefers cobbler.)

The last of the denizens is Lily Watson, a spirit medium with more things to tell each month than the rest of us combined, though one thing we never heard from her, nor would we ask, was whether she had a significant other in her life. We all hoped not, but none ever spoke up, for though all three of us had an eye for Lily, none of us had a voice.

It would never come up, anyway, at our meetings, for spooks are the sole bond shared, and in the intervening weeks, the four denizens lead totally different lives. The only one I ever meet outside The Tron is Ian at his shop on Candlemaker Row. Mike, of course, I'd see much more frequently from the corner stool in the front room, which I've bought a hundred times over (the stool, not the room).

On quiet Mondays, Mike himself used to listen in to the stories we told, which was a good thing, for if one of us had a doozy to share, its shivery resolution generally fetched the company a round on the house.

Other folk joined the Jamesians from time to time, some I knew by name, some I gave a nod to, but probably couldn't introduce them to you by name even if you bought me a round (not that I mightn't improvise under those conditions). But the irregulars we most welcome are tourists. We get our fair share of them, thanks to Mercat Tours, whose black-cloaked guides, usually attractive college coeds, shepherd visitors at night (of course) through the streets and closes of Old Town to visit haunted houses and sites. These "ghost walks" begin at Mercat Cross on the eastern edge of St. Giles and finish at The Tron, where wee drams help these itinerant customers combat the chills they feel from the weather, plus what they've heard during the ghost walk. With the bartender's help, some wanderers make their way to the back room, where they're welcomed and rightly so; their presence affords the denizens a chance to trot out their personal best, and if we're lucky, the visitors return the favour and provide us with a nightmare or two when we toddle off to bed.

– III –

The first Monday of a freezing February night. Snow piled up in the streets to mid-calf.

The Tron was nearly deserted. Only the back room showed signs of life. There was a young, good-looking couple enjoying cold platters Mike prepared for them (he'd sent the kitchen staff home early). A stranger in black sat at another table nursing a pint of ale. His heavy overcoat dripped snow on the floor. Mike stood in the archway keeping an eye on both rooms. Every so often, I noticed him glare at the man in black.

Harry, Ian, and I sat at our usual table, a big round oak affair with decades of graffiti scratched on and in its surface. We were loath to begin; Lily hadn't yet arrived.

"She'll show," wee Harry declared. "She never misses a meeting."

Ian shook his head. "I doubt she'll slog all the way over from Cramond. The wind has teeth."

"Hate to start without 'er," Harry mourned. "I've got precious little to say this month. What about you, Ian?"

"Oh, I've got a bit of a thing to tell. Happened to Hamish, my younger brother, not that he's a spring chicken. He come to visit, asked the loan of my bicycle—"

"Let's give her a little longer," Harry said. "Doc, anything t' contribute?"

"Well, my poltergeist still does inconvenient things, but its nature is to nettle me; there's nothing fearsome about it."

Harry waggled a finger. "The meeting's not started, give us the details."

"The latest mischief is it hid the remote for my new DVD player. I was just going to watch *The Innocents!*"

Being good friends, they both made appropriate sounds of condolence without insulting my intelligence by wondering whether I'd merely misplaced the damn thing.

"How long's it been gone?"

"Three days, Ian, but I found it tonight, just before coming over."

"Where was it?"

"Under the bed. I was pulling on my overshoes when I heard this *clunk;* I knew what it was soon as I heard it, and there it was in a spot I'd looked at least fifty times. The remote was still rocking, as if it had been dropped from a height."

"Probably was," said Ian with a sage nod.

The man in black suddenly chose to address me. "Doesn't your DVD have control knobs in front?" Spoken mildly enough, but there was no mistaking the irony. For some moments, I'd been reading negative vibes from him.

Mike grunted. He seemed to resent the newcomer's intrusion, but, deciding courtesy was always the best policy, I signaled for a refill, then turned to the speaker and replied with a physician's studied affability.

"*Mea culpa.* I recollect black-and-white TV with rabbit ears antennas. I never minded hopping up and down to get rid of ghosts—the double images, I mean, as if you could see the actors' auras. But I'm old now. I prefer to sit in one spot and aim my remote. Is that a problem?"

"Not at all," he said, rising, "but now that you've mentioned ghosts, you *are* the Jamesians, aren't you?"

"Indeed we are." My heart wasn't in it, but I stood up and shook his hand. "I'm Wally Kimble; everybody here calls me Doc. Would you like to join us tonight?"

"If nobody minds."

I did, but the Jamesians always welcome visitors, and that goes double on a night so inhospitable to tourists. Perhaps this morosely irritating fellow had a bit of spectral darkness to share. Morose he surely was, from his Hamlet-black shirt and trousers to his sharp nose, indrawn cheeks, pinched lips; imagine Basil Rathbone at a funeral and you'll picture him fairly well.

Harry waved him to a seat and uttered his invariable welcome. "The more the scarier."

I sighed. "We allow him to say that once a meeting."

"Once only," Ian added.

I performed the introductions. "Harry Glamis, and this is Ian Napier."

"Where's Lily?" the man asked, and pretended not to notice our reaction.

Just then, Mike reentered with a snifter of Glenkinchie, which he set down before me with more force than necessary. "She said she'd be late, you should start without her."

The most Mike normally said at our meetings was, "Another round, gents?" Something was, as The Bard might put it, amiss. Anyway, I figured Lily called The Tron and left her message.

I turned to the newcomer. "You know our distaff denizen, then?"

"Quite." With a curt nod, he took his sopping coat from where he'd hung it and started to drape it over a chair at our table.

"Leave it!" Mike barked. "You made enough of a mess already."

Mike was often prickly, but confrontation with a paying customer wasn't typical. It was cold enough outside, but the weather in The Tron suddenly turned Antarctic.

The man in black arched an eyebrow and said crisply, "Your friends may be used to your lip, Mike, but *I'm not.*"

No one budged. The young couple stopped talking. After a long electric silence, Mike apologized sourly and left the room.

A first for everything, I thought. *Good thing he sent the kitchen staff home; they won't be hit by the aftershock.*

Ian tackled the awkward pause with a question. "So what do we call you? Mr. Anonymous?"

With his black coat repositioned where he wanted, the man sat down across from me and said, "You can call me Mack."

"To Mack," said Harry, raising his glass.

I hoped Mike hadn't heard. To be politic, I added, "And Mike."

"Mack and Mike." Harry giggled. "Sounds like a vaudeville team."

"Slainté!" Intoned by all.

Small talk seemed in order, so I told Mack I was amazed he'd braved such weather to join us.

"It's a right night, Doc, for blood and ghosts." The way he said it brought the blizzard closer. Though he sat at our table, the congeniality of the Jamesians was lost on him. A dictionary could have used his picture as the definition of "brooding."

The Jamesians have never been guided by *Robert's Rules of Order (Revised;* yes, I *am* compulsive). Still, our meetings always begin with a brief recap of the club's *raison d'etre,* with stress placed upon the nature of the permissible stories. Each month, we'd flip a coin to see who'd deliver the introduction. This time Harry won. You'd think that with only one new person present, he might have abridged his remarks, but after Harry retired from the track, he was hired as a sportscaster and became involved in an incestuous affair with his own voice.

Harry's monologue met with inattention from Mack, though his remarks did capture the attention of the couple at the other table. They asked to be included in our group. We were glad to have them, so Ian pushed closer to Harry, I moved nearer to Mack, and we all called Mike for another round. (Don't try to keep track of the evening's drinks; you'd need a calculator. Only two gents could have kept up with us, both writers: a fellow named Godwin and a newspaperman, Steve Knickmeyer, who could not only drink me and Godwin under the table, you could also throw in Faulkner, Hemingway, Dylan Thomas and Bacchus Himself.)

The young pair were backpack tourists; each hung traveling gear over their chairs. I judged them in their early thirties. He was stocky, with wide brown eyes, prematurely white wavy hair, and a lopsided grin. He introduced himself as Geoffrey deLannoy, a Brit, but though she spoke like a Yank, her origins were local, I was sure of it; tall redheads like her are all about town: astonishingly fiery hair in curls halfway down to her sacrum; eyes blue as the bright waters of Leith, pale complexion, ruby lips.

Judging from the gold band on her left hand, the pair were a matched set, yet her name was Lawrence, not deLannoy: Melinda Lawrence.

At the table where they'd been sitting, there was a black cloth guitar case canted against the wall. She set it near as she sat beside her . . . husband? Significant Other? (Ah, for the days when the "eff-word" was more offensive to young ears than "commitment.")

Harry indicated the guitar case. "Traveling musicians?"

"*Un bel di.* I'd practice more, but Jeff complains I already spend more time with my instrument than his." A laugh both musical and earthy.

"Mellie, behave," her mate chided, though there was nothing stern in his tone or the way he looked at her. "Gents, I'd say I can't take her anywhere, but you can just imagine what she'd come up with if I did." He grabbed her face between his palms and gave her a kiss I didn't think Brits knew how to manage.

"Geoffrey, we're in public!" And she blushed.

I will never understand modern women. Or, come to think of it, any of them. (Always excepting my late wife, peace to her heart and spirit; she graced the seasons and the years.)

— IV —

"Shall we talk about death? And what comes after." Coming from the funereal Mack, the sentiment seemed all too appropriate.

"You make an interesting presupposition," I said.

Harry groaned. "Here we go again."

"It's suitable," Ian said. "Since Lily's still absent, let Doc have his say."

"Well—not without a refill." Which met no resistance. Mike came and went, curiously subdued.

"I assume," said Mack, "that by 'presupposition,' you're questioning whether ghosts are the natural byproduct of human mortality."

"Indeed—" Which is as far as I got.

"There's more than one theory," Mack usurped. "The traditional one is that ghosts are souls who have not yet passed on. Which assumes there is somewhere we pass on to."

"Hope it's not like Hoboken," Melinda remarked. Her mate shushed her.

"Another theory," he continued, "is that haunted houses soak up *psi* energy, or *chi*, if you like, the energy implanted in walls and other building materials by strong emotions experienced in the haunted spot." He not only looked like Basil Rathbone, he sounded like him. "So instead of an integrated soul surviving death, what we feel, hear, or see is just the spiritual residue of a suicide, murder, or other traumatic experience."

"Integrated souls," Ian interrupted. "Curious you mention that. Have you heard of a chap by name of Drew Beltane?"

"I have. You know him?"

"*Knew* him," Ian corrected. "My cousin from Ardrossan. Died a few years back investigating a haunted house in Pennsylvania."

"Aubrey House," Mack said. "A place you'd have to be mad to set foot in. I read about it in a book that outlines your cousin's Theory of Fragmented Survival . . . the soul dies out a bit at a time, so ghosts may just be fragments of the people they once were."

"Usually the worst fragments," said Ian.

"What's your take, Doc?" Mack asked.

My turn at last. "Since you're kind enough to ask, as far as the Afterlife is concerned, I'm a little to the left of atheism. Still, when I was a doctor I tended many a deathbed, and felt that coldness—what can I call it?—imagine a vacuum sucking energy from your spine. When you feel that enough, you come to regard it as real. Defining it, though, that's another matter.

"So now you know where *we* stand, but the only thing we've learned about you is your first name, or maybe it's a nickname. Where do you come from, what do you do, and how do *you* feel about ghosts?" I tried to be smooth about it, but something about him set my teeth on edge.

The bleak equivalent of a smile. "I've neglected my manners. Mack *is* a nickname; my real handle is Hugh and I come from Connecticut. I'm a farmer, not the kind with a duck, duck here, a goose, goose there. I grow barley."

"In *Connecticut?*"

"That's right. And as for my opinion of ghosts, I believe we're like the blind men and the elephant. Remember? Each of them felt a different portion of the beast and thought he had the entire idea of what an elephant is. They were all wrong . . . but they were also all partly correct. Life's so complicated, shouldn't we expect the same thing of death?"

Ian had his fill. "All right, lads, that's quite enough philosophy for one meetin'. Give ear to what happened to my brother Hamish, and *then*, if y' must, talk to me about ghosts."

The monthly meeting of the Jamesians was officially under way.

"For twenty-nine years," Ian began, "Hamish lived in Maxton, North Carolina, where there's a Reverend who claims he was born eight years after his mother was buried, but that's a story for another evening. I'm going to tell you what happened last fall when my brother borrowed my bike.

"When my sister-in-law died of a massive coronary—fat and fierce she was, little wonder—Hamish retired and moved to Glasgow. He was always going on about how much he missed Scotland, and how little of it he saw when he lived here. So he borrowed my bike to do a Grand Tour from the Borders to John O' Groats."

"Powerful lot of peddling," Harry said. "Would've taxed me at the peak of my career. Your brother must be in good shape."

That made Ian laugh (an uncommon phenomenon). "That tub o' lard?! Surprised they didn't make 'im buy two seats when he flew to Heathrow."

"Why Heathrow? Why didn't he go direct to Glasgow?"

"Because, Doc, Heathrow cost him less. He come the rest o' way by train. Hamish is so tight, his ass squeaks. Begging your pardon, Miss Lawrence."

She chuckled. "No need to apologize."

"Anyhow," Ian continued, "a bike, no matter how strenuous, saved him car rental, which meant he'd have more to feed his face. That's one item he never denies himself. And so last autumn, he set out on the road—roads. The thing began late one day when he was a goodly push from the inn he was aiming for in Clachaig."

The Brit interrupted. "Mellie and I were in that district last week."

"Then you know it's a place to be wary of."

– V –

Sunset's high relief offset the ruined edifice. Nine miles still to Clachaig. Hamish decided to rest. He dismounted with a weary wheeze. Cycling was a younger fellow's sport.

According to the leaflet he took from a holder on a post outside the arched entry, the place was called Dunharrow Kirk, *but a pile of stone this big weighs in heavier than a kirk, a right cathedral it is.* Hamish propped Ian's bike against the post. *Nobody in nine miles likely to bother it.*

He studied the leaflet and learned most of the building dated back to 1137 AD and was in ruins ("Never venture past the rope barrier. The ceiling is eroded and pieces still break off."). But one end of the structure had been shored up and turned by locals into a modest museum.

"Suggested donation, one pound, to defray the cost of sweeping and dusting on Saturdays, and other maintenance. Donations are honour system; deposit coins (paper money blows away) in the receptacle secured to this post."

Well, it's Monday, nobody'll be the wiser, he reflected, entering. *I've only got paper pounds; I can toss one away or drop it in the can, either way it's sacrificed to the wind. No, thank you.*

The light was swiftly dying. The museum, a great stone rectangle on the building's eastern face, was dim, and it was difficult to read the inscriptions on the white cards affixed to the exhibits. He was glad he'd recently bought a new battery for his flashlight, but when he snapped it on and played the beam about the room, most of what he saw wouldn't have been worth the pound: artifacts, souvenirs, and ephemera commemorating persons and events of interest to none but locals, though Hamish rather doubted that, as well.

There were three things worth noting, though. One was a fair-sized slab of stone that, according to the card, had been dug up by a nearby amateur archeologist. "Part of an antique circlet still viewable at the dig (directions obtainable at Clachaig Inn), this monolith is at least as old as the stones of Stonehenge." *And you can walk right up and touch it . . . not cordoned off, like the Brits do.*

The museum's second unusual feature was an uneven crack in the wall running from floor to ceiling. A twilight breeze sifted through it. It was a leper's crawl. Souls otherwise shunned by the worshippers were permitted to come within earshot of Sunday services, and through its narrow access were able to take Communion, Dunharrow's origins being Roman Catholic.

The leper's crawl made his skin crawl. Hamish stepped away backwards from it, and turned to look at the museum's largest and most ominous artifact, a black stone coffin that stood upright, towering over him nearly nine feet. Within rested (*I hope!*) the remains of the man depicted on its exterior, a helmet on his head, a sword gripped between both gloved fists.

"William, ninth Baron of Percuit Hall, a loyalist supporting the king of the same Christian name," the leaflet stated. "Known as the Bloody Baron, he kept tally of all those he slaughtered, and when he succumbed to the plague, he so regretted that he'd slain one less than a thousand, his confessor feared the Baron would summon up one last burst of strength and throttle him so he could go out with an even number."

Hamish aimed his flashlight at the face on the coffin's lid. Stark it was, and grim, its moustache stern parentheses about the cruel set of the mouth. *No wonder the confessor was scared!*

There were three windows set high in the stone walls, one on the east side, one a little to the left of the leper's crawl on the north, and one southward. Each was thin and narrow; none of them let in much light. As he switched off his flash-beam, it occurred to him that there were better places to hang about at sunset than a deserted museum dominated by the Bloody Baron Percuit.

Hamish stepped through the western archway, and there was the great cathedral cavern. Its stained-glass admonishments were sinister in the last rays of the sun. He uttered a curse at the barrier ropes cutting him off from the artwork. This was an area in which he possessed both knowledge and discernment. *If I tread ever so lightly,* he thought, *I may at least examine the nearest panes of glass. . . .*

Unfortunately, the careful tread of a man as stout as Hamish Napier is excluded from the definition of "caution," as it is recognized by eroding stonework.

His third footfall dislodged a great chunk from what remained of a flying buttress; one last time it flew, and its descent was briefly arrested by his bald head, which it bounced off on the way down.

He hit the ground right after the stone.

It was pitch-black. He groaned and sat up. Somehow he'd managed to keep a grip on his flashlight, but, too disoriented to think of using it yet, he blundered this way and that, bumping into walls.

He'd wasn't sure where he was. His thumb accidentally brushed the button of the flash; it clicked. He found himself back in the museum. The bright circle of light illuminated the Bloody Baron's coffin. It was open.

And empty.

Hamish heard an odd rasping noise behind him.

Like someone sharpening a knife.

And then his flashlight flickered and went out.

He tried to tell himself the latter might be a lucky thing. *If I can't see, maybe he can't, either.*

But Hamish didn't believe it.

What he *did* believe was that he was going to become the Bloody Baron's thousandth victim.

Ian paused, possibly for dramatic effect, but mainly to drain his glass.

"What did your brother *do?*" Melinda exclaimed.

"Well, lass, he couldn't get out how he come in, not with a fierce warrior's ghost whetting his knife behind him. What would *you* have done?"

She thought about it for a few seconds, then snapped her fingers. "Make for the leper's crawl!"

"Right y'are; that's what m'brother did. Not that it was easy to fetch it in the dark, but he flailed his arms along the northern wall till a hand slipped into the crack, and now he had just a few feet o' stone between him and the cool night air."

"*Only—?*" (There had to be an only.)

"Yes, Doc. Only 'twas a tight squeeze for man o' his girth, and he got stuck. He was neither in nor out. So there he was, stuck in stone like a fly in amber, waiting for the Baron to cut 'im apart, when he goes and hears a new sound. Like the rustle of women's skirts, only it come from behind him. Two guesses what it was."

Now it was my turn to feel my skin crawl. The old story of the lady or the tiger was bad enough, but to be caught between the Bloody Baron and a leper's ghost was, if you'll forgive my understatement, quite the dilemma.

"Now, Doc, the next time y' want t' talk philosophy, explain t' me what use it would have been t' Hamish at that moment."

I was at a loss for words, but Melinda wasn't. She was practically bouncing up and down on her chair (a meritorious spectacle). "*Please* tell us what happened to your brother! He . . . survived?"

"Lassie, I apologize. I wouldn't have made so free with the story if anything had happened to him. Hamish has faults, and I make sport of them, but he has a goodly set of virtues as well. And as proof of that, he had both sense and sensitivity there in the leper's crawl, and that's where he stayed, waiting it out till morning. Behind him, right enough, he felt the Bloody Baron's icy menace, but knew if he stayed where he was, he'd be safe. Now who wants to tell me why?"

I had no answer. Nor did Harry, Hugh, or Geoff the Brit, but Melinda did.

"The leper protected him."

"Aye. The way he tells it, the leper's ghost did not touch him, but there was something gentle about its aura. Hamish was comforted; he knew he could hold out till morning. The crawl's a holy place, y' see? Created in compassion for the afflicted. It was a long night, o' course, which give m' brother time to think. So as soon as it got light, Hamish squirmed his way out of the leper's crawl, but before he got back on the bike, he found a pebble to weight down the pound note he dropped into the donation can."

– VI –

The Jamesians (denizens and first-timers alike) now voted whether to include Ian's story in our "official" archives. The yes was unanimous, for though the presence of a gentle ghost slightly skewed our titular definition, we felt the Bloody Baron balanced things out.

Harry opened the pocket journal that, for the time being, he was in charge of; maybe next month it'd be in my care. It passed from hand to hand, which is the closest we come to organization. He neatly inscribed the date and Ian's name, then said, "What shall I call it?"

The story-teller always has the right to name his tale, but having talked more than his wont, Ian opened it to the floor and Melinda suggested, "In the Leper's Crawl," which was heartily accepted.

Harry, trying to pin me down, said, "Well, Doc, that was a ghost story, right enough."

"Maybe, maybe not. He saw an open coffin and heard sounds behind him. All possibly due to natural causes. There's no hard evidence."

"Not as hard as your head!"

Harry was clearly nettled, so I took the opportunity to visit the men's room. On the way back, I looked for Mike, but he wasn't at the bar. Strange. I poked my head into his office. I found him there, sitting behind his desk and leafing through a sheaf of old letters. He spied me and shoved them in a drawer. "Refills?"

"Mike, forgive an old fussbudget, but are you feeling off?"

"I'm fine."

The Anglo-Saxon mantra, I thought. "Was thinking maybe something was bothering you. Or someone."

"Y' got me, Doc. I don't like Yanks."

"Since *when?*"

"I don't like that Yank."

"Hugh?"

He exhaled enough air to fill a balloon animal. "No more Mack. First-name basis now, is it?"

"I don't much care for him, either."

"Well, you're a class act."

"I am? Does that mean the next round's on the house?"

Mike laughed. "Y'r also a son of a bitch."

When I returned to the table, they were talking about "bad vibes."

"I wholly get what your brother felt," Melinda was saying. "There are places here in Edinburgh I don't like to walk past."

"Such as?" Ian inquired.

"Right over there by St. Giles, for starters."

He nodded. "By the northwest steps."

"That's the place! What happened there?"

"The worst hanging in the history o' capital punishment."

She poked her companion. "I told you there was *something!*"

I asked where else she didn't like to walk.

She turned to me. "There's this house on Melville Terrace that gives me the creeps. Just south of the Meadows . . . which also gives me the shivers."

Ian wasn't familiar with Melville Terrace. "Harry?"

"That's the other end of town for me. Doc?"

"Yes, I live south-side. I think I know just where she means. Big pale grey house, second from the corner." She nodded. "I avoid walking past there myself. A long time ago, the man who lived there blasted his brains out. As for the Meadows, its history is plenty grim. They buried plague victims there . . . dug long trenches to hold I don't know many hundreds of bodies, and if they didn't fit first try, they broke the arms or legs so they would."

As his mate shuddered, Geoffrey hoisted his refilled mug and said, "I count myself lucky that Mellie's the sensitive one on our team."

"For sure," she muttered. No one else caught it. Then she addressed Ian. "The most nerve-wracking place we've been to so far is that valley your brother was in."

Lines creased Ian's brow. "A place I don't like to speak of."

She laughed. (*Easy sound to get used to*, I thought.) "Come on, Ian! Next thing, you'll be warning me about He-Who-Must-Not-Be-Named!"

"It's like Shakespeare's 'Scottish play,'" he explained. "Actors don't say its name and only quote from it when they're in a production."

Harry laughed. "I was in a production. I played Macduff's son. While we were in rehearsals, I got into an argument with the little woman." (His wife was at least a foot taller.) "She says to me, full of spite, '*The!*' (He pronounced it *Thuh*.) I says, 'The?' Whatcha mean, 'The?' She smirks at me and says, 'I'm quoting the Scottish play!' Well, that cracked me up, and the argument was over."

I could see Melinda was disappointed at Ian for stifling her. (By the way, I call her by her full first name because I noticed her lips thinned whenever Geoff called her "Mellie.") Well, Ian's reservations notwithstanding, we owed her the courtesy of letting her contribute, so I decided to draw her out.

"You're not so far off, you know, when you mention He-Who etc., Voldemort in the Harry Potter stories. Part of the third movie, *Prisoner of Azkaban,* was filmed right where you're talking."

"I didn't know that."

"Anything you don't know," Harry said waggishly, "ask Doc. He's got the D. O. S. degree."

"D. O. S.?" Geoffrey was mystified. "Never heard of that."

"Doctor of Obsolescent . . ." Harry glanced at Melinda and lamely added, ". . . Stuff."

"Guilty as charged," I nodded. "That valley, Melinda—why did you find it so nerve-wracking?"

"We camped out there overnight. Well, I did. Geoff slept in the station wagon. I had a blanket roll, and believe me, I needed it, so I stretched out on soft turf. But I couldn't get to sleep."

I suggested she was unused to the night-noises you hear in the woods, but she shook her head.

"No, I love the forest, but that place is unnaturally quiet. No birds, no animals, I didn't even hear crickets, or whatever they're called over here. The only sound was the wind, and after a while, I would have welcomed a ghost."

"Y' say that *now*, lassie."

The redhead argued with Ian. "Oh, no, I mean it. A ghost might frighten me, but fear's a healthy human reaction—fight or flight. That's better than what I felt, sleeping there where soldiers cut down I don't know how many men, women, and even *babies.*"

I said, "Thirty-eight were butchered in the massacre at Glencoe (sorry, Ian). King William ordered Captain Robert Campbell to put the MacDonalds to the sword, but he didn't do as thorough a job as legend would have it. There were about two hundred folk living in the valley. Most escaped, though many fled into the snow wearing almost nothing and died of exposure. But history becomes myth and the long and the short of it is, 'the Campbells slaughtered the MacDonalds.'"

She shuddered. "I could almost smell the blood."

"Melinda, if you're that sensitive, why did you stay there overnight?"

"I don't know. Guilt, I suppose."

"I see. You're a Campbell."

"Directly related to Captain Robert, I'm afraid."

"He was a victim as well. It haunted him the rest of his life."

A sharp, hard laugh. "So the Campbells claim." I glared at Hugh, but the coldness of his gaze made me look down.

"I was browsing in a bookshop in Dunkeld," Geoffrey cut in. "I found a book of folk songs for Mellie. One of them is about the massacre."

"I've already learned it. Shall I sing it?" Harry and I said yes, and Ian shrugged. The man in black excused himself and left the table. (One never really purchases malt beverages; one rents them.)

Melinda took out her guitar, strummed a few chords in a minor key, and in a voice obviously borrowed from an angel, began to sing:

O, cruel is the snow that sweeps Glencoe
And covers the grave o' Donald.
O, cruel was the foe that raped Glencoe
And murdered the house of MacDonald.

She paused. "Do you recognize it?"

The three denizens nodded. "For many years," I said, "I thought it was an authentic folk ballad."

"It isn't?"

"No, lass. Chap named Jim McLean wrote it back in 1963."

"Doc," she said, playing a chord, "you *do* know damn well everything!"

Now excepting for that brief bit o' prickly between our bartender and the farmer from Connecticut, it had been a pleasanter meeting than any of us might have anticipated, considering the great blizzard that discouraged less hardy (more sensible?) souls.

But everything was about to change. Just as Melinda started in on the mournful verse of the ballad, a whisper of cold air trickled in and a new voice overrode the music.

"Since when are the Jamesians a folk-singing society?" There she stood in all her sensual glory: Lily Watson, six feet and an inch, eyes as grey as frost and close-cropped auburn hair, a thick winter coat concealing slim, shapely contours, once seen, never forgotten.

Except I had. I'd forgotten she was coming, and judging from their confuddled faces, so had Harry and Ian.

Now when it comes to ghosts, I like to play Devil's Advocate, as you've noticed, but when it's a matter of distaff psychology, a man with any wisdom will "ree-garday lew" and get out of the way. (Long ago in Old Town, chamberpots were tossed out of high windows and the tosser would call the Scottish equivalent of a French phrase meaning, "Watch out for the water!")

Which is my convoluted way of explaining how I felt when Lily joined us and found her admirers "stol'n awa." When it comes to the interplay of genders, human nature is curious, indeed. Neither woman was available to me, Ian or Harry, except, perhaps, as wistful fantasies, yet that never stopped us from savouring the thousand nothings we always made of Lily's smiles and irrelevant glances. Yet here, in a heart-throb, I'd transferred allegiance to Geoffrey's oddly uncommitted companion, and Lily knew it as soon as she and Melinda exchanged one casually murderous glance. Not a word was exchanged, yet everyone in the room, even the Brit on his own wave-length, knew the lasses were at war.

Melinda was armed with an acoustic guitar, so she won the first skirmish, forging ahead with the verse of the ballad of Glencoe.

Her foe stamped snow from her boots, shook it from her coat, but Melinda played louder, so Lily went through the archway she'd entered from, though as she did she tossed me a glance like a gauntlet.

Muggle in the middle; I squirmed, if not visibly, metaphorically. I remembered Anna Russell's take-off on *Hamlet*'s "To Be or Not to Be" speech: "Did'ja ever have the feeling that you want to go, and yet you have the feeling that you want to stay?"

I fought it out with myself, decided Melinda was ultimately ephemeral and followed Lily to the front room. But I didn't stay there long. Just long enough to hear an elliptical exchange between Lily and Hugh.

Lily: "What are *you* doing here?!"

"You asked me to come."

"A long, long time ago. A *long, long* time. What kept you?"

A long pause. "Circumstances."

A longer pause. "Who was she?"

"N'importe. She's gone."

"Condolences or congratulations?"

"You're angry."

"You're *so* astute!"

More than I needed to know, and less, but Lily noticed me listening, so I rejoined the Jamesians.

The ballad was just ending.

Compliments were forthcoming, as was a pint of beer Geoffrey brought the singer. Harry began to request an encore, but Lily took her place at the table and said, "Nice music, but who wants to hear a ghost story?"

"Something new?" the changeable Harry enthused.

"Yes and no," Lily replied. "Let's have a round and I'll tell you. Mike?" The last called out; her voice, less melodious than Melinda's, possessed a throaty plangency capable of producing what Boccaccio termed "the Resurrection of the Flesh." (Well, I don't always think like a physician.)

Mike did the honours with the respective snifters, mugs, and cups. Old MacFarmer reclaimed his place across table. The guitar was back in its case. Mike stayed in the room; eyes and ears were focused on Lily, our resident medium.

"I've worked this case several days . . . nights, actually. I cracked it yesterday, but had to stop off there on my way here tonight."

"In this weather, you're doing business?!" Ian's tone was admiring; he was more like his brother than he cared to admit.

Lily nodded, then sipped her scotch. Her eyes widened. She turned to Mike. "My God, what *is* this?"

"Octomore." I didn't think him capable of a whisper, but whisper he did.

I don't know if Ian or Harry knew about Octomore, but I did, and I was pretty certain Lily did, too, for she knows her single malts. Octomore was an old farm that once produced what distillers acknowledged as *the world's most heavily peated whisky—ever.* In 2002 (October third, to be precise), the Bruichladdich distillery, two miles away from the site of Octomore, revitalized the legendary scotch, producing 800 cases, and no more. If you can afford to buy it, be warned, they fetch a princely sum.

That's what Mike served Lily. From the expression on her face, she was both pleased and displeased.

All right, here's how it was. Lily's audience consisted of me, Ian, Harry, Hugh from Connecticut, Geoffrey, a conflicted, but interested Melinda, all of us at the central table. Lily stood halfway between Hugh and Mike, who perched half on, half off a chair by the arch to the front room.

Lily began. "The place I came from tonight used to be Number Seventeen Inverleith Row."

"Number Seventeen's long gone," I protested.

"No, Doc, the buildings either side were torn down and rebuilt, and the numbers changed. Number Seventeen now, appropriately enough, is Number Thirteen."

She set down her glass and told her story.

– VII –

"A visitor leaving the botanical gardens will notice a squat five-story building across the street. Long ago, a solitary, sour old Major lived there nearly twenty years. Mrs. Trevor, who was directly beneath, often complained about the sounds of revelry that were heard from his apartment, though no soul other than the Major ever entered or left his rooms.

"One morning Mrs. Trevor told the landlord she would no longer tolerate the noise. 'The raucous laughter and weird music are bad enough, Mr. Johnson, but if I hear shrieks again like I did last night, I'm calling the police.'

"The landlord decided to have it out with the Major. He mounted the stairs and rapped at the door, but there was no answer. He opened the door with his passkey and there was the old man on the floor, his face mottled crimson, his features contorted horribly. His cold hand clutched a bell with odd markings.

"Since the Major had no relatives, burial was swift and cheap. Ignoring Mrs. Trevor's claims that she still heard noises up there, Mr. Johnson hired a woman named Mary Muir to clean the apartment so he could rent it again.

"Mary went upstairs, but didn't come back down. The landlord finally went up to warn her he wouldn't pay more than the contracted sum. But he found her cowering in a corner, her eyes bulging, her hair turned stark white. The Major's bell lay on the floor beside her. She died in a madhouse."

"Lily," I broke in, "you're telling us a story most of us have heard before—"

"By way of preface. Do you object?"

"No. I've got a question, but it'll wait."

"Very well. Let me continue. The landlord reluctantly decided he'd better close off the top floor, but a young divinity student named Andrew Brewster came forward and said he felt compelled to employ the power of faith to rid the house of unholiness.

"Mr. Johnson was concerned for the young man's safety, yet he was unwilling to lose the rent the flat generated, so he arranged for the youth to keep vigil that night, only with the precaution that the landlord would wait on the landing outside the flat.

" 'Brewster,' he said, 'Take this for safety's sake,' and he handed the student the Major's bell. 'If you see something strange, ring it once. If you're in danger, ring it again and I'll be with you on the double!'

"With that, Mr. Johnson took up his post and the divinity student sat down in an armchair, the bell clutched tight in his fist. Ten tense minutes elapsed, and the landlord heard the bell . . . and then, *immediately* afterward, it rang again. He leapt across the landing and burst through the door, but it was already too late.

"Brewster, bolt upright, his face a picture of pure terror, was stone dead, but as the story goes, his hand twitched and the bell rang one last time. The landlord rushed from the room and didn't stop till he staggered outside, heart pounding like a trip-hammer.

"After the police came and went and took the body with them, workmen sealed the room, and that's how it stayed for well over a century. Those who know the story wonder what the Major, the cleaning woman and the student saw that frightened them all to death.

"Now, Doc, your question?"

I said, "The way I heard it, the landlord gave the divinity student two different bells. I never heard about a single bell with peculiar markings that belonged to the Major. How'd you find that out?"

Lily fished in a canvas bag she unslung from her shoulder. "Here it is, have a look."

She put a black bell on the table. It was big and had a large wooden handle, the kind you see in drawings of town criers. Markings circling its base were too small to discern except up close, but I was reluctant to handle the thing.

Ian asked, "How'd you get this?"

She replied, "The owner of Number Thirteen wants to turn the top floor into a penthouse apartment. He'd heard the legend, but scoffed at it till he set foot inside. Fortunately for him, he's a sensitive and immediately sensed something not to be trifled with. Which is when he called me in to help."

"You should've told him No!" Harry almost shouted.

"But I'd heard the old story and frankly I was curious."

"Weren't you also just a wee bit worried?"

"I was scared as hell, Doc! But I'm no fool. I never sat in there alone, and I never let down my defenses. I let the energy register on my skin, that's all. As soon as I felt it build, I stopped the session P. D. Q."

"If that's all you were doing," Melinda asked ever so sweetly, "how *did* you solve it?"

Lily looked down at her (figuratively, literally). "Pure deduction. I wasn't even at Number Thirteen when it came to me. I stopped there tonight to take the bell. Who's clever enough to tell me why?"

I'd figured it out. "The room was a red herring."

"Nice, Doc, though not entirely accurate because the Major obviously dabbled in the dark arts for many years. But that's what tipped me off. It suddenly occurred to me that he'd lived in the room nearly twenty years before it up and killed him. Whereas Mary Muir and the divinity student were hit fast. Conclusion?"

"It was the bell."

Lily acknowledged the answer, though she would have preferred it coming from me, Harry, or Ian, not Melinda.

My curiosity was almost as intense as my wariness. Gingerly, I picked up the bell, taking care not to ring it. I inspected the markings. They were words in Old French. Translated it read, "Swift the summons, swift the coming."

"You needn't handle it like a hand grenade," Lily said. "I broke off the clapper." She dropped a tear-shaped lump of lead on the table and said, "What do you suppose they saw when they rang it?"

"Take my advice," Ian warned her. "Pitch it in t' North Sea."

– VIII –

Harry noted the story in the journal, naming it "Number 13."

Mike rose and patted Lily's shoulder. I saw a narrowing of the eyes, not just hers. "Nice," Mike said. "One round comin' up on the house, then it's time to settle up."

"So soon?" This from the man in black.

"There's a blizzard out there," Mike growled. "Time to go home."

Watch out! my intuition warned me, but I summoned up yet more courtesy than I felt towards Hugh and asked him, "Why do you say that? Do you have a story to tell us?"

"Not exactly." Hugh hauled up a black leather case I hadn't noticed; he fiddled with its clasps, snapped it open, rummaged within, and withdrew from its depths a huge bottle of amber liquid.

"This," he proclaimed, looking directly at Mike, "is the sole remaining bottle of the finest single malt I've ever known. I made it myself."

"Oh, did you now? The *finest* single malt?" Mike took up the challenge. "And just where's it from?"

"Connecticut."

A miracle Mike didn't kill him on the spot. *"Conn-ect-i-cut?"* he repeated with stunningly untypical understatement. "Where did you get the barley?"

"Grew it himself," Ian volunteered.

"And the peat?"

"Imported."

"And the water?"

Hugh smiled; an unsettling sight. "Ah, Mike, America's a *big* place."

"It is, is it?" With that, Mike plunged into a catechism beyond the expertise of scotch *savants* at that table, and I include yours truly.

He asked: What temperature did Hugh keep the kiln? Long necks, curved or straight? How many parts per million Phenols? What percent "the angel's share"? Was it caramel free? Chill filtered? The nose? Apples? Apricot? Nutmeg? Vanilla? Lemon meringue? Kiwi? The barrels? On it went, on it went, but the man from Connecticut parried every riposte, and indeed the pair were fencing, the foils envenomed.

"All right," Mike growled, finally giving up, "maybe your stuff is total swill, maybe it's drinkable, but if it is, how do I know it wasn't made right here in Scotland?"

"Take it home with you, Mike," he suggested. "Savour it at your leisure. I can't wait a month for the next meeting. I'm going home Tuesday, but if you've a mind, I'll meet all of you here next Monday night and Mike can tell us how it turned out."

"I don't see," said Ian, "how this has anything at all t' do with the Jamesians."

"Oh, didn't I mention?" Hugh asked. "My single malt is haunted."

That didn't sit right with me, Harry, or Ian, and I couldn't fathom Lily's expression, but it was the prosaic Brit who voiced the question.

"What do you mean, haunted?"

"Come back in a week," Hugh told him, "and find out."

"Our flight leaves Friday," Melinda mourned.

"Sorry about that."

The hauling on of overshoes, the tucking in of scarves, the tugging on of gloves. Mike went to the bar to tally up the tabs, and took the bottle of Connecticut single malt with him.

A flurry of currency and plastic. Winks and pats on the back and reassurances we'd (most of us) return next week to find out what the hell the Yank was talking about. Melinda gave me a

good-bye hug I won't forget till my dying day, and at last The
Tron was empty, all but myself and Mike. I'd deliberately strag-
gled to talk to him.

"What do you want, Doc?"

"You're not going to drink that."

His jaw set. "That did not sound like a question."

I folded my arms in the most formidable professional attitude
I could muster. "Now look, Mike, I stay away from other people's dirty laundry, and you know it. But ever since Hugh in-
truded on our meeting tonight, alarm bells have been going off
in my head."

"Get to the point."

"All right. I don't know how far back, but something bad
went down between you, him, and Lily. That's your business, not
mine. However, I'm damn well not going to stand by and let you
drink whisky that might be laced with arsenic or cyanide."

"Ah, come on!"

"Mike, I'm dead serious. Give me the bottle. I'll have it analyzed. If it's harmless, I'll get it back to you by midweek."

His answer was to wave me out impatiently, but I waited for
him on the snowy Royal Mile. He emerged, snapped the locks
shut, gave me his most dour scowl, but it didn't take. "Ah, damn
it, Doc, leave it to a shrink to make things more complicated
than they are. All right . . . *here!*" He handed me a paper sack
with the bottle in it. "You know where to find me." He tramped
off east and turned south toward Nicolson Street; I had a vague
idea that's where he lived.

I went the opposite direction toward George IV Bridge; I was
feeling peckish, as the Brit would put it, and there was a fast food
joint near Greyfriars that stayed open all night and in every sort
of weather; I had mind and stomach made up for haggis, and
don't give me grief about it.

– IX –

It was too deep to trudge very far the next day, so I didn't get to Edinburgh University labs till late Wednesday. I tracked down Jock Williamson, one of my old students, and he did me the favour. I had the bottle back Friday afternoon, its level down an ounce or three; Jock was thorough and conscientious, especially when it came to single malt. I didn't tell him its origin, though. I just asked him to make certain it was in no way adulterated or dangerous.

It wasn't.

"Pure scotch," Jock told me. "Eighty-six proof, moderately peaty, wildflowers and a touch of honey in the middle taste, but there's an astringent finish I can't identify. A little like Talisker, but I rule out the sea; to pin it down, I'd have to run more tests."

"But it's not toxic."

"No more than any good scotch, Professor."

I thanked him and tried to pay him for the time he spent, but he wouldn't hear of it, so I promised to buy him a meal after he was done for the day. I put the scotch into a paper bag and trundled it over to The Tron.

Mike did the expected told-you-so's but as he did, he washed out a pint bottle, filled it with the single malt from Connecticut, and handed it to me. "For your trouble, Doc, but don't say thanks. It's probably worse than horse piss."

It may surprise you, but I didn't try the scotch that day. I meant to, but I had time to kill before making good on my promise to treat Jock to dinner, so I went to the National Museum and took another look at the eight miniature coffins that were found in a cave on Arthur's Seat (the volcanic peak that overlooks Edinburgh from its place in Holyrood Park). I've a theory about those coffins, but that's another story.

Dinner with Jock cost me a bundle, but I enjoyed it. Feast or Famine (a restaurant on Rose Street) serves up a brave rack of lamb, which we washed down with F&F's own version of pale India ale. For dessert there was brandy, black coffee, cheese and scones, so is it any wonder that when I tottered into my bed-chamber at one in the morning, all I did was to open the bottle and smell its nose?

I put it on the night stand, too tired to screw the cap back on, and fell across the bed with my clothes on.

It was not a comfortable slumber.

Sometime before daylight I stumbled to the W. C., washed my hands, splashed my face, finally got undressed, turned out the lights, and quickly got under the covers, for the room was icy.

Sleep didn't come easy. Half-formed thoughts tiptoed through my brain, and none of them were cheerful. I passed into a troubled doze, but part of my mind would not shut up. It kept trying to make out what the voices were saying. . . .

I sat up, awake all of a sudden. The room was silent. I reached over to the nightstand and switched on the reading lamp before I lay back down.

I woke just before noon, not the least bit rested. I went to the kitchen, found the remains of a bag of haggis from the night before, ate it cold and went back to bed.

It was like that all day, listless time awake, an exhausted nap with vaguely unpleasant dreams I could not recall when I sat up.

I forced myself to go out to dinner. Good that I did, for the crisp air cleared my head. The storm was over, but there was still plenty of packed snow crunching under foot. I walked along the southern border of the Meadows and turned northwest on Lauriston. I soon came to a rich selection of Indian restaurants. I picked one and had chicken dopiaza (cooked with onions and tomatoes in spicy sauce) and a tall bottle of Maharajah. It was early when the meal was done, so I continued up Lothian Road, and when the air got too chilly for me, I went into the Caledonian bar and sipped coffee and armagnac till they closed.

I lucked out; there was a cab right outside the hotel door. It brought me home at midnight; I went straight to bed, switching on the reading lamp before pulling the covers up to my chin. My slumber again was troubled.

My friends know there's only one religious law I insist upon, and that is never to telephone me before twelve on a Sunday.

Well, the damn thing rang at ten of noon. Normally I wouldn't have touched it, but for once I was glad to be roused from bad dreams, so I picked it up and hoarsely said hello.

"Doc?"

Whispered so I could hardly hear.

"Who is this?"

"Mike."

Did I know anyone named Mike? Wait a minute . . .

"Mike? From The Tron?"

"Can y' come?"

"Y' need a doctor?"

"No, what I need—"

I waited. And waited. Finally I said, "Go on, Mike. Say it. Whatever you need, I'll help, if I can."

"Doc, look, I hate to admit it, but maybe I need—ah, damn it!—therapy."

No wonder it took him so long.

I scribbled his address on a Post-it, told him I'd be there ASAP, hung up and tended to morning necessaries. A mouthful of orange juice, two bites of toast, then I put on overshoes and topcoat, stuck a cap on my head and grabbed my old medical bag, which force of habit kept fresh-stocked.

Halfway out the door, I went back and shoved the bottle of scotch into the bag.

He lived northeast of Newington on a dead-end block that aimed for, but didn't quite make it out to Dalkeith Road. His house, which consisted of bricks mortared on a base of great granite slabs, looked sturdy as its tenant—or that's what I thought before he opened up the door.

Mike's eyes were blearily unfocused. White stubble blurred the definition of his jaw. His hands jittered and fidgeted. The colour of his skin worried me the most: grey as the house's granite foundation.

"Mike," I blurted out, "what have you done to yourself?" This was neither good medicine nor psychology, so I apologized and resolved to let him set the tone and direction of the visit. He led me to an ample parlour that had two overstuffed beige armchairs and a sofa that doubled as a cot (which fact I established by the rumpled sheet that streamed like ectoplasm from its interior).

I sank into a chair that swallowed me up like a Venus flytrap.

Mike, flopping onto the sofa, protested, "Look, Doc, I'm not gonna lie down on this thing, understand?"

"Whatever makes you comfortable." I unzipped my bag. "I want to check your vitals."

"What?"

"Heart, lungs, blood pressure, pulse."

"Thought you were a shrink!"

"Before I went into psychiatry, I was a surgeon, and a damn good one."

"Never mind that stuff. There's nothin' wrong with me a wee

dram and a good night's sleep won't fix. I called because I've got to talk to someone, and you're a man I've always trusted."

"Thanks. Talk to me."

Mike rested cheek and chin against his left hand. "Not easy for me, Doc."

"What's not easy? Talking about feelings?"

"Talking about anything."

His face was half in shadow. Daylight in February is short and puny. Though it was still the middle of the afternoon, the sun was already giving up the fight.

"Heard the discussion you had last week," Mike said, "the one about what happens after we're dead."

"If anything."

"Doc, you're a man of science. You know we decay, we nourish the earth and grubs, but what happens to the energy that drove the engine? Nothing's wasted, that's a basic principle of natural law."

"What are you trying to tell me?"

"I think we get recycled."

I nodded. "*Many Lives, Many Masters.* Ever read it?"

"Doc, I didn't call you here for a literary discussion."

"Why did you call me, then?"

"Conscience. 'The evil men do lives after them.' "

"Mike, tell me in seven words or less what's bothering you."

"I'll do it in one. Glencoe."

He'd heard Melinda singing the ballad, and ducked into his office. "I hate the damned song."

"I'm not overly fond of it, either."

"You'd hate it more if you were a Campbell."

"As a matter of fact, I am."

"But your last name—"

"Is Kimble. My great-great-multiply that-grandfather went to court and changed the spelling."

"In that case, Doc, maybe you know what the worst thing was about the Glencoe massacre."

"The bloodshed?"

"Now come on, Doc, this is Scotland. Our history's steeped in gore. Why did this particular atrocity result in such public outrage and political repercussion?"

I knew the answer, but he was talking, and I wanted him to keep on going, so I let him tell it.

And he did: how the MacDonalds were suspicious when a military company from Fort William appeared in their home territory. But Captain Campbell gave them a song and dance that allayed their suspicions, and then, said Mike, "They quartered with the MacDonalds. They were wined and dined and treated like family. One soldier even contracted to marry one of the clan's daughters.

"But then they rose up one night and butchered their hosts, raped their wives, slaughtered their children and grandparents, and even though the king's orders exempted old men, one eighty-year-old fellow was cut down. They'd betrayed the sacred bond of trust between guest and host; that's what prompted such a great public outcry. And ever after, the valley's haunted, and so are descendants of the betrayers."

"Mike, this is an old tragedy. Why does it trouble you now?"

"It reminds me of something I shouldn't have done."

"Does this involve someone I know and someone I met recently?"

"You don't miss much, Doc." He told it simple and swift. How he'd met Lily stateside while he was a bartender in New

Haven. What began as flirtation turned passionate, obsessive, finally scandalous as she ran away with him to Scotland, leaving behind her husband, a farmer named MacDonald.

"Ah, Doc, I was a poor choice for a mate. Too much drinking, too much gambling, and I raised my hand to her once too often. She walked out on me, as well she should have, though I still love her."

"It must have been a shock when Hugh turned up last week."

"That it was. I still can't figure what he hoped to accomplish."

"Bury the hatchet?"

"Not bloody likely. A mean, vindictive man. Peculiar reputation, too, with his neighbours."

"What do you mean?"

"The kind they used to hang people for in New England."

I didn't want to encourage this line of thought. "Mike, come on, how could he have mischief in mind? He brought you a gift. Which reminds me, how was the scotch? What will you tell him tomorrow night?"

Mike pushed himself off the sofa and stumbled a step or two to a pole lamp, which he switched on. It wasn't high wattage, but it dazzled my eyes. Then he crossed the room to a well-stocked sideboard and picked up an empty bottle. "How'd you like the scotch I siphoned off for y'?"

"I smelled it; it's got a promising nose, but I never actually drank it."

"That's a pity. Those rumours about Hugh dabbling in magic must be true—for much as I hate to admit it, there's no word t' describe his damned single malt but 'spectacular.' Bottled in quantity, it'd win awards. God help us, a 'classic' from Connecticut!"

He dropped the bottle in a wastebasket.

"Doc, what did you do with *yours?*"

I fished it out of my medical bag.

For the first time that afternoon, Michael Campbell smiled.

I measured out two decent snifters apiece, with a wee bit more to top off. Mike's assessment was accurate. Perfection is a will o' the wisp, of course, as anyone who pursues it discovers, but a few moments in life come close, and as I sipped Hugh MacDonald's improbable American libation, I reveled in a taste, texture, body, and flavour as breathtakingly complex as the best woman I'd ever known.

Daylight departed with the last savoury sip. Mike's head lolled on his breast. I rescued his empty glass before it hit the floor. I had a mind to check his vitals while he was helpless to protest, but didn't wish to rouse him.

Besides, my limbs felt heavy, so I succumbed to the lethargy of satiety and shut my eyes.

I've always been able to sense the time of day or night quite accurately; I judged it now to be a bit short of 5 A. M.

The coldness was fierce. This was no banking-off of heat in an Edinburgh home; it was Highland winter, where even the wolves cringe when slivers of ice blow sharp as needles.

Under a pile of rough blankets, I trembled. Thick wool could not cast off the chill. There was more at work than the North Wind. I had my head under the covers, but all around me was dark, as well. I smelt the aftermath of cooked sheep and black pudding; there was an acrid tang in my mouth.

The covers were suddenly thrown off me, and I heard a voice in my ear whisper, *Rise up, Wally, 'tis time!*

My eyes opened. I saw too little and too much, for some darkness is worse than being blind. Dostoyevsky knew it, Camus knew it, you'll find it in Balzac, and you'll find it in the valley of Glencoe.

If you've never had an out-of-body experience, you won't know what it's like to be in two places at once, but that's what I was experiencing: split-screen.

Ghosts . . . no, I've never seen them, awake or asleep, but just before nodding off I've sensed them. Not skeletons, not white mist, not corpses with or without winding-sheets, no, they're always dark and dense. You don't see them so much as feel a black hole of concentrated danger, and if you don't fight back, they'll suck you in and fill you up.

That's what was happening to me. All around me they were, ghost after ghost after ghost. Without and within it was midnight; cold stars like crocodile tears pinpricked the shrouding sky. On every side, surges and riptides of movement; the ghosts were approaching the tents and wooden halls where the Mac-Donalds slumbered unaware.

Where they crept, so did I, for I was both part and prey, at one with them. Mike was there beside me, too, though nothing of the man revealed itself, not body or breath, only the harsh imprint of his guilty spirit.

Then we were there, the two of us embedded in this fell company, for the ghosts had control of our limbs, and we had work to do: the tearing out of tongues, the slashing of guts, the hacking apart of chests, the mailed fists that tore out hearts and lungs, the ripping open of stomachs, the slicing of livers, the chopping off of privates, the rapes of women before their throats were cut, and then one swift stab, meant to be merciful, killing both mother and unborn child.

O, Thou whom some call merciful, why did you have to make the MacDonalds so *fertile?!* If you had a human heart, Your Godship, a baby's dying scream would make it burst.

* * *

Mike bumped into me. We could see each other. In his eyes, both pain and bestial pleasure; I hoped he saw something different. Recognition crackled; he clutched my arm like a life preserver, throwing us both off balance. Down we went. I lurched into the broad wooden front of a sideboard and hugged it like Salvation's Cross.

Bottles rattled. Glasses struck the floor and splintered.

I released my hold and stood unsteadily.

Edinburgh dawn.

Mike was sprawled face-down on a tatty throw rug.

I knelt beside him, but it was too late.

Police came and went, and I gave evidence at the inquest. The verdict confirmed my opinion.

His heart had burst.

– X –

Robert Louis Stevenson once called Edinburgh's weather "treacherous." He was right. When I tottered out of the police station Monday morning, the sky was sparkling, the air was charged with ions, and the snow was melting so fast the streets of Old Town were a swamp.

Under such circumstances you'd think natives and tourists both would stay home, or at least in their hotels, but something indomitable (or perverse) in the human spirit comes into play. When I walked into The Tron that evening, I'd half expected it to be closed in respect for its bartender, but the place was packed. *To be fair to management,* I conceded, *there's not been much commerce lately.*

In the back room, a bunch of noisy young fellows was in possession of the Jamesians's traditional table, but I didn't mind that, nor their blustery good spirits; I had plenty need of that this night.

Harry and Ian were in a corner booth; a chair was pulled up to it, which they waved me to take. No sign of Lily, or the Connecticut Yankee, not that I expected him to show his face. As a matter of fact, we never did see him again, nor Lily, though I seriously doubt they went off together.

I sat down and asked the lads whether they'd heard. An appropriately lugubrious nod from Ian. Harry said Mortimer, the relief bartender, told them the facts but no details.

"I was with Mike. Should've insisted he go to hospital."

"Morty called it heart failure," said Ian.

I sniffed. "Show me a death that doesn't apply to. Mike's ticker blew apart like a hand grenade."

"Good God!" Harry's eyes widened. "What did it?"

"The official ruling is myocardial infarction, plus his spleen ruptured, and the colour of his liver was alarming, but what really killed Mike was that bottle o' single malt. It almost fetched me, too, though I only drank it once. Mike had been at it at least two nights."

"Was it poisoned?"

"No, Harry, not in a way that'd hold up in court."

"Then how?"

"I've got an educated guess, but no one can prove it."

Ian, I suspected, was thinking along similar lines, but as usual let me do the talking. "Had either of you drunk the stuff, I doubt it would've had any effect. Its power was rooted in the old grievance, MacDonald versus Campbell, and in Mike's case, it was compounded by guilt. I believe black magic was involved."

"Quite a suggestion from our gadfly rationalist," said Ian.

"Aye. I feel like that Kipling character forced to set aside western pragmatism and acknowledge voodoo."

"Welcome to my world." Ian gave my hand a reassuring pat, for him the equivalent of a bear hug.

"So here, lads," said I, "is my notion of MacDonald's recipe for haunted single malt. The barley was grown in Connecticut, but the peat came from abroad. He hedged about the water, but I'm sure that was also imported."

Harry's fingers drummed the tabletop. "Where from?"

"Think about it, Harry," Ian suggested. "Think about it. . . ."

Yes. Think about the long harsh Highland winters, think about the deep roots of the forest. Think about generations of blossoms crimson in the short summer, wilting and mixing with the earth in winter. Think about the long mulch of centuries as they distill, convert and recycle old bones, sinew and blood.

O, cruel is the snow that sweeps Glencoe
And covers the grave o' Donald.

The bartender approached us.

"Gentlemen," he said, "in memory and honour of Mike, The Tron would like to serve you all a wee dram."

For the first and only time in the history of the Jamesians, its denizens declined the offer of a round on the house.

Strindberg's Ghost Sonata

TANITH LEE has a gift for mingling both the macabre and the beautiful in her award-winning fiction, which includes *The Birthgrave*, *Companions on the Road*, *Dark Dance*, *East of Midnight*, *Drinking Sapphire Wine*, *Red as Blood* and many other novels and stories, as well as shorter fiction contributed to *H. P. Lovecraft's Magazine of Horror* and other genre periodicals.

Like Orson Scott Card's earlier ghost story, Tanith's contribution derives from the literature of theatre, but instead of Shakespeare, Tanith's story depends on one of August Strindberg's oddest short plays. Its title is usually translated as *The Ghost Sonata*. . . .

by TANITH LEE

Sonata: A composition for one instrument or two . . .
usually in several movements . . .

Oxford Concise English Dictionary

The Student

– ONE –

It was Christmas, and he was dying.

Blya Sovinen lay on the ice of the embankment. Above him, the grim stone statues of warriors, and—far below—the partly frozen belt of the River Vlova.

All around, others were occupied as he was, with death. Men, and several women, stretched out or seated quite decorously under the plinths of the damnable statues.

The night was freezingly cold. A white night of winter—the pale blue sky, bright as an early dusk, this effect caused by the icebergs floating offshore to the north and west. The moon hit them, and cast an umbrella of light back into the ether. But light scarcely mattered. It was so cold in the city, they said, fires froze in braziers. Oh yes, it was a night to die.

He himself was spread under the statue of Kurlinsay, the ancient king who had saved the city from invaders many centuries ago. Blya, when he had first looked up, had seen the icicles depending from Kurlinsay's upraised spear and gauntlet. But that had been, surely, three hours before. Blya had heard the bells from the Gethsameen sound three times.

How long it took to die, he thought drearily. Even so long to lose consciousness. Others had been luckier. Their faces for an hour back were blue and empty already.

Something pressed like wetness against Blya's cheek and eyelid. It was unwelcome, intrusive, and too alien even for the infernal night.

His eyes flew open.

Warm light scalded down.

He felt blinded and scorched, and writhed in an agony of rage and distress, his mittened hands pressed to his eyes. Generally the police did not intrude on the process of departure—

And a voice: "No, friend, we are not *police*. No, no. Let me look at you."

"Let me alone!" Blya howled. But *his* voice was little more than a croak.

Then, a woman's tone, soft as a feather, whispered by his ear. "Ssh, baby. There. Look, Oska—*he can be the one.*"

In a torpid horror, like that caused by some paralysing drug, Blya found himself staring into the face of the young woman who bent over him. She was smiling with a sort of joy. The man was only a shadow behind her, though he too had sounded quite young. Something clinked against Blya's clenched teeth.

"Drink, dear friend. It's only vodash. It will do you good."

"Let me—be."

"Never, friend."

What were they? Were they insane? Or—had he passed un-knowing into some limbo actually policed by demons?

Despite himself, a trickle of the fiery, water-coloured alcohol ran into Blya's mouth. He swallowed it. Rather than cough or choke he lapsed back on the ground, feeling the base of the hero's plinth grinding into his cap, his hair, his skull. He was cry-ing. *They* took no notice.

They were devils with gentle hands. They drew him up, there among the other wreckage, the drunks with ice forming on their beards, the ice-white mother and her azure baby, she who alone watched with dying and contemptuous eyes.

"This way, friend. Not too far, Take some more vodash. That's it. This is Zophi. All's well, now."

This city he had known for two years flowed by in a dream. The route was easy and familiar. They guided him—half carrying him like a large toy—off the Heroic Vlova Bridge. Then along North Vista, one of the city's wider avenues. Blya's feet trailed in the road, in snow that was slushy where the braziers burned (no, not all frozen after all), and slick as vitreous between. Torches like torn banners up on their poles. By the great houses, set back from the street, bloomed ranks of lamps. They soon passed the Cathedral-Church of the Gethsameen, whose opened doors gave on a golden cave. He had the impression of priests processing round and round, bearing the icons of saints in scarlet.

"Holy Mother, I was resigned to Hell. Why didn't you let me die?"

"What's he saying, Zophi?"

"Some foolish thing. Hush, baby. We'll soon be home."

Off the North Vista lay the city domicile of the old Tzaers, called the White Palace. Behind wrought-iron gates, garlanded with fir boughs and silver ribbon, was the little ice-lake. In the midst of this stood the palace, made also to resemble ice, in milk-glass and marble. It had been hollowed to a skeleton by its festive lights. Carriages were parked all along the lake shore, and on the causeway lanterns moved to and fro.

"Or is this Hell?"

"Ssh."

Blya fainted—why not long before?—at the turning into Weavers Alley. He knew no more until he woke in the house. *Their* house. A tenement called *Perfection*.

- TWO -

Blya lay in a stupor for a long while, dimly aware only of warmth, which at first nearly hurt him, then made him burn with fever. Some strange part of himself monitored all this pedantically: He even experienced visions or hallucinations—perhaps fever dreams—of talking with professors at the University, who demanded a firm analysis of his condition from him, and chided him when apparently they thought his opinions too sketchy.

He had studied at the University for one year and eleven months before utter penury drove him out on the streets. He could by then no longer afford books or writing materials, was cast from his lodging on Smite Street, and sold his only coat for a loaf of bread. Most of the bread was stolen from him anyway by militant beggers in the Narzret District. (He had been significantly robbed before. To that their attack was minor.) Hunger stopped his concentration in the classes. One tutor, the always-angry Polinov, struck Blya on the side of the head as he sat drooping from famine on the bench. "Wake up, Sovinen! You're not here to sleep but to learn the greatness of this world." He had been too fuddled to reply. In his twenty-first year, Blya anyway would never have struck back at Polinov, an old man; a wonderful teacher with a heart of granite, and wit only for his subject.

Now Polinov, in Blya's dream, did not hit out; he only declared in ringing tones: "Wait until she sees him." And the other students laughed; only Blya did not know what Polinov meant.

External to his fever-exercised brain, Blya Sovinen was thin as a rail, pale as ashes, but beautiful to behold. Even his sufferings had not yet cancelled this beauty, for he was young, and, in the past, had not been badly nourished or cared for. Jet black curls poured about his face on the pillow. Black brows and lashes indelibly marked his eyes which, when they occasionally undid themselves, were the light blue-green of a spring river of the Stepi. His body, despite being so thin, was well made and strong enough, though slender in natural build. His hands were those of a musician or scholar.

"He's like the picture of a young saint," Timara exclaimed to Zophi, leaning over the delirious man. "Santus Yivan—or the Angel Mihaly—"

All of the girls and women, one by one or in groups, came to flutter or mutter over him. The men of the tenement—called Perfection in the days of the Tzaers—also came to view. They were generally more judgmental.

"Oska—is he good enough? Yes, handsome—exceedingly—but will he *do*?"

Or, more sternly, and not using a pet name, "*Ossif*—will he even *live?*"

Perhaps all this visitor activity was what infused Blya's fever with scenes of interrogation. Perhaps not. Coming back to life when he had been so near the threshold was very difficult—worse in fact, because he was young and not unvigorous. His body pulled one way like a cart horse, his inclination, long ago disgusted by the world's vicious surprises, the other.

But life won.

As a rule, given the right conditions, it does. In one form or another. . . .

At last Blya woke up fully, dazed and cool, his limbs like boneless lead, and saw a crowd of his saviours gathered there, looking at him like an audience.

It had been only two days and nights since his abduction from the Heroic Vlova Bridge. Since *then*, spooning soup between his lips, or water, or Vodash the Water of the Grain, they had become, all these people, nearly his parents.

He stared back at them in the candlelight, through the haze of the rich warmth of the stovepipe that angled up like a white worm in the corner.

"What is this place?"

They told him, almost in unison, like a speaking choir: "The Perfection Tenement."

"On Copper Walk," added one of the older men.

"Why am I here?"

"We brought you here."

Blya's eyes, not dazzled but foolishly clear from recovery, roamed over them. Some were young, and a few quite elderly. A little huddle of old women over there, grannies in head dresses from thirty years before, and two old men, one with a triangular popular guitar across his back.

But a girl came forward, not more than sixteen, a pretty, happy-looking girl, carrying broth in a cup.

"I'm Mariasha—and you are Blachi!"

The pet name for "Blya". "How do you know my name?"

"Oh, we asked you. And you said."

Probably it was true. In the delirium the professors had asked his name from him, over and over.

Now they propped him high on pillows. He found he could

just manage the broth with both hands. It was good, and had meat-juice in it, even wine, he thought.

Yet they were not wealthy. And this was a tenement, some ancient mansion now carved up in apartments for the working-class. They had put Blya into one of the nicest rooms, a chamber where a pipe ran from the main stove below. They gave him broth and wine. They gazed at him with a sort of *joy*.

Were they crazy? Perhaps some mad sect dedicated to the Virgin, to Christ or some saint?

It was the season of Christmas, the Twenty Days of Light. Maybe they always went out at this time and rescued some poor unfortunate. A charitable act.

No sooner did the broth land in his guts, than sleep put its heavy soft hands down on him.

Someone took the cup.

Laughing quietly, congratulating him and each other, all the people were ambling from the room. Mariasha murmured, "Sleep well, dearest."

He had no choice, the body again making its demands over heart and intellect. Blya slept.

It was morning when he woke again.

Outside, and through the house, he could hear human noises—arguments and calls, children crying or shouting, the clank of pans, feet running up and down stone stairs.

The air in the warm room smelled of flowers.

Blya saw that a pot of lush blue hyacinths had been placed on a small table across from the bed. Their scent was intense, nearly alcoholic. How had anyone grown this plant in winter? Perhaps, having a powerful stove, it had been possible to force the blooms—

He was not sure he really liked the perfume. It reminded

him of something read in the previous months, read in another
language, and finally watched on stage in his own. A peculiar
and haunting work that, although it stirred now along the
backrooms of his mind, was so muddied by other associations,
he repressed it like a scream. He thought very clearly, however,
*A collection of persons trapped like suicidal spider-flies in a
sticky and deserved web of their own making—which also
snares evil things and innocent things, randomly perhaps, and
without pity.*

Then the door opened, and in came a huge woman, fat and
majestic, who paused to look Blya over, with, curiously, both approval and *dis*approval.

"Here *he* is," she said.

Where else was he supposed to be?

Behind her stood a youngish boy holding up the gurgling urn
of a self-bubble. The aroma of black tea conquered the scent of
the hyacinths.

"There now," said the woman. She loomed over Blya as he
struggled to sit up. "I am Olcha, the house-mother of the Perfection tenement. My word is law here." She seemed quite playful.
Playful as a cat is likely to be with a newly-caught mouse. Cruelty
and opulence coexisted with great smugness in her round red
face.

The tea was served him, and a cherry conserve, and a piece of
dark bread only just cooling from the oven. Blya stared at the
bread. The urge to weep stumbled behind his eyes and throat.

"Yes, this is for you, handsome little goblin. Eat up and get
strong."

Blya held the bread against his lips, kissing, not biting.

But the house-mother of Perfection swung off round the
room, and with an awesome whisk of her fat arm, raised a cover
from a rotund copper bath. "Koresh there will bring the hot wa-

ter, soap, razor and towels. The bath will do you good, wash the last poisons of the fever from you, make you wholesome and pleasant."

Blya thought of the house-mother of his own previous wretched tenement near the Smitings. She had been bleak and indifferent to all her charges, letting the house self-bubble go cold, refusing to see to rats or to keep other unwanted visitors out—nor did she like to let wanted ones in. Only those able to bribe her got any service from her, and any who reported her to the landlord she herself then accused of horrible crimes, and so had them thrown out.

"Why?" Blya said, as jolly Olcha pirouetted like a padded aproned elephant through the room.

"*Why*? To make you fit for society."

"Why this kindness, Mother?"

"Oh, we are very kind here," she threateningly said.

He had the sudden, unassailable notion they would feed him up, wash and groom him, in order to cook and devour him on Christmas Night.

He smiled at this sadly. At least it made some sense to him. Altruism always had its price. He had never met disinterested generosity in his life, save from his father and mother in boyhood. But even they had wanted him ultimately to bribe them, with unqualified affectionate respect, and by ceaselessly studying and passing examinations, and so becoming a scholar of whom they could boast.

Reassured by the macabre idea of providing a good dinner for the house, Blya began to eat the bread and drink the sweetened tea. Presently when the boy—Koresh—came back with hot water, Blya took a bath.

Clean clothes, a shirt and trousers, a jacket, even a waistcoat of old, darned silk, a scarf, a new cap, undergarments of once excellent material—all these were laid on the bed by Koresh. *Of course*, Blya thought dreamily, intoxicated by warmth, tea, and hyacinths, *when they put me in the oven, they'll redeem these clothes. That's all right then.*

But also he thought, *If I grow well, then I'll see the true danger and madness of all this. I'm not sane yet myself, but presumably it will come. God help me, then.*

The Days of Light, the twenty days of Christmas, moved four steps further along the calendar of the city.

Blya Sovinen grew stronger. He got up and wandered about his alotted apartment and then, partly driven out by the scent of the hyacinths, about the tenement. He found cramped seeping passageways, stairs, side chambers and cupboards, and abrupt open rooms of great size, usually untenanted but always full of objects—elder caskets and chests, chairs and cabinets green with mildew, emptied wine crates, heaps of fusty curtains, and so on. Cornices traced the upper reaches of these areas, and whorls of carved leaves and roses indicated where once, years back, chandeliers had hung glittering with crystal and flame.

The *shut* rooms, the cells of the people who lived in Perfection, he did not naturally attempt to enter. But sometimes doors stood wide open, and seeing him the inhabitants always called out some greeting, bleary or cheery, depending on their condition. Some insisted he visit them. They played cards and often sang, if the old man with the guitar was present. Every one of them seemed to know who Blya Sovinen was, and that he was new among them, and extremely welcome.

Surely, for so many people, he would furnish only a small meal, a slice or so of meat?

There were also grand bathrooms in the house, three of them, with marble tubs. Two latrines existed, perched out sidelong from the walls about cesspit tubes that ran down into the paving of the yard to the sump. On the roof, looking east towards the Vlova, a single gargoyle reared, a sort of dragon, but its head was off, and snow had swamped it.

The snow had fallen again while Blya lay unconscious. The city was muffled in a thick white counterpane, from which black smokes rose to an ivory sky. At night the sky was silver, and slits of windows shone dull red and amber, but the bells blasted the atmosphere with ringing accolades to the forthcoming birth of the Christ.

In the evenings a bell rang also in the tenement. Koresh rang it for the house-mother. They all trooped, all the tenants who wanted and had paid, to a communal supper in one of the big old ballrooms on the second floor. Cauldrons of cabbage and onion soup, pancakes and flat black loaves of bread, dishes of sausages made in the Bocsash District, and once a pink salmon caught between the city and the port, and *once* beaming drops like static golden tears—kaviah. Fruit sometimes appeared also, persimmons and apples and bitter black slahs to be eaten with goat cheese and crystallized honey. Vodash constantly passed about the table, and on the third night, an iron-tasting yellow wine in a gigantic bottle large as a two-year-old child, and known as a Bible.

What luxury, in this house named Perfection.

Blya assumed a cellar still existed here, overlooked from the days of the Tzaers. He reasoned the house-mother Olcha had valuable connections with grocers, butchers, and fishermen. But doubtless too they had saved for the season. The mystery in it all was only his inclusion.

As when passing apartments, in some of which twelve people resided, he was always made welcome at the feast—in fact boisterously *dragged* down to the dining hall if he was shy, as on the first night he had been. "Payment? What nonsense. You're our guest, Blachi."

Everyone spoke to him as if they had known him for years, needed therefore to ask him nothing beyond what he wanted for his comfort—loved him and valued him. It was so bizarre he had given over questioning it. Either they were deranged or he had died, and entered a curious half-Heaven or luxurious demi-Hell. They even brought him books, when naively he mentioned his lack of them, and sheets of paper and ink, pen, and pencil. They all knew his name.

Conversely he knew nothing about any of them, not even properly remembering half their names. And though they told *him* at once anything *he* asked (aside from why they valued him: "Blachi, you're too modest—why should we *not* value you?"), the ninety or a hundred persons in Perfection had so many complex and varied histories, that he could not individually retain them, or barely. They became for him an entity. It was twenty-seven years of age, or fifty or nineteen, or eighty-two, had worked on the tramlines at Ursusk, fallen through ice at the White Palace lake and been saved, or fought in the Rebellious War, eaten a bear for a bet, and borne sixteen children, fifteen of them now dead, and the sixteenth a rich kept woman on the West Vista.

Occasionally he caught odd snatches of their own conversations. Many of them seemed to be waiting for a visitor—a female in each case—wives, daughters, sisters, he deduced.

Blya's awareness staggered among informations. But they all knew who *he* was. All of them looked at him with affirming affection.

At night he went to bed in the stovepipe room with the hyacinths on the table. Their odour slid him in moments to dense, drugged slumber.

But as he grew stronger, (four days and nights, then six), Blya came doggedly back towards his sanity, all the saneness a volatile young man of imagination and sorrow could possess.

Until then he had not attempted to leave the tenement. That morning he did.

Timara and Mariasha came up to him among the hanging washing in the yard.

"I must tell you a story, Blachi."

Back into the house, with velvet hands they led him.

"This was once a magician's house!"

"Have you heard, Blachi, of Nezchai?"

Blya nodded. He had *read* of Nezchai, an alchemist said to be of part-Mongol extraction, and comparable in some ways, perhaps, to the mighty sorcerer Volkh—who had been not only an exponent of the magic arts, but a shapechanger and werewolf. Volkh was still said to have defended the city of Keev against Infidel invasion, rather as Kurlinsay had defended this one.

Nezchai too had been able to take on the form of a wolf. But in those days—three hundred years ago—wild beasts had often ambled the streets of this metropolis, which was then built more of wood, while the vast River Vlova was straddled only by a wooden bridge which several times burned.

"However," Blya said, consideringly, "I never heard Nezchai kept a house here."

"One of many," said Mariasha.

They had led him up to the attics of the tenement. Even here a few persons made their home. But all were away working, like bees. The last coil of the stovepipe ended in the upper wall. Socks, mittens and coats hung steaming in the heat, giving off the smell of wet wool. Outside the narrow windows lay the landscape of the snow, only here and there a whitened tower or tall roof rising above it.

Mariasha and Timara sat on a carpet near the pipe. He sat with them, not knowing what else to do.

"The house was different then. It was built of wood, but the centre was a stone tower. Part of the tower still lingers in a central wall, and part of the roof of the tower still hangs above this attic. That's why we brought you up here, isn't it, Masha?"

Beyond the grimy window glass, thin snow was falling again. Blya watched it, hypnotized.

He thought, *I can't escape them. Someone will always prevent my leaving. Till they're done with me.*

Taking it in turns, sometimes speaking excitedly, or else dramatically, the two young women told him of Nezchai.

It seemed there had been groves or a wood in this area then, and the house stood alone, clear of the original walls of the wooden city, though later urbanity drew in on it. Wolves wintered in the trees, and on white nights Nezchai became a wolf himself, pale as frost, and joined them.

"Sometimes he *mated* with one of the females."

"But she never bore a cub. He was a man, after all."

Miles off from the wooden city was the great port the Petran Tzaers had built on the northwest coast. The port and the city were linked by the great loop of the River Vlova, and down the river from the sea, even in winter when ice formed at the edges of the water, came ships with slaves to man the sewers of the city, cut logs, and work at the urban building, or other tasks.

"One afternoon," said Mariasha, "the low winter sun was setting lower yet, and the sky was clear, a luminous grey-lavender, with high translucent, cream-coloured clouds lit up by the sunset dripping back on coastal ice-floes—"

Blya stared over at her. Was she quoting from some book?

"And Nezchai was walking, as a man, in his black furs above the bank, along the ancient road where now North Vista runs."

"He saw her on a ship."

"Saw whom?" Blya heard himself blurt, like an infant eager for the story. Why had he done this?

"Ah. He saw a woman," said Timara, smiling mysteriously, "so beautiful, even though she stood there among the filthy, ragged, weeping slaves—"

"So *beautiful* that he, the mighty Nezchai, felt his belly light with desire and his heart sag with melting pity," whispered Masha.

How thickly the snow descended now. Blya could not take his eyes from it. And yet, against its twirling patterns, which made the attic space seem to be flying always upward— imagination placed the picture of the wintry river, the antique ship, the girl gleaming there like a diamond.

Such was Nezchai that he spoke a word, and the moving vessel instantly stopped still as if turned to marble.

Only the people on her could move.

The slave-gangs cried and moaned, and the master of the ship rushed up on deck. He spotted the sorcerer at once, positioned on the shore, black in his coats as ebony, and the rings of power flashing on his fingers.

"*How have I offended you?*" screamed the ship's master and all the sailors, and as many of the slaves as knew the language of the city, and grasped what they were in the presence of, plummeted on their knees howling in fear. But the girl stayed motionless, her eyes cast down now, her hair, which was itself black as a raven's back, mantling her round.

Nezchai only walked down the bank, the ground itself making for him a special track, and when he reached the ice below the bank, a raft of it carried him carefully out to the ship.

I will have her, said Nezchai.

She is only a slave, Lord Magician. She comes from the savage forests to the east, where humans exist disgustingly, like animals.

Nezchai said nothing. He folded his arms.

The master shouted to a pair of his sailors to let her down over the side, onto the ice.

When this happened, the young woman raised her eyes again to the sorcerer. They were dark blue, the shade of Baltic corundum.

She was dressed in rags and dirt like all the rest of the captives. But when her feet reached the ice she said quietly, in a stumbling and heavily accented way (yet even so her voice like sweet music), *Don't remove me from my people.*

Nezchai took her hand and the bloodied cord that bound her wrists dropped in the river.

You have no people, he said. *There are none to match you. You shall be mine always. My treasure.*

I have been raped and whipped and starved, she answered, without any emotion.

What is any of that to me? Nothing can flaw your perfection. I doubt you are even a human thing after all.

No, I am not, she replied, *while I live.*

On the soft whirling of the snowflakes, Blya saw her image standing there. Her exquisite face was turned towards him, not to the magician. Her indigo eyes were fixed on his.

Blya's head nodded abruptly, as if he had dozed asleep. The shock—it did shock him—propelled him to his feet.

Some curious spell had been shattered. In bewilderment he saw that Mariasha and Timara were only taking down, in businesslike fashion, the dried socks and other garments from the strings across the beams. The two girls were laughing and ordinary.

He gaped at them, unsatisfied, knowing, *without* knowing either how—or what—they had nevertheless cast some skein around him, cerebral, perhaps psychic. A web.

"What became of her then?"

They turned and smiled on him.

"Oh, if you drop off to sleep, so bored with our story-telling—"

"Why should we bother to tell you more, my darling?"

Blya Sovinen had never shown violence to any man in his life, let alone a woman. But he strode across the attic and both girls, to his consternation, burst giggling and squeaking away from him, as if all of it were a rather chancy game, but one which all three of them knew well.

"*Now* he wants to hear the rest!"

"*Now* he is interested!"

Blya stopped. He felt dizzy. He put his hand on the wall and said nothing.

Then Masha stole up and laid her head against his arm. "*She* came to live in the house. With wicked and indefatigable Nezchai. *Here*. At least, on this spot, before his house was destroyed by evil spirits and flew away in bits through the air, leaving only the tower, which then mostly collapsed. This—our mansion—was built on the site of Nezchai's, two hundred years after. But he was gone by then, down to Hell, they say, for all his terrible deeds."

"So did she too die?"

"Yes, but long, long before," said Timara, also stealing up to his other side. "She was only mortal, despite what she said. Only a short while did she stay as his possession before she died. She was yet quite young. About your age of twenty years."

"Of what—" he hesitated "—of what then did she die?"

Mariasha spoke: "Of beauty. It was too great for her to bear in her fleshly form."

But Timara murmured, "She died as we all do. It isn't *death* that kills us. It's life that does us in."

* * *

Blya sat in his room until the irritating, irresistible bell began to ring for supper and many fists beat on his door, and then a herd of them came in to take him to dine, his parental stranger-friends from the tenement.

His eyes had been wet with tears.

He had kept thinking of it, this girl who died of beauty or of life. What had been her name?

Fool. It was a story.

– THREE –

He understood by the eighth day that truly they would never let him leave. He had gone out to the yard two or three times, but someone always appeared and led him off somewhere, even to the house-mother's kitchen, where they sat him by the larger self-bubble, and he watched Koresh and a thin girl scrubbing plates and pots. Once Blya had even sought one of the two yard latrines, and hidden there, looking out through the tiny eyelet in the door to see when the area might be vacant. At first there were endless arrivals and departures—people going to their work, or to shop for provisions. Others wanted the conveniences, and one man, old Zergoi, rattled on the door, calling cheerily, "Are you ill, child?"

"No," Blya replied sheepishly, "just a touch of the winter trouble."

Later, when the yard had been utterly depopulated and no one was either at a window above, or loitering in the wide doorway, Blya darted out and hurried towards the yard gate. The instant he reached it Staivn and Ossif appeared from the snowy walls beyond, carrying between them several huge logs in a sling. "Give us a hand, Blachi."

Had they lain in wait?

Blya said, "I wanted to go to the market."

"Oh why do that? Koresh or Mother can get you anything you want. That way you won't have to pay for it, either."

Helping swing the heavy fire-logs in along the tenement corridor, Blya said very bleakly, "You won't allow me to leave the house."

"Decidedly not," said Ossif, surprising Blya by such frankness.

"*Why* not?"

"Because we love you. You're dear to us."

"*Why?*"

"Don't stall with those logs—you're worse than a bad donkey, Blachi."

Staivn said, "Has no one ever loved you, Blya, that you can't accept this gift? Are you so unlikeable? We've never found you so."

"Am I your prisoner?" Blya said, as they heaved the logs into the store beside the colossal white stove.

Staivn laughed. "We're all prisoners of something. It could be worse, couldn't it? The prisoners of the ancient Tzaers used to rot in green dungeons, gnawed by rats. The present authorities use similar methods. Much nicer to be the prisoner of your friends."

The tenth night of the Days of Light was Christ's Eve, the Night of the Dead. Blya, on the eighth day, conceived a different plan. For surely some of the people in the house would go out to visit a local graveyard, to put paper flowers, cakes, and vodash on the graves in respect. He might be able, under cover of this, to slip away.

Trying to prompt some of them to suggest or intimate the intention of honouring this custom, Blya wandered again about the tenement. (In his room, the pot of hyacinths had achieved a thick threnody of perfume, somewhere between the delicious and the decaying. It was impossible to sit there long, and at night when he slept, he felt the fleshy blooms striking like blue velvet hammers in his brain. He woke always with a headache that dispersed only once he was elsewhere in the house.)

He believed he was quite sane now.

The notion he was to be a Christ's Eve dinner for the tenement's citizens had left him. Whatever this was, it must be far worse.

He climbed the long shallow flights of stone stairs up to the attics, passing as he did so girls with baskets of washing, Yori the cobbler stitching shoes in the room he shared with five others, and then Zergoi, playing the triangular guitar, leaning on a bannister.

All greeted Blya, none detained or coerced him. None spoke of going out to honour the dead on the Tenth Night.

Blya thought, *Perhaps, from the attic roof there is a way down to the street, unseen and unexpected—*

As he came up onto the last flight, which was narrower and the steps wooden, an alien sound went through the air.

What was it?

It was like a guitar string snapping—or a pane of thinnest ice cracking right across, with a high, dull, metallic yap.

Blya paused.

Above, the landing was shadowy, for the windows up here were small and caked with dirt inside and snow out.

He had thought this part of the premises uninhabited by day—his main reason for finally roaming up to it. The denizens of the attics worked all of them from dawn to twilight at various manufactories and mills to the east of the city over the river. Some worked through portions of the darkness too, creeping back at midnight like mice, drunk with exhaustion and vodash— yet on such nights they slept lower in the house, to save themselves the stairs.

But now, after all, a figure was there, standing above Blya on the landing.

The weird breaking note quivered again, plucking at Blya's nerves.

Miles below he had heard all this beneath the murmur of Zergoi's guitar, yet now even this seemed to be fading away, not as if the recital ended, more as if the lower house were metaphysically detaching itself from the upper.

A deep silence enfolded the attic region. And she came out along the landing, and stepped onto the stairway. She moved as if rather unsure of the stairs, as if she were not yet *used* to stairs, having lived all her brief young life on flat surfaces, with the only tall things being trees or mountains she did not think to climb.

Her hair was unbound, and so long it drew around her slender shape a thick black pencilling, almost, he thought, to her knees. She was pale as an ermine, and her eyes were lowered. In her left hand she carried a little dish and seemed to be studying it with her cast-down gaze.

Blya stood back against the bannister to let her pass.

She descended towards him, step by slow, graceful, cautious step. At the last moment, as she trod down onto the stair he too occupied, her face tilted up. She stopped quite still, looking at him. Her eyes were an extraordinary dark blue, like polished coals made into mirrors. Her loveliness was dreadful. It was unbearable.

As if she knew, her eyes flooded with tears of shame. She glanced away from Blya, who stood there speechless, not four feet from her, unable himself to move. In a blank despair, a sort of horror, he watched her further descend the wooden steps.

She had given off no human warmth; the skirt of her dress, brushing by him, had been insubstantial.

At the bottom of the stair, in the split second before she turned the corner, she vanished.

There could be no doubt she did this. You could not tell yourself you had imagined it. One breath she had been there, then she had exhaled herself back into some dusk otherness, with the smooth downstroke of a soundless sigh.

That eighth night all of them, *all*, crammed into the ballroom for the evening feast. Even the poorest members of the tenement, though obviously they could have paid nothing into the communal purse. Or perhaps they had—what could Blya know for sure? Blya looked at them, this hundred or more, this entity and mass.

Elderly road-sweepers rubbed shoulders with clerks and neat seamstresses. The lamplighter from the northwest streets sat beside a plump whore, chatting, doubtless each knowing the other from their dissimilar street-walking. Combined now with the refined attention of some was the coarse pathos and uncouthness of others, slurping wine from saucers, taking off boots and cutting their toenails and flicking the debris behind the stove, chuckling that the house-mother paid no heed, or else lachrymose as another large wine-Bible lumbered with the vodash down the long tables.

They all, whatever their calling or condition, seemed delighted with each other, and the world.

The big room had been decked too with boughs of fir. Silver-papered nuts hung from candlebranches now each with two or three candles burning in them, some tied with bright red crepe to prophecy the sacrifice of the Christ. Yet this was the eighth night still, the celebration two nights early . . . were they then celebrating some other thing, special to the house, though now incorporated with Christmas?

As the first Bible flagged, another one appeared.

No one chided Blya for his set, brooding face. Rather they

kept toasting him. All of them used his name, or the pet name "Blachi" he had not heard since he had been a child with his parents.

He sat between Ossif and Zergoi, who filled his glass with the wine, and then, when the food began to come, ladled off cuts of salt beef, sour cream and dumplings onto his platter.

What have they done? How is it possible?

"Cheer up, sweet prince," said Ossif at last.

"Let him alone. He's our blessing," amended Zergoi.

From her large chair among the benches, the house-mother rose. She raised her goblet. "We salute the night!"

They clambered to their feet and roared, and drained their glasses or mugs.

Only Blya Sovinen remained seated.

Then, when they all sat down, he got up and walked along by the table to stand next to the mother, Olcha. She looked up at him, her face already dewed with sweat from the hearty meal. "Yes, handsome goblin, how can I assist you?"

Blya turned his own face away. Disgust stifled his thoughts. He did not know what could be said, and grasped none of it. As he strode out of the ballroom, Mariasha dashed up from her place and ran after him. She caught up to him in the passageway. "Blachi—Blya—come back! Share our happiness."

"There's no happiness."

It was dark in the passage, the flaming light of the dining room excluded by the corridor's coiling progress. They might be standing inside a worm, its inner walls dripping moisture, echoing stupidly with far-off laughter and cries from hidden outer places.

"Blya, there *is* happiness and joy. Oh, you've made *us* so happy. And don't you think we *deserve* a little happiness in our poor lives?"

"No. None of us," he whispered, "*none* of us do."

"But Blya, how can you think *she* could be content to live always in *oblivion*. Isn't it better to bring her back to us? We're like her family, Blya. Since I was a child, I've known her, *seen* her. *Felt* her go by me. Sometimes she speaks. Can you imagine that? Her voice is just like in the story, accented and hesitating, and full of a pure music."

"She's dead. She died three centuries ago."

"Yes, of course. In a way. But we—and those before us—and now *you*—give her life."

"It's unholy. Worse than that, intellectually wrong. And how can *I* have given her life?" But as he said this, Blya blindly guessed the truth of her words, and his heart sank like a stone into a frozen river.

"Sometimes she fades away. Three hundred years—it's been such a time for her. After she died, mighty Nezchai couldn't bear to lose her beauty. At first he embalmed her dead body by his arts—"

"Horrible!"

"But the finished body was hard as alabaster and the face had no personality. The eyes—shut. It gave him little pleasure and eventually he put it away in a vault where, they say, in the end . . . the rats . . ."

"Christ—Christ—don't tell me any more—"

"Then naturally I won't. But this I *will* tell you. He had to have her still. And though he could not restore her flesh—by his power he brought her back to him. His magic was so strong—it outlasted even Nezchai. And now, whenever it seems she flags, *we* bring her back. It happened when I was a baby. She faded then. Like a lamp sinking for lack of oil. The whole house was full of fear and crying. But they found a young woman that time in the city, and Orena came here, and *she* was summoned back by this new young life—Orena's youth and vitality and good looks. Blya, that is what guides her here. Like a traveller to a beacon—like a moth to a flame. And love. Love most of all. *New* love. Do you see? She becomes accustomed to us, to Orena, too, as to others in the past. And so, again we must wake up the fire. And you—*you* love her? Yes, you must, or how else have you brought her into the house again? Even when you were hearing the story, you fell in love with her then. We hadn't seen her, any of us, for a month—it was like a year to us. The tenement is named for her, I suppose you realized. Perfection. *Her's.*"

Blya's ears were singing and drumming at the loud angry stamping of his heart. He leaned on the moist wall, dimly aware that others had now followed them out and filled up the worm of the passage, like shit, he thought, gathering in a cloaca.

Nevertheless his mouth formed words he could not resist.

"What's her name?"

"She? Oh, she's always called The Swan. For her grace and paleness, her long throat. Nezchai called her that. Decades after he was dead and all the first house blown to bits and carried off by demons, *she* was seen here, wandering among the huts that people lived in on the waste ground. All loved her, Blachi. How could anyone not love her? Not want to *keep* her. She is *ours.* We must have something beautiful in our lives. We must have something."

"She isn't your—possession."

"No. Our treasure. As she was Nezchai's. Our secret, too. None of us would betray it, even under torture And nor could you."

"I," he said bitterly, "*I.* Your insect."

"Only *love* her, Blachi. Keep her alive. It's so simple."

"*She's a ghost.* She is a ghost and you shut her out of Heaven."

"Oh, and is there a Heaven, Blya Sovinen?" Mariasha's voice

was tired and flinty. "How can we know? We're only shown this harsh world, and then an open grave. If she's able, through Nezchai's possessive sorcery, to evade *that,* why shouldn't we help and have her? Like—like a hyacinth in winter, when no flowers grow."

Blya raised his eyes. At the twist of the passage, just before it bulged back into the ballroom and the feast, balked the fat house-mother, smiling. She held a slice of beef in her hand. She spoke across the rest, who respectfully listened. "Evil, not beauty, killed The Swan. But it was *love* trapped her here. Love, Blya Sovinen, however selfish, warped and lunatic, however soft, kindly and adoring, is always stronger than evil. And therefore far more terrible." Lifting her hand, the Mother crammed all the meat into her mouth and ate it in one gulp.

– FOUR –

The ninth and tenth day he lay on his bed in the hyacinth smoke (which now smelled to him of burning houses and dead rats coated with scented blue powder).

He refused to go about the house.

But oh, he heard all the others coming and going, and now and then, perhaps deliberately vocalized outside his door: "I have *seen* her!" "She has returned." "More lovely than ever." "Last night I met her in the annexe by the fourth cupboard, and she said quietly, '*It is night now.*' "

He was reminded of reported visitations of the Virgin, said to have occurred in the Narzret District a year before. She had reappeared at some sacred spot. This washerwoman or that drunk had seen her. A two-month wonder.

But this, in the tenement, would not end so swiftly.

Blya asked himself what he had done and been made party to. And also he prayed, as—for five years—he had never done.

"Oh God. Correct this error. You supposedly see even the sparrow's fall. Each of us is numbered upon the eternal nacre of Your carapace, like stars upon the endless skies."

But once Blya Sovinen, then sixteen years of age, had heard a priest say, "God will always listen, but rarely will He answer."

Besides, it was no use.

Food and drink were put outside the door. Whenever he went to collect it (despising his own hunger), no one was ever there. Only the beehive hum of the house explained to him it still intransigently existed. His prison. And once he had chewed a crust, drunk down the tea or alcohol, Blya slept, and dreamed of The Swan. She walked slowly towards him, in an antique gown of hyacinth blue, holding her little white dish in which something golden seemed to lie. And in his dream he always went to her. He took hold of her. Nor did she vanish then. She laid her perfect head on his shoulder, her hair glimmering over them both like black rain or a river. He *felt* her body on his, her *warmth*.

He loved her. As Masha had said, how could he not?

What had she been to be so beautiful? It was her beauty which had trapped her, for it was her beauty which caused this vampiric love from all who were able to recognize her, regardless of their gender or sexual inclination.

No wonder she had begged the magus to leave her with her own people on the slave ship. *They* apparently had *not* been able to see her properly. Not to see she was a piece cut from Heaven, a treasure on earth never to be let go.

Other dreams came.

He married her in the Cathedral-Church of the Gethsameen, he and she crowned with willow and gold wire. He made love to her on a huge white bed, never quite seeing all her loveliness unconcealed, never quite reaching the climax of lust, detained by her serene sad face upon the pillows, void as a fallen star.

When the tenth night came, Christ's Eve, the Night of the Dead, he had forgotten all about his former plan to slip away.

Zophi, Masha, Timara and Staivn entered, having barely rapped on the door.

They behaved as if this had all been agreed between him and themselves, a pre-arranged treat, for which he had omitted to be ready out of playfulness.

"Look! Here's the hot water. Shave quickly, Blachi."

"Here's a greatcoat. It was one of Yori's son's coats—but he's rich and away in Archaroy—it will fit you."

"Now, the comb for your hair. Such tangled locks."

They laughed and bounded round him.

He let them make him do things. It was all nonsensical. Listlessly, he said, "Are we to go out then?"

"Up to the roof, dearest Blachi."

Zophi and Masha told him how, since it was the Night of the Dead, plenty of people from the tenement, who had no urge to visit anyone in the city graveyards, would climb out on the house roof to hear the bells from the Gethsameen and other churches, and to watch the processions of lights.

"Have you ever seen the candles and torches from high up?"

Dully, Blya answered he had not.

Last Christmas on this night, as he remembered, he had still not been badly off, and had got drunk at a cheap restaurant on East Vista, with two or three other students from the University. He then went to bed with a wild blonde girl. In the morning—Christmas Day—he had sat alone in his lodging, his aching head anointed with oil of rosemary and lavender, working at his studies. In the evening he wrote a dutiful letter to his mother and father. (This year he had had some superstitious plan of writing them another, by now post-mortem, letter, and carrying it on this very night to the graveyard of the Santa Ukatrin. Here he would have pinned it up on a post already thick with other such communications to the dead. But that wish had been mere self-indulgent folly. What would he even have said to them, now they were dead, and everything had changed? That he was a fool, and deserved nothing better than a death on the Heroic Bridge?)

But as for last year's Night of the Dead, he had a memory only of the lamps and lights streaming up and down beyond the restaurant windows, as he sat over salt fish, pickles, and black vodash. And there had been lights under the window, too, where he had gone with the blonde.

How wonderful she had been, that girl. Alluring enough, with slanting Eastern eyes, but freckled and with big ugly feet. So divinely human. Flawed—like an emerald.

"There we are now. He's quite ready."

In another place and time, Blya recalled he had loved the blonde for her imperfection. And though next day he had forgotten her until now, *now* he wanted her back. Conversely, he had never wanted to reclaim his parents, even when dead. They withered, like their last gifts, from the vine of his life, as dead things must—

"There we are now," said Timara again. "Now we've tidied him, what a charming young being he is. No wonder . . ."

"No wonder," glowed Zophi, "he proved quite irresistible . . ."

Staivn had wiped and folded up the razor.

I should, Blya Sovinen thought. *But I should—what?*

All up the stone stairs, moving among the throng of the others, toting their bottles of drink, their cakes, and their own candles as yet unlit. All the way up the wood stairs to the attics. He was sick with dread that suddenly, as before, she would be there in front of him, in front of them all. The Swan.

But she did not—*manifest.*

Had they been mistaken? Had he? Some strange mesmeric communal hallucination brought on by their determined greed?

In the attics, among new, down-hanging forests of steamy socks, stockings and shirts, Mariasha gently blindfolded him. *They know, even now, if I could I'd escape them*—But Zophi said, "It's not just you, Blachi. Lots of us can't bear to look when we're on the roof stair, it's so dangerous, more a ladder—but safe enough if the surefooted ones guide you."

A madhouse. Climbing ladders blindfolded or with eyes squeezed shut. Like life. Or death.

They guided him up the stair, which was indeed a sort of ladder, and also so meanly made that with every step, two-thirds of each foot poked back off the tread. You must go on tiptoe, and not breathe. He counted fifteen of these stairs, then he was assisted out into the clear crystal ice-breath of the night. The blindfold was drawn off. He stood up. Sections of the city lay spread below, from Copper Street to North Vista. Startlingly near, the Vlova snaked in a sugared rope, beyond darker walls from which some of the snow had dropped away. (The river was partly frozen solid, it would seem, though the muscular current would keep a central channel free.) A galaxy of veiled windows, street-lamps and torches dotting like amber and garnet beads the better thoroughfares, did not rival the glittering ice-quills of the stars above, where some enormous diamond bowl might have been shattered in the air. *Numbered . . . like stars upon the endless skies . . .*

Blya drew breath. The cold stung his lips, flayed his lungs. The night itself was clean.

He looked over the parapet. The rail was neither very sturdy nor raised much higher than his knees, yet every one of them crowded all about, sometimes even slipping on the surface of the roof, which was flat here. Over the pyramid of a Dutch gable, the dragon gargoyle craned headlessly from the snow.

Copper Street, directly below, was formless, these slums darker than the places nearer the Vista.

Staivn and Ossif had produced pocket watches.

"In one moment only—the bells."

And abruptly then all the churches across the city woke to their midnight tumult, clanging and ringing together and out of tune, one colossal bellow of bronze and iron.

At once the processions began everywhere below.

"Do you see, Blya?" asked the soft voice of Mariasha at his side.

Out of a thousand, thousand houses, tenements, huts, down steps, cobbled hillocks and stairs, over bridges; lamps and lanterns, torches, candles, tapers—the torrents of the lights came pouring.

Like golden threads running on some vast unfathomable machine of great magnificence, some clockwork device perhaps inside the brain of God. Together and away, around, beneath, above. Every street and alley, valley and rise of the city, fluttering as if on fire, weaving woof and weft to make some garment of flame, or coin some new serpentine currency for the use of angels.

"See how beautiful it is, Blya," said Masha's low voice, muffled a little by the bells and by her fur hood.

And Blya saw the beauty of the streams of fire, webbing and threading back and forth.

Yes, after all, beauty was easy enough to fashion. Men created it, he had once thought, from a memory of the ethereal world beyond the earth, to which, once liberated, they could go back. . . .

"Why do they do this thing?" Mariasha now murmured, her

voice lower yet and remote too, and strange. "When I see it I ask then, why?"

"To honour Christ," he said, unthinking, hypnotized by the threading fire as before by the falling snow.

"Who is Christ?"

Blya turned.

All the others had drawn off to the edges of the flat roof. They were motionless, hands clasped, some of them, as if in prayer or supplication. Their faces were stamped with all the expressions known to mankind in transports of enlightenment. But Blya did not even glance at their faces.

It was not Mariasha beside him.

The Swan stood there.

Her eyes were wide as his. *His* eyes seemed to stretch his bones, like two open mouths that tried to roar or scream.

Yet he heard himself say coldly, "Did the enchanter never tell you of Christ? Nezchai lived in Christian times. Did *no one* ever say?"

"Perhaps they have said," she replied. Her voice was sweet. Like music.

Blya stepped back from the apparition called The Swan. He went quickly over the roof, over to the opening. He nearly ran, and mostly slid, down the uncanny ladder-stair, landing in the attics, catching at and pulling loose the woollen stockings and shirts, like hollow feet and torsos of the truly dead.

– FIVE –

The house-mother Olcha was positioned between Blya Sovinen and the door of his room. Her fat bulk that had, he surmised, nothing *yielding* about it, blocked his way, a fearful *military* bolster.

"Let me by."

"Ah, clever goblin. Not only handsome but wise."

"*Let me—*"

"To catch her interest, our white Swan. Then to fly away. What can she do but pursue you, Blya of the curly hair? Honey to her you are, honey that makes even a butterfly stick."

"*God help me!*" he shouted.

The words hit the ceiling of the passage.

She was not discomposed—or at least, seemed not to be.

Her voice was like that of a human wolf.

"Once *I* was the bait for her, Blya Sovinen. *I.* Yes—this bulbous slab of meat. Once I was slim and charming as you, my baby. Years back—ten, fifteen years. I was Orena then—what? They *told* you? Pretty Orena from the sinks of the city, still good enough to offer to our Swan. Didn't you think, *thoughtful* little *boy*, that 'Olcha' is the familiar version of Orena?"

Blya put his face to the wall. "What am I to do?"

"You spineless, shell-less crab—what can any of us *do?* Your best. That's what you must do. What more is plausible?" She stood back in a barrage of skirts and malignity that long ago— just conceivably—had been lissom and hopeful and not unkind. "There's your door. Go in. Go in, shell-less crab, and *hide* under your stone."

Marvelling in a wintry horror, he went by her and through the undone door.

The room was solid with the putrefaction of the dying hyacinths, which seemed to have cast a web all about from wall to wall, as the pure processional lights of the Night of the Dead had webbed and woven the city. They had been benign. This, poisonous.

He slammed the door, crossed to the pot of flowers, lifted it to smash it, pointlessly, on the floor. Remembered the theatrical drama he had read and witnessed, it seemed so long, long ago . . .

the other web *it* described, which had formed of smallminded, awful wickedness, remorselessly trapping not only the cruel, the stupid and the unjust to punish them, but also the only innocent, and the supernaturally evil.

Then the pot fell from his hands, smashing as he had thought he meant it to.

The Swan was in the corner, quite near the pipe of the stove. She still carried her little dish, with something gold shining in it. Her sorrowful eyes met his. To be so beautiful—it must be for her as if, he thought, she had been drenched in vitreol—

He crunched over the broken pot, the flowers, and reached her and said, "I am irredeemably in love with you. It's too late. Everything is over." And this was like what had happened to him before, after the play.

But The Swan put out her right hand and touched his face. He could not feel it. Of course not. She was a ghost.

The Swan

– ONE –

As soon as the sun gained its nadir, the trees of the forest became animals and spirits. It was possible, even in daylight, however, to see what kind of creature each might really be, and so be extra wary of it.

For example, the thin high pine in whose serrated trunk might clearly be spotted the snake-head and folded wings of a dragon. Or the little birch in the glade, damaged by recent lightning, and so beheaded of its bare winter crown, that even so resembled the clawed hand which, after dark, it became, rumaging along the ground, scratching and snuffling after unwary beasts and men.

Thirteen years old, the child had been numbered as a woman for three years. But also she, too, was not quite human. Her mother had conceived her, as sometimes happened, while the male partner was away at a long summer river fishing. Many of the men went to the fishings. They lifted whole colonies of blue sturgeon and black salmon from the waters and salted them for winter provisions. Several men came back, too, and found their women carrying progeny that could hardly be theirs. Some killed their mates as faithless. Others shrugged, carefully marking the stay-at-home man who had probably sired the baby, to see if his genetic virtues were worth raising in the home hut. Now and then a wife went straight to her house-bonder on his return. This the child-woman's mother had done.

It seemed the bondwife had been out tending a village cornfield in the clearing, with other women. But she was overtaken by an unusual sleepiness and had, in the late afternoon, lain down between the standing stalks. She woke alone and alarmed as the last glow guttered through the trees. Worse, standing up, the woman found a wetness between her legs and on her skirt, not blood. In the crimson shadows, plainly showing among the young cornstalks, were uncouth footprints, webbed, like those of some water bird or—more likely—demon, coming toward her and going away. Sensibly the woman rushed at once to her nearby village, and brought back everyone she could to witness these prints. They were quite obvious still in the twilight, though by morning they had faded.

The woman told her returned housebond humbly that he might kill her if he had to, but he had still better wait till the child was birthed. Otherwise the demon might be angry at the waste of its seed.

Later a travelling priest, one of the Volkheshy, tramped through the village. He bent to tap the woman's distended belly, and told them all she would bear a magical child; on no account must she or it be slaughtered. In the future it might prove significant.

The Volkheshy were feared and respected. They alone could wander about the Lesha, the Great Forest, free from danger through their knowledge of gods and powers of sorcery.

When the child was born and began to grow, it was seen anyway that it was a very bizarre thing, slender and proportionate, a female, but not made like the usual villager of either sex, who was stocky and grew low to the ground, mid-dark of skin and hair. The demon's get had a white skin and hair black as the black feathers of certain birds. Her eyes were of a colour seen only in the sky of high summer nights, when the sun did not quite sink—or on winter nights, when the ice floes to the far north threw back moonlight on the earth's ceiling. None of this was believed to be attractive in her. But certainly it confirmed her mother had not lied.

Now the girl ran through the trees in order to escape impending tree elementals let loose at sundown. She understood besides if she met her true father, the water demon—who undoubtedly lived in the swamp an hour's journey off—he would at the least push her over and do to her the selfsame thing he had done to her mother. At *worst*, he would abduct her. She would be sunk in the mud and thick green swamp water. Here she would live in captive misery, or else simply drown.

The anomaly of her position had always been totally commonplace to her: to be unhuman yet bound by human laws of obedience, superstition, and survival.

It did not, any of it, seem strange to her. She never questioned. None in the village did. They made offerings to sky, lightning, wind and fire, to the Lesha, to the earth—the last, holding clods of soil in their hands, eating them even, for emphasis.

That her human foster father had already routinely forced her, and thereafter carnally used her on countless occasions, never mentally jarred against the to-be-avoided rape by the *demon* father. (Nor the fact that, during visits from her two uncles, hunters of prowess who always brought gifts of bear and squirrel meat, greycat or wolf pelts, she was loaned to either or both of them like a warm blanket.) Such duties befell all daughters among the huts.

Nothing in her was ever uneasy with her *mortal* life. She did not ache or pray for change. Only her given name sometimes troubled her. In the ancient tongue of the Lesha it meant White-Feather-Black-Feather-Sky-Blue. But generally she was called a name to do with her blood-father's webbed feet.

She reached the hut that night unscathed. It was just twilight. The single space was full of turgid murk, and on the open hearth rested a black bronze cauldron, full of ingredients such as dried meat, cow's milk, wild civia, grass. Three crocks stood about, with liquid fat burning a low, yellow flame. By this obfuscation everyone had learnt long ago to see.

Webbed had gathered roots and berries in the forest. Now her mother rose and tipped the leather bag out on the floor, searching through the haul, clucking and clicking over it.

No one else was there yet. Webbed sat down to clean off roots with a flint.

"Something comes," said the mother, presently. Webbed looked at her. "Old Woman say so. Bad. This night, all we go out."

"Out," repeated Webbed.

She knew what her mother referred to—not the threatening idea of the *coming* something, but the grim, tiring ritual that must be enacted if the Old Woman decreed. It had been performed twice before in Webbed's lifetime. Once she had been only six: too young to attend. She had seen her mother steal from the hut, and her elder sister, then not house-bonded elsewhere. Her foster father had turned on his side, feigning sleep. Men were not permitted to attend this semi-religious, magical act. The second time Webbed was eleven, and she too had had to go out. She was still a virgin then, which made her extra valuable at the rite, though why she never knew. Nor did she puzzle over it. Now her value that way was over.

"Hush," said her mother. Not because Webbed had spoken. *Hush* too was ritual. It meant, *Say nothing*.

The human father, who had been herding animals, then drinking khoumis with other men, did not arrive home until another hour had passed.

They ate some food. One of the village cows had been slaughtered, and a slab of meat was added, by the man, to the brew in the cauldron. This obviously did not cook enough to be tender. The father was strengthened by the bits of half-raw meat, and mounted the mother in their corner of the hut. She showed pleasure, naturally. It was a sign of his favour to take her, when he had a youngish daughter still to hand.

With the ritual in the offing, really it was fruitless to sleep. But Webbed was worn out from her berry-gatherings in the forest, which had started just after dawn. Therefore she did sleep, until her mother roughly yanked her arm. Then, without a pause, Webbed got up, retied her hair by its scrap of dried gut, and followed the older woman from the hut. (As she did so, in the night-low ebb of the hearth, she saw her father turn hastily again on his side, not to see.)

Even late summer here was cool by night, for the sun by this time of year was all down. Outside the huts, under the still palish northern sky, the gathered women were like bears or cats or deer themselves, closed in their skin and fur garments.

The Old Woman led the procession from the village, towards the furthest of the field-clearings. The trek took half an hour. All the forest was by now full of phantom animals and elementals, but the Old Woman, waving her stick topped by a wolf skull, brushed them off. She was the daughter of one of the Volkheshy, and so she had this talent. Also she could foretell, which was the reason she had ordered them out tonight.

"Something coming," muttered Webbed's half sister.

"What is?" another young woman asked.

"She not say."

A fact. The Old Woman had not.

In the chosen field she called a halt. It was an eerie spot, under the wide sky but with the soaring black trees ringing it round, full of unseen eyes watching, and vaguely heard demon-mouths whispering.

The corn had failed in this field. Which was why the Old Woman had brought them here.

She went about the women, young and old, tapping some of them with her wolf stick.

At length she selected three, an elderly widow, a young mother, and a girl of twelve.

They all knew what must be done, apart from the twelve-year-old, who became frightened, rolling her eyes when she, along with the widow and mother, was tied by a tough rope of bog-grass to a hefty rock lying partially embedded in the blighted field.

The other women quickly assembled to beat these three "draught-beasts" with twigs and pine-switches, shouting loudly they must pull the plough. The young girl began to cry. But she strained as the others did to hoist the rock from the ground. Eventually it came out. Then the three women were made to drag it round the entire circumference of the field, the rest running along with them, still calling and shouting, casting down pebbles they had picked up on the way, or tiny skulls of birds or rats, in the uneven track—the furrow—the rock randomly made.

When the circuit was complete, the Old Woman went forward and yelled at the field: "Evil that threatens be closed in as this blight is by the furrow of the plough. May the sun burn you up as this field is burnt. May the lightning strike you. Mother Earth swallow you in her moist black mouth."

The other women shouted some of the words too, even the elderly widow, who was exhausted, and the sobbing girl.

Webbed also shouted the words. She did not think about it. Such things were needful, happened. She felt only a faint anxiety about creatures in the woods, and her own overbearing tiredness.

A silence dropped from the sky when the shouts were done.

Drained, they stood gazing at the Old Woman. But she only spat on the ground, then turning, raised her staff and shook it again, glaring at the ring of forest to the west.

Usually she was able to dispel elementals quickly. But now her caws and shakings went on.

The other women, Webbed too, becoming perturbed, looked where their witch did.

A weird flutter of brownish-reddish light was leaping towards them through the trees.

Only the youngest two or three women shrieked. The oldest, she who had ploughed, groaned and said, "Not tree-things. Is torches—"

They had one moment more to be perplexed, even reassured. No man of the villages would dare come after them at such a time. This guarding spell was female, taught only to girl children by the earth herself.

The moment passed.

Out of the trees ran big, bear-like forms, men after all in thick, shining furs, the torchlight lashing bright above and around them. Many waved sticks, not capped like the Old Woman's with a skull, but which instead suddenly let out sharp farting cracks of sparks and thin smoke.

Astonished, the women saw Old Woman spin around. It must be some new magic to disperse these monstrous intruding strangers— But no. No, it was not magic, or if it was, an unrecognizable one. For the Old Woman spun and fell and lay prone on the field, one foot in the rock-furrow, and a rivulet of blood, very dark but unmistakable, crawled out from under her body.

The new running men, who had no fear of women's rituals, waved their guns, those sticks which spat fire and pellets of maiming or death. Most of the villagers had heard of these, dimly. Few had ever seen, or seen and lived to recount it.

The women dropped back together in a huddle, defensive, pointless, instinctual. Webbed found herself back to back with her own mother, who craned her neck to mumble the reminder in Webbed's ear: "Remember. Your father was demon."

A parting gift. Next second the mother, too, was felled, clubbed on the head and brained because she had tried to claw. She was too old anyway for the slave-takers with guns, who wanted only the youngest women and men from the forests, for the hard labour in their port and city.

Webbed saw her mother trodden on, along with the widow who had helped haul the plough to prevent all this. Then a huge stinking hand covered her own nose and mouth. She was lifted, only half conscious, up into the bear's embrace. In another language she had not yet learned, the slaver laughingly said, "This one's a find. I stake first claim to her. Maybe I'll wed her even, if she washes up nicely."

He did not keep her in the end. He raped her for a dozen nights and afternoons in the travelling bivouac of the slave camp, then lost her at cards to another man, who in turn gave her in exchange for some other woman they had found, who had coppery hair.

In reality, Webbed could not be anything but a slave. Though it was a shame, several of them had said it, that the lucrative days of sending pleasure-slaves to the Tzaers, and other princes of the cities, were gone. In a Christian era, such a habit was out of favour. Conversely, she was too good for the harsh work the rest must endure. Perhaps some fancy brothel might like her, and pay a fine price. To this end, several of them took it on themselves to teach her proper speech, whipping her when she was slow and stupid, as mostly they found she was. The whippings only scarred her back a little. Not enough to spoil her for future use. Some fine fellows even liked such scars, they had heard.

What Webbed learned, along with the beginnings of their civilized tongue, was that what physically they did to her— therefore what her father and others had done—was neither a formality nor an acceptable act. Indeed, neither the sexual intrusions *or* the starvings and beatings for punishment. They told her this, although by an obtuse means. The punishments, they explained to her carefully, *were* punishments, things she would only have to suffer if she failed their expectations of her—*not* necessary customs of a family or group. As for the rapes, they would have to go to a priest to confess this use of her as a sin, a bad and vicious error *they* made, being too weak to resist. They discussed the confessions sometimes, and the grim penances they dreaded—kneeling on stone floors, praying, in cold chapels, the giving up of meat, vodash and wine.

That they thought her *tempting*, physically appealing, even beautiful, filled Webbed with utmost horror. Not because of the resulting assaults—which even if she had learned they were sins, she still put up with almost unthinkingly, as always—but because she thought these new men must be degenerate and insane to be attracted by her.

How could they want her? She was not like proper women in appearance. Her father and uncles had made do with her because they had nothing young that was better. If her sister had still been in the hut, she doubted they would have bothered with Webbed. And even these slave-takers, though taller and less gross in their looks than any villager, were still identifiable to her as human men. That was, debased, mentally limited, unwholesome in smell and action. Made of clay, in fact, as mankind must be, unless, like herself, formed by demons.

In the camp, she stayed, whenever possible, among her own people. But as most of her village had by then been split up with other slaver parties, those taken from other Lesha villages now predominated. These did not know her, and shunned her for her peculiarities. This was as it must be. Humbly, she crouched at the edges of their lives, forlornly consoled by sane ostracization.

But confusion clouded her days. It was worse than ill-treatment, to which she was accustomed. Worse even in some ways than her bewilderment at exile.

However, when they emerged from the forests at last, going up river firstly, on rafts and cranky boats, blind terror seized Webbed, as it did most of her compatriots.

The earth had become a sort of Hell. It was enormous. Its horizons stretched to unguessable limits, where, to the absolute despair of the forest people, it tumbled away into plains of sky slung with colossal mountains of cloud—which often seemed about to crash down on the land. Some of them had even done so in the past. They were visible far off, clouds that no longer moved, being broken from their fall. (The slavers, who had come across this sort of agoraphobia before, mocked the villagers, saying Yes, yes, those mountains over there had certainly once been clouds, shot down by guns. Then they would threaten to fire at the real clouds. The threat would induce compliance, when needed.)

Rapids also smashed the passage of the river, and frightened the slaves with their turmoil. Here boats and rafts were dragged ashore. This river was not as yet the mighty Vlova, but a mere eel which would, only finally, gush into it. Nevertheless, to the forest people, it was terrible, and must, like any water, be full of spirits and monsters, waiting to drown and devour.

Long months they had been on the journey. There were many stops. Other peoples began then to be seen, at fairs, in villages and towns along the river's course. When Webbed and her remaining group of slaves ultimately found themselves sailing slowly down the winter Vlova, further education took place. All knew they had entered a world of devils, taller and finer made, alien—for the earth had not constructed them.

But the slaves were quite numbed by then. Their rudimentary minds had been slapped into utter vacuity.

Therefore, though the vast Vlova appalled them, its southeast-north flowing loop miles wide beyond the port and paved with white winter ice, the black inner channel concealing malignity, they barely responded. The most refined cruelty could not perhaps have done this. It was too much ordinary experience which had shattered their souls.

An evening came, luminous, full of the danger of the low-flying clouds. Out of the landscape rose another landscape.

It was a city. They did not see this. Instead it must be another crashed cloud, fixed in unlikely shapes of stone and wood— presumably a cloud's original material. Here the demon-people had come to live in an enormous band, and had lit fires in the air, on poles. The sun set across the river like a scarlet mask. On a bank, black on the sunfall and the snow, one more black-furred alien stood, surveying the ship.

How had he been, Nezchai, able to see her such a way off in the middle of the crowded ship and the snow-flounced river? Well, he was a sorcerer. Besides, he owned a very ornate spyglass of faceted topaz.

– TWO –

Nezchai the sorcerer lived in a mansion built of foreign Javan wood, hard and black as vitreous. The manse was itself formed round the spine of a high, and slightly leaning, tower, a shaft of slated granite pierced with windows only at its top. By night, most of these might shine out. Sometimes the colours changed, yellow to rose, or to purple.

Inside it was a draughty wind-groaning house, with earth or stone floors, empty of almost everything but ancient books on shelves or stands, stone tables and wooden stools, carved chairs with cushions of ruined velvet, chests, vials and jars, bottles and crystals. Precious gems glinted and smouldered everywhere. An owl, or maybe a pair of them, had a roost in the tower-top, but also flew about inside the mansion, catching mice as a cat would, then letting loose agglomerated cones of condensed fur and tiny bones. The flights of these owls, or owl, seemed inexorably gliding and silent as time.

There was one human servant. He *was* human, squat and obese, swarthy of skin. Yet by now Webbed was wary of him, for she saw he was afraid of her in an unknown, sophisticated way: similar to, though not as magnified as, his fear of his master.

Other servants also plied the house of the magician. They were invisible, and did things which distressed but did not shock her, for she had grown up in a forest similarly populated by elementals. Often objects would drift through the air, or be hurled. Things broke. Others did not. Book pages were turned. Or else different books, coiled up in linen jackets, sprang off, or hung down from the stands, or over the stairways. There were noises and voices, too. Just like the Lesha.

Strange reflected glimmers came and went on the ceilings—perhaps cast up from the river, though surely it was too far off.

"You will sleep in here," Nezchai told her, speaking clearly so she could follow. "Five hours each night. That is enough."

The room was narrow, and the bed, for a bed it was, also narrow. It sloped curiously, the head much higher than the foot. There were coverlets of fur and quilts stitched with worn antique pictures in bursting gold and silver thread. Seed pearls scattered the icy stony floor. The only two fireplaces were on the lower storey, in the wall. The human servant kept these flashing with fire, and sometimes threw in unguents that produced a glamorous smell. But Webbed's bedchamber was cold. Nor did she employ it properly to begin with. She took the covers from the bed and slept in the corner, rolled in them like a scroll in its linen case. One of the invisible servants must have reported this. Nezchai told her she must sleep in the bed. He picked her up and placed her on it, in the proposed position. After that she slept on the bed.

He seldom touched her. He had not raped her. Nor did he punish or strike her.

She did not mind the food, the haunches of deer broiled in the fireplaces, the goose stews, the pickled cabbage and plums, and hot bread.

"You must eat twice a day. I will show you how much. There is water to drink every day. It's clean, from the well in the grove. Drink wine in the evening from this beaker. It belonged to an Egyptian queen and is made from a single emerald. Two helpings, out of that jug."

He told her she must walk about the mansion all day, except

after meals, when she must sit as still as she was able for one hour, which the spirit-servants (whom he named *Striyi*) would measure for her. They did this by delicately chiming a little bell hung from a beam at her sitting down, slamming a lid on a great urn of pickled fruits and cucumbers when the hour was accomplished.

Frequently she would be summoned into Nezchai's presence. The human servant was always the one to conduct her, though sometimes the spirits rolled about as he and she climbed the tower, nearly visible now and then on the stairs, like ribbons or balls of pale, tangled hairs.

The owl, or one of the owls, slept during the daylight hours. Once the low sun dropped from sight, the owl, or both owls, separately evolved, floating about the big tower-top room, skimming indecipherable gadgets and potions with raddled wicked feet.

Nezchai did not always look at her. But usually he did. He studied her. He *read* her, it seemed, like one more book. He felt her hair, now often washed with perfume, weighed her in an upright balance. And occasionally he looked into her eyes through a magnifying crystal, as he would examine a jewel.

Only twice did he require her to strip her clothing, the warm wool and furs he provided in winter, later the lighter garments put out for summer.

She was shocked the first time—not by the cold, for there was a brazier of charcoals burning in his alchemical laboratory—but at the infringement of her basic secrets. Her father and uncles had never made her bare any of her body, save for the essential part, and then they had not looked at it, only navigated an entry. The slave-takers *had* looked her over, but only in portions. One had wanted to see her breast (one breast was enough), another her vagina, and so on.

This with the magician was plainly not a prelude, however, to sexual rape.

The very first time, he studied her for perhaps five hours, walking round her, seating himself, drinking wine or water, gazing. He took notes, writing in dark ink and eccentric characters, on a tablet of goatskin, then gooseskin fixed with ambergris.

All this while Webbed stared into nothingness, shrivelling, deranged with a voiceless revulsion—and—what could it be?—*anger*? She had seen the rage of others, but did she know what *her* anger was?

The human servant did not intrude. A Stri kept the brazier active and hot.

After he was done with her, she hid herself until the following day in a cupboard in her room, where only marks in the dust showed where things might once have been stored. She stood among these phantoms and wept, as she had not done since earliest childhood.

He was teaching her words by then, for he read *to* her endlessly. Although she hardly ever knew what any of the matter of these readings comprised, sentences, phrases, solitary monosyllables had begun to take root in her. She was learning expressively to vocalize. She now spoke to herself, fumbling not in the forest jargon, but in the allegorical syntax of the sorcerer . . . *Shameful gold, debased metal like a moon, fire to water that changes into a shell—*

The second time he told her to remove her garments came years later. That summer evening she tore them off and threw them down.

"Yes," was all he said. Then, "You haven't changed your plumage, my Swan. Still white, still perfect. The same weight and almost the same age. How *will* you age, I wonder? Is it possible you even can?"

Swan was his name for her, from the beginning. She had absorbed the name gradually, like the other words.

Swan thought, *Acid to volcanic flame. Night is falling in crow wings.*

He only watched her nakedness, during that second perusal, for one quarter of an hour. By then she could judge time quite ably in the new way, from the water-clocks dripping all over the house, or the clockwork icon of gold and chrysoprase he kept in his tower, where an eye of rubicelle moved round and round a white owl face marked with numbers—which she had come to be able, also, to read. Though she could not count higher than twelve.

Of all humanity, Nezchai was to her the apogee of otherness. (As indeed he was to humans, who thought him actually *abhuman*—worse than the forest people had ever thought Swan, in fact.)

There was something direly significant in this. She had never fitted among humanity. Now, in the globe of human sorcerousness that was Nezchai's world, she felt her chastisement for having ever been born.

During summers, the mansion sweated and was hot. The walls smelled of the river down the long slope, and of struck tinder, the flint rasping on the tinderbox.

The odour of the volumes and scrolls also increased in summer. It drifted like pollen. Flowers and berries exploded on the banks of the Vlova, visible from windows, and in the groves beyond the house colour was rife where, in winter, lay only monochrome, and wolves perambulated like silver cogs in some other faunal clockwork. She had no urge to pluck a berry, let alone a flower. Besides, it was presumably forbidden.

In the house, anyway, bizarre flowers grew. They were brought to Nezchai, like the jewels and books and other curios, from everywhere on earth. She had thought he lied when he spoke to her or read of other countries of the earth—that he made them up to amuse himself. (Nezchai had told her some god had done precisely that, moving over nothingness, and talking lands and creatures into being.) One blue flower came from a situation he named *Holland*. The perfume was very strong. It looked like a sculpture of wax rather than a flower.

Ships moved along the river. The moon rose and sank. The sun crossed the vast sky (which, sheltered in the house, she was growing to accept) or balanced on the sky's high summer border, never quite disappearing, but dull as her mother's battered bronze cauldron.

Having no true life, Swan, who had been Webbed, began to form inadvertently another life, *not* true, but accessible and functioning.

Even so, meaningless.

It hooked itself, like owl claws, on language, words and concepts—which doubtless she did not understand, yet which, for herself, she formulated to strange (applicable?) meanings.

As in: "Going to the river, the man cast down a net in which came up a pike of solid gold, decorated all over with precious stones." This, to Swan, (or Webbed) transformed to a miniature event, a miniscule golden fish that swam in a dish, a sort of pool of the river where the men had fished in the forest. With this image, despite the views of the wide Vlova and the statically-reeling city, she was content. But no—not *content*. Such pictures were like the cupboard in which she had taken refuge. A small retreat from chaos, refuge from the inimical. (For she *was* human, whatever she might think. That very process of denial and miniaturization was the one by which all mankind, even the maguses, retained their wits: shrinking eternity to the stars of the sky, and

God to a wise elder man who sat there, and life to a single spurt from womb to grave.)

The Swan swam through the years in the sparkling, darkling sobriety of Nezchai's mansion, remembering how he rode to meet her on a piece of ice, the ship stopped dead in the river.

In sleep, summer and winter, spring and autumn, she dreamed only of her mother's hut with the smutty hearth. Even of her father's nasty fumblings. Even the drunken uncles reeking of khoumis fermented from the wild horse-deer of a neighbouring village. Sometimes she heard her mother mumbling, "Your father was demon." It had been a gift, that final announcement. Knowing *herself* the webbed Swan managed to persist in limbo.

Language grew in her like plants, but otherwise she was silt and the slush of forgotten ice. Bread was never enough to live on, though no one, not even the Christian atheist Nezchai, had told her who might have suggested this. Not bread alone. You could not flourish on that. Nor on words, unless they sprang from a Word. *The* Word. No. She could not live.

– THREE –

Swan dreamed a new dream. She had been called up to the magician's chamber in the tower. When she had entered he told her, for the third time, to take off her clothes.

Six years had passed by now. Among the forest clans she would have been long wife-bonded to a man. She would be growing old, like her mother. Here that had not happened. One more discrepancy.

Even so, she did begin to feel age. Wandering up and down the enormous mansion, even allowed, since the fourth year, into the single walled grove adjacent, or sitting in a chair while the invisible servants hurled things or fluttered the pages of his books, Swan became tired. She sat down and slept at hours not prescribed by Nezchai. Sometimes the Striyi servants, even the human man, played tricks and woke her—slamming the lids of jars and barrels, spilling water over her feet. But eventually they relented, or were bored with it, and left her alone.

It was during just such a nap that she dreamed of the magician's summons and his command that once more she strip.

"But I am old now," in the dream she said.

"Old? You're a maiden. You are a gem. Gems age in centuries but not appearance."

She did not, even in a dream, know quite why she would not do what he wished. Her reluctance was personal to herself, therefore irrelevant to her. But she could not, did not.

Then Nezchai crossed the room and put his hands on the ruby buttons of her collar. And in that instant, Swan felt herself turn into what he had told her of, a white and gleaming polished stone.

He started back. She had never seen him discomposed, let alone alarmed, before.

Inside her nacre armour she half smiled. She thought, *I can never be touched again*. This saddened and energized her. Autonomy, though random and not quite comprehended, was startlingly valuable.

When she woke, she lay on the tilted bed, where someone, probably the sorcerer, had placed her.

She was not, as in the dream, made of pearl. But she could barely move nevertheless.

One moment she was freezing cold, the next very hot. It was as if the two great seasons of winter and summer rushed back and forth through her body, replacing each other every few minutes. Oddly, in this fashion, she was never too uncomfortable for too great a time. Between the dual states were intervals of relief and equilibrium, the cold growing warm, the heat cool. Spring? Autumn?

Nezchai stood at the bed-foot, reading over her some lesson or incantation.

The words for once were lost on her.

Then he put down the book.

"Have you drunk water outside the house?" he asked her quietly. He had forbidden her to do this. Of course she had not. Only once had she disobeyed him—even in a dream.

"No."

"Has anything bitten or stung you?"

She pondered vaguely. In the forest of her childhood small animals and insects often did such a thing, yet here . . . After a while she recalled that a little black-green fly had settled on the back of her hand as she stood at a window of the mansion, looking at carts on the distant track by the Vlova. She had felt a sharp itching pain, as if a heated pin had been driven through her skin into the vein, and as she started the fly spun away on gilded wings.

She tried to tell Nezchai this, but found the act of speaking very difficult. She mumbled, "I was made naked."

"That? That was long ago."

Presently he bent near, measuring her heartbeat, the rhythm and colour of her blood, staring into her eyes through a prism. He had always analysed her. She was not dismayed. She fell asleep.

When she woke the next time, she lay in a bath of liquid gold, up to her neck in it. She thought this was quite logical. She was changing into pearl, and would need to be mounted in a golden boss, to hold her securely for his future scrutiny.

Still she was not distressed. She breathed slowly and heavily, and on the floor flowers in a pot gave off a blue marzipan of scent.

The sorcerer tried many methods to retain his treasure. A bath of mercuric silver when the gold failed, partial immersion in tar, and liquified pummice from the bowel of a volcano. Tiny bats bled her and white maggots cleaned the wounds with their teeth. Needles of gold and steel were put through pinches of her skin at various points—the inner crook of the arm, an earlobe. Elixirs were mixed. She drank them awkwardly but always obediently. She had no interest in anything apart from the movement and patterns of light on her ceiling—the possible reflections off the river or the bank, or of lamps there after dark, or on the track below the groves, or fireflies crisscrossing the summer nights.

Her bodily functions were attended to by the invisible servants. These beings were quite gentle now, and unlike a human nurse, never impatient or enraged at the work. Having grown in the forest, she had never much cared anyway if another saw her urinate or crap; it had always been happening.

However, these functions ceased soon, as she put aside the chore of eating and drinking.

Swan was not restless. In the ripple of the ceiling she beheld people from her past, even enslaved villagers from the trip west and south.

One night she heard him raving in the room high above in his tower, something that had never happened, blaspheming some god she had not learned about or been properly aware of. Despite that, the *tone* of resentful blasphemy was unmistakable— she had heard it once or twice in the village. A man spitting at the sun, a woman cursing the demon that had broken her best pot. The man was struck by lightning a month later. The woman, though precautionally beaten, sickened and was good for very little.

Swan felt no unease for Nezchai. He was nothing to her, only a fact, like the immovable coming of day or night. Always alone, the tolerance of her village towards her had upheld her. But even this, of course, had emotionally not amounted to much. Lying on the bed, in the end, she stopped concocting nostalgia from the ceiling. Then she took an interest in the rippling for itself. Abstract and ever-altering, like the words Nezchai had read which she never really grasped, it absorbed her, teaching her a whole fresh library of concepts, feelings without any name— needing none.

She was evading Nezchai, slipping away through his clutching genius like water through the fingers of a boy. She was dying.

Then she was dead.

She never heard the raucous dumbness of his fury that night he lost her. Half the city claimed to have done so, and to have seen horrible waves of glare and shadow cast upward on the sky by his tantrum.

How long passed after? Accounts varied. A day, a year. Not long.

Why had he so uncontrollably wanted this trophy? His control elsewhere was phenomenal, legendary and feared. Nothing much was known of Nezchai's own youth. Maybe something then had left him prey to such avarice and villainy, this collector of books and gems.

For The Swan . . . as if in deep sleep, dreamless now, but following on some *magnificent* post-life dream instantly mislaid. Only its *sensation* lingering, already melting, gone. Hollow then, rushing through a nullity into a tiny keyhole of dull light that abruptly exploded. Like a golden fish landed on a rotten shore, slung down and forced to yield three alchemical secrets.

She found she stood in the world again, inside midnight and the flickering brazier red of Nezchai's tower, that stony, upright penis of his will.

And she could remember nothing of the place he had dragged her back from—less than nothing. Only the conviction that it had been full of things that, like the sublime awarenesses preceeding death, were nameless and inexplicable.

But what ever had been? What had she ever *wished* to have explained?

She *did* know what he had done.

Nezchai had reclaimed not merely her phantom appearance, but her *true* ghost, the soul firmly meshed inside it. He had pulled her like thread through a needle's eye, and glued her down again where he wanted.

Presently she noticed the magical symbols drawn on the floor.

He saw the frosts and blooms of the afterworld still littering her. On garments, and caught in her hair, as if she had been swept through a storm of butterflies or leaves.

But he only slammed shut his volume of spells, frowning with his triumph over every god who dared to exist.

For a few minutes he walked all round her, as he had done long ago. He ignored now the tinsels and ethereal cobwebs. Besides, they faded swiftly in the roar of reality. Then only she was there. But that was all he wanted.

"I have you back, my Swan. My jewel. Do you remember me, and where you are?"

She had not forgotten him. She had forgotten nothing worldly.

Perhaps in those moments, too, he thought he would outwit also his own death. Such things had been heard of among his kind. Perhaps, with the cranky sentiment of the cruel, he reckoned he had spared her something, and that, if he lived forever, she would have his eternal protection.

She was clothed in a perfect facsimile of her best garments. (The tactile original of the gown lay in a chest.)

He seized a broom of iron twigs and brushed the symbols off the floor.

Then she was free to move about as she wanted. Of course, all she did do was what he trained her to in life. She walked weightless to the door, and though not bothering to undo it, glided through and down the stairs.

In the mansion the invisible Striyi servants, still invisible, may have marvelled that now some of her abilities matched theirs. Certainly they no longer attempted tricks.

As for the human servant, he ran away. But first he burst into tears and kneeled down before her apparition. "Forgive—forgive—I am lost—shall burn in Hell—forgive me!"

The Swan glanced at him remotely. *No* one was preferable to her now. She was finally barred even from her longing for the society of proper humans.

He took her disconnection as a curse. He fled the house, and hanged himself in a wood behind the Gethsameen. The priests buried him in unsanctified ground. He was a suicide, and had been well known as Nezchai's minion.

– FOUR –

Did she mourn her loss of the other world? No. Did she pine? No. Was she ever anything save *there*? No.

Soulless in her phantasmal en-souled shape, The Swan drifted to and fro, a stray feather from the wing of an owl.

While he, like any cunning, clever, solipsistic child that gets its own way, spoiled, lost interest gradually.

Oh, he liked to see her. To meet her. To regard her. She was like all the trophies of his house.

He grew elderly, for now time was moving on, though it had

seemed to pretend to hesitate, earlier on. Time discarded elements from itself—an owl, both owls, a wolf, a pack, a tree in the groves, the dark colour from a man's hair, the semi-tautness of middle-age from a man's face. The mansion was knee-deep in dusts of life, fallen pages, seed pearls, dropped hairs, desiccated thoughts.

But she did not alter. Could not.

Untouchable and untouching, wafted here and there, in and out.

Various persons on the road below saw her at high windows above the trees, a distanced figure still of discernible beauty, like some princess from an ancient tale. A handful saw her out on the bank, among the overgrowing groves. *Like a blue marsh flame* they said.

Did she watch the building projects, the city massing and extending itself, like huge lungs inhaling, towers rising, churches, houses clustering close, the making of the great Vistas—the North one partly running below Nezchai's mansion, as if pushing it away.

No, she did not watch.

Sometimes he still called for her. She always did as she was bid.

"I saved you from a grave," said the man in the carved chair, whose hair was white string, his ringed fingers, despite all the potions, twisted by their crippled bones. "I shall not die," he assured her.

Did she ever speak?

Yes.

"Why does that ship sail by?" she asked the wind on the river-shore. "Why does that dog bark?" She knew the names of countless things. She did not know why she asked, even so, or even why she talked at all. Occasionally she spoke in the old way:

"Stars drop deep in the river. A lion" (she did not know what lions were) "carries the spire of the sun on his back, whose rays change dew to opal."

Once in nine million heartbeats of a heart that no longer could beat, a wisp stirred in her of memory unremembered. Then came a feeling of unpredicted sweet and shining *otherness*. The legacy of where she had been before he reclaimed her? Why not. Others know these moments, and they are not even ghosts.

And she was more than a ghost. She was a prisoner and a slave beyond all prisoners and slaves. An outcast from an unknown country.

Nezchai, in popular belief, was one hundred and twelve years of age when he perished.

Stories abounded as to why it came about. He had outstripped even his own villainy in some novel and outrageous sorcery. He had offended the Devil himself. Or offended so many various demons and sprites they banded together to overthrow him. Or else God, looking down, had simply said, "Is that wasp still crawling there?" And stamped on him.

It was near summer's end. The sky was extremely pale that night though the sun was fully down. It was pale like a plate of blue china from the East, and plaits of stars visible from horizon to horizon.

(In the making of the new great road, many of the trees had been chopped down, and parts of the bank levelled. All this had taken place only some three quarters of a mile beyond the slope where Nezchai's wooden house stood among its wolf-groves. Wolves no longer came there, had not done so for twenty years or more. Neither had the workmen paid much heed to the house, which looked only eccentric and ramshackle. They were miserable slaves, anyway, ignorant of cities. Only watchmen sometimes noted the lighted windows in the tower. But they wore their talismans and said their prayers. The metropolis had grown used to the sorcerer, perhaps judged him less.)

That night, too, there was a sense of impending storm. Not about the city, only in the vicinity of the house.

Old Nezchai had drunk deeply and become uncommonly boisterous, laughing and calling up illusions to perform acrobatics, and to dance.

Near midnight even so, he stiffly climbed the stair towards the tower-top, to spend time with his spell books.

On the way, the mage became aware that his rings struck sparks off the stone wall. A smell both pungent and metallic filled the tower.

Entering the room above, he flung a handfull of powder on a tall lamp, that caused it to flare and lave the atmosphere with olibanos. The magician soon stood reading at a stand, often employing his emerald magnifying glass. But gradually he was conscious of noncorporeal comings and goings all around the space. It was as if half-visible patterns lifted in the plaster of the walls, or out of the floor, or off the shelves of phials and volumes, to swirl about. Tired eyes might mis-see in this way, but the eyes of Nezchai, though no longer as sharp as they had been, were never afflicted by such megrims. Magic was loose in the tower. A magic not of his making.

Even as he began to stare, a long, low hissing sound drove in through one of the windows. The shutter was leaning there on the wall, and it banged, and further showers of sparks flew up.

Nezchai went to the window. As he paced across the room, his very clothes, brushing the furniture, caused further sparkling pyrotechnics. Outside, above, the blue china sky was sullenly boiling. Vast clouds were running in across the river, resembling a high, abnormally sculpted, opaque fog. And in them wild twisting shapes and frills of white lightning. Elsewhere all about, the city lay becalmed. The approaching tempest was only here.

With the years of her captivity, The Swan had grown into her weariness and despair. But these negative states in themselves sometimes brought respite. For when unobserved, she would fade, literally, away. Then she sank into a kind of medium devoid of everything. It was a psychic grave. It was like sleep, but totally vacant, and granted her small tastes of peace. Forgetting it was not the state of death, she came to desire it very much.

When he summoned her, however, she had no choice but to return at once into both consciousness and appearance. So strong was the sorcery he had fashioned, so obdurate, it dwarfed even Nezchai himself. Flung from his brain like a knife, now it was an object of will in its own right.

Nezchai called his slave from her fading-place in order to protect her from what now encroached on the mansion. That was, in order to keep safe his property. For the same reason he sent the Striyi scurrying throughout the house to transport the most valuable items into the security of the tower. Nezchai had no doubts by now the onslaught of weather was unnatural and directed solely at him. He had no idea from whence it came. Who would dare? Not even the Tzaers bothered him. Rather, from time to time, they sent him little gifts. Whatever came, nevertheless, the tower, and everything in it, would withstand. It was built of mighty stones and shored up by occult craft. He was right, mostly, about the tower.

The Swan was aware of all the divergent currents as she rose along the stair, sometimes treading like a flesh-and-blood woman, sometimes levitating. That some of the whirling semi-visible entities were unfriendly she also sensed, though none showed any spite to her. They seemed actually indifferent to her.

At the instant she entered the tower room, all the windows blew inward together.

The Swan paused, impervious, in the inrushing gale of thin and thick glass. Murky vapours poured after. Yet the storm had no louder noise than a low grumbling.

Nezchai had scrambled up on a stone table. He made sweeping gestures to the night, and shouted in his cracked flute of a voice. The floor was littered by books and vellum he had grabbed up, cast down, and now things were smashing on the shelves, and liquids and fires dripped and trickled.

The mansion shook.

With a series of terrible moans and grunts, pieces of its walls unlocked themselves from the central core, the tower.

A whirlwind filled the room, smoke, flame, glass, feathers, papers, liquids, broken wood, chips of stone, and Nezchai gave a loud bellow, like that of an animal felled with an axe. His powers were useless. His eyes were red, his blackened teeth bared, foam bubbling from his lips. There on the table, impotent at last, he shook his fists as the helpless did, and howled in a mania of rage and fear.

Then the whole wooden house disbanded and galloped upward, flying past the tower windows and its open doorway. Another list: long timbers and fireplaces, paving from the floors, panels and hangings, chests and chairs, cupboards without backs, or fronts, and all the jewels and bottles spangling and shattering like erupting stars. Even trees burst out of the courtyard and shot away Heavenward, fired from some sorcerous subterranean cannon.

The tower itself rocked, and with a ponderous booming slowness, half its length dissociated from the other. A fountain of flints and shards gushed down amid the ascending upward stampede of other stuffs. Nezchai tottered as the table also snapped in two. Wailing, he began to fall through the wound in the tower towards the earth. But next instant the huge fists of the storm had clasped him. *Up* then he, too, spiralled, kicking and shrieking, up and up in the flying debris of his mansion, until he grew tiny as a fly, and the clouded sky gulped him. Into some vortex he had been taken, and much of the wreckage with him. Although bits of it were still to be seen, roiling in the cloud, the lightnings smiting on them like swords. And with this cargo the storm gathered itself higher and higher, one huge fishing net, and rumbled away towards the west.

Final a-physical atomies, seen, unseen, semi-seen, followed it in an ultimate up-pouring. The invisible servants of the house went with them. They were glad, maybe, to have found a community at last.

Sighing, creaking, the night grew still. Its lid was all pale blue again, and the polished stars again gleamed out.

Ships rocking lightly at anchor, further along the river, revealed their ordinary pinpricks of lanterns. There was no evidence of disturbance or alarm. Dogs barked somewhere, and from a single church a single bell lamented some grief that had nothing to do with this.

In the dismembered tower, which had been swept clean of every other thing, only the ghost of The Swan remained.

– FIVE –

Did she have one minute, one hour, a night even, of belief his destruction might set her free? No. Any hope of it? No. She knew. The cage he had built for her would outlast the maker.

Though she was now unwatched and alone, able to fade to her resting nothingness, these escapes were no more available to her than sleep to a living thing. Had she been sheer ghost—a husk, an echo of life—she could probably have faded right away forever. But she was soul-trapped. He had bound her to the world, and her soul itself fettered her there. For where else did souls come, but to that same world, trapped by flesh and the chains of others?

Only death could let her go. But death had been outwitted. Perhaps Death had shrugged, not minding to lose one among so very many.

Mankind found her again quickly enough.

The first was a boy playing a pipe on the bank. He was off a ship. He saw her manifest, a blue flower among the trees above. He got up, bemused by her loveliness, and when she winked out like a blown flame, ran to the ship to tell them all.

They came and went, people.

Along this stretch of the river, and the North Vista, eventually grand palaces would rise, one with a man-made lake. A bridge would cross the Vlova, guarded by statues of heroes. Meanwhile huts and hovels went up among the last trees, were lived in, confiscated, felled, haphazardly rebuilt.

Foreign itinerents camped in the area of Nezchai's legendary mansion, using the bisected stone tower as shelter or else hauling slabs out of it for other purposes, so more of it crumbled down.

They, too, saw her.

The foul, stinking, butter-yellow candles of their scrabbling lives magnetized her, poor moth. It was not that she wished to be among them. It was the spell, always that. A sound—a cry—a call—the badly-played waver of a pipe. She had been propelled from her essential place by Nezchai's summons. Now by theirs.

The Swan did not question any of it. She never had.

But they, seeing her ghost, *they* haunted *her*. They were desperate always to look at her, watch her, *keep* her. They made her offerings, gross or full of pathos—a skinned hare, a silver ring . . .

Stay with us.

What beauty did they have in their wretched lives? None. They reached greedily for hers. A family treasure.

Like Nezchai, they encaged her.

She was *theirs*.

After unmeasured decades, the site was cleared. A fine house, the second mansion, was erected on the spot, among other such buildings, and the groves, what was left of them, were subsumed into a fashionable Italian garden. The stone tower was kept, augmented as a sort of inner chimney. A prince and his family settled in the house like fat, noisy birds, among a plethora of ill-used servants and slaves. If they had heard of the sorcerer Nezchai, they were too intelligent to believe he had been real. Or, if real, accomplished.

There had been a prolonged lacuna for The Swan. She had faded and rested some while. She was drawn from her peace this time in a quiet and hideous way, to burnished wooden floors and statues of Greek gods, a conservatory with trees like rhinoceros hide, stabbed at the top by dagged plumes.

Life (the spell), had netted her once more.

She appeared first to a romantic son, a drunkard and idiot, who took his inebriated scribblings for fine verse, and had published the rubbish to some misguided acclaim. (It would be long after that truly vibrant and ideally glamorous life was thought necessary to draw her, a legitimate mistake made by those who reckoned themselves of little worth. It was *new* life, that was all. A new face.)

The drunk described her after as a blue crescent moon. But he had followed her through the house—it was late. "She had a small white dish, and in it a golden pike swimming. It was made of gold, I mean, set with precious jewels."

The drunkard-poet took the fish for her pet. It was not. It was her misplaced, vernacular, half alchemical symbol for her own condition. Dragged from liberty in limitless sea to be questioned, measured and admired.

The great innovative stove, a white iron monster, ornamented and painted in a barbaric style, sent its tentacle through the central house, passing along the route of the ancient tower. Stairs also ascended along a similar path. The stairs were the way she took, the poet's azure ghost.

But high above, near quarters where servants slept, she dissolved into thin air.

Somehow—the spell, also?—they knew to title her The Swan.

So she remained with the family of nobles, drifting in and out of their rapid history, until there came a night of thunder and shouting. Red light of burning stained the river and along the snow. The Rebellious War had begun.

Her main manacle, the poet, shot himself in drunken terror. The rest escaped from the city and were cut down somewhere in the birch forests beyond. Released, The Swan sank to her rest.

Which was not long. The house was soon busy again, split into its rooms, *teeming* with people now, all aching for some beauty in their sordid and sorrowful existence.

This time a group of young women saw her first. Among them were the mothers of Zophi and Mariasha.

"She's like the Virgin!"

"Ssh. Don't blaspheme. But yes—beautiful . . . holy."

"So pure. She can never have—"

"No. She is the spirit of some chaste saint."

"Or a rich lady before—"

"Ssh. Don't talk of *them*, our oppressors. But yes, she has that look. Refined and pristine."

They came to see her, all of them. They came to keep her, all of them.

Their treasure.

Theirs.

The one thing that could not be rent from their struggle of living, that had nothing to do with it.

She faded to rest, but they rested in her.

Haunted.

And when she flagged, as now she did, worn out by their infatuated, ceaseless demands to see her, the cacophanous clamour of their delight, they, too, hauled her back, their golden fish, out of the ocean of nullity. They did it first accidentally, by bringing in a new and vivid person, a man or a woman. Then noticing it worked on her, the fresh life luring her. So then arrivals were primed by the story all had somehow learned of The Swan, from legend, or from the drunkard's scrawl. The arrivals duly fell in love with her, and so—back she came to one more rancid candle, one more music badly played.

Houses and alleys and slums and winding avenues now stood between the mansion on Copper Street and the river, with its fringe of palaces. What had seemed quite near was pushed far away.

From attics, unknowingly attracted there by the remnants of the tower, The Swan looked across at the Vlova. It ran like a platinum scar on the city's belly. But once more she never left the house. Human pressure was always on her. Even in her fading-place, even there, she sensed their dreams feel after her, stroke and pinch her to wake up and come back to them.

Nevertheless, flagging she was. Could it be possible at last, envampirized and drained utterly by the hunger of human things, even her *soul* could fade? Could die? Oh, how she longed for it. Drearily she sometimes spoke to the tenants of the house, sentences which to their ears had portent and profundity. But nothing had meaning for her but the idea of unravelling and peace: freedom.

Sometimes she even mentioned death. But they never understood. Her syntax still was not exactly theirs. In any case, how could such wonder wish to end? And how could such sweetness be anything but eternal. Like the wonder and sweetness of the Christ. She could not truly die. She could not leave them. For-*never*.

The Hyacinths

– ONE –

"Poor ghost," he said. He quoted inadvertently something he could not recall. But next he covered his face with his hands. She had told him all her history—either that, or he had read it from her phantom brain. Or—could it be?—imagined it only. No, it was true enough. What else. This despair.

The Swan had moved off again. She had sat down, as if she were able to sit, or needed to, in the mended chair across the room.

All over the floor, the broken pot and the broken hyacinths, their petalled tenements snapped, buds spilled like blue peas—

He was sorry.

He sat down also, on the side of the bed.

Naturally they had given him a room where the stovepipe ran. For the pipe partly adhered to the course of Nezchai's ancient tower. A magnet, for The Swan. (Perhaps iron filings were as unwilling as she, to be sucked in to *their* magnetic lodestone.)

Blya Sovinen thought, *What can I say to her? She doesn't want to hear how I, too, adore her, want to possess and keep her—worse than mere lust and sexual desire, this gnawing itch to coerce and cage. What can I say?*

"What may I call you?" he humbly asked.

At that she raised her eyes and stared at him.

Softly she said, "I had a name once."

"What? Tell me, do tell me—"

"Webby—Webbed. Web-Foot."

Blya caught his breath with revulsion. Perhaps she saw, or she did not.

She said, "There was another name, feathers and white and black and blue—"

He felt himself begin to cry for her, and was ashamed, and clenched the tears away behind his eyes.

On her lap, between her two quiescent hands, the little dish. In it the golden fish swam up and down, glittering with minute jewelry: the symbol of her worth and slavery.

"You are like a hyacinth," he said slowly. "Like a flower."

She looked up again at that, puzzled.

"The flower of night," she said remotely, "the giving way to the sun that rides on the back of white horses, and the lion bearing a diadem."

He said, "I can't think what I should call you. It's all quite wrong. What would you want to be called?" She gazed at him. Suddenly, like a piercing ray of light through cloud, a peculiar intelligent exactness sharpened her face. "Nothing," she said.

Blya lowered his eyes. He knew not to look at her was not enough to release her, even temporally. His fascination, his love—if such it could be termed—bound her here, for now, for always.

After a while they—others—knocked loudly on the door.

He called out harshly, "I'm with *her!*"

Their noise fell off in murmurs. They were jealous. But then came the voice of Olcha who had been Orena, arch-envy incarnate, herding them off like naughty children. The "New One" must be given time to cement the spell.

The new one.

I, he thought. *I.*

The night was stretched over like a canopy. They sat, then lay beneath it. He had invited her to lie down on the bed. "I won't touch you—I *can't*, can I? Can't touch you? But rest here."

Patiently she did as he said. He understood she did not *rest* anywhere but in her fading-place. He wished he could release her to it, but even if he should doze, no doubt some part of him would act sentry, tying her in the room and the tenement. Anyway, he could not fall asleep. He lay studying her, her exquisite profile, her eyes turned to the ceiling. Did she see the curious, deceptive reflections rippling there still? The urge to ask her was very strong and he choked it down. She should not be asked a single thing. She had told all, or he had *absorbed* all, breathing it in like perfume from her phantasmal body and hair.

Hyacinths. But hyacinths that could not decay. Rats had eaten her embalmed corpse. He must not consider that or he would surely go mad.

He stared on and on. He stared through her, though she was not at all transparent, and seemed real as any other element in the room, until or if he should try to make physical contact. Or she with him, as she had at first, when she put her hand upon him. Why had she done that? Did some remnant of compassion linger in her for her torturers, all these never-ending bands of slave-takers. *Don't ask. Let her be.*

No one else had tried to disturb him. Them.

Earlier there were riots of noise from below, their rejoicings, he thought. Later the inhabitants of the house went stumbling to their beds, singing, cheerily arguing, one vomiting on the stairway, chided and derided. Later again, quiet weighed down the tenement, heavy as lead. Outside, bells thinly gilded the night, far-spaced, it seemed to him. Tomorrow was Christmas Day. He thought the city saved itself now for all the great racket of the morning, all the shouting and ringing that betokened Christ's birth. Yet dawn did not arrive. Night went on and on. He had no watch—that, too, had been sold long since. Perhaps the night would never end.

She made no movement, did not speak. But in the faint illumination that somehow remained after the oil-lamp burned itself out, he could see her still, lying by him on the bed, her eyes closed now, as if she slept.

"Swan," he said, reluctant to use this label of a name, this title of her enslavement, "Swan, let me tell you my own story."

Astonishing him, for he had expected no visible reaction, the woman on the bed turned calmly on to her side. She put her slender left hand under her cheek, and lay now looking directly into his face. This gesture was so human, it hurt him. It was as if she were his lover—or his wife—accustomed and fond, ready always to listen.

He told her, then, how he had come to be in that house, picked up off the bridge and used as bait for her.

"It was because of a previous night. The night I went, to see the play," Blya Sovinen said. "I'd been a student at the University less than two years, and had never heard anything from my parents, in return for my dutiful letters. But they had saved up money to send me for my education. Doubtless this was to serve their own ends, but I barely considered it at the time. It was what I was to do. And so my letters were full of my virtues, how hard I worked and how much I had already achieved. I must confess, I didn't love them, either of them. My father was a hot, fixed man who beat me often, *beating me into shape*, as he put it. And my mother was a cold woman who had no interest in me outside my possible skills. She was only happy in the little blind church, where she spent most of her time kneeling before the icons, more real to her than anything else. But, to come to the play in the city. That night I went to the play—I had just got on the street, rushing to the dilapidated theatre on Sunny Avenue—do you know the one? Oh—but you wouldn't know the one. A poor venue, with hard wooden benches like rails, or else one stood, but I had enough money, which I'd put by, to sit on a bench. This was a drama I especially wanted to see. A while before I'd read it, and in the original Scandinavian language. The play *haunted* me." Blya smiled, apologetic at the use of this word. "But on the street, as I went along, a man met me. He'd come all the distance from my village. It seemed my father and mother, who had never allowed me to love them, were dead from some illness of poverty and cold. And all the money they had accrued over many years, was put aside, as I'd done it for my theatre seat, for *me*. The messenger, an honest, savage man, a kind of ramshackle priest, had been entrusted to bring it to me. Which he duly did. There on that street he thrust it, sheaf on sheaf, into my hands that seemed to have lost all feeling. He said he was glad to be rid of it, the temptation had been enormous to thieve it, but he had triumphed. Huge pale bills they were, I remember still, written over and drawn with the heads of Tzaers, and of those who have replaced them. Never in all my life had I seen money quite of that form, and never so much. It was frankly meaningless to me—you will grasp that, I think. For money means nothing to you. But suppose I compare it to something you recognise? For example, the ability to be *free?* Yes. Yes, you know now what the money represented. But you see, I could not feel it. I stood on the cold ground, which I could experience bitterly through my threadbare boots, listening to the priest's story of death, and personal triumph over avarice. In the end I had the presence of mind to thank the man, whom I didn't know, though he claimed to be from my home village. I then made him a generous gift—I did all that as if I were some sort of machine. But at first he refused me, as if affronted. I had to insist, and then he took what I offered with a muttered curse. Only after this point I began to realize, rather vacantly, I could live well—in my own type of liberty—from what I'd received. I might easily pay all my fees for the continuing period of my education. And besides, I might live in reasonable comfort—better, in fact, than on my father's former, intermittent handouts. Yet these things also meant at the hour absolutely nothing. However, I'm sure they would have come to do so. Because, without any sort of financial help from my father at all, I would soon become frankly destitute. Yet I wanted to get away from the proud messenger of death and riches. I did not have the gall to say to him I was hurrying to a theatre. Instead I announced I had a sick friend I must look after. To my credit, neither did I have the cheek to pretend I required time alone to grieve. After I left him, I glanced back once, and noticed he scurried into a tavern."

Blya said he ran then to the theatre. He found his place on a bench quite near the stage, and had no sooner sat down there, when two other late arrivals also hurried in and sat beside him. They were, he thought in the low light of the theatre, a mother and daughter, dark-skinned and good-looking, poorly dressed and wrapped in modest shawls. He made room for them a little. And suddenly a spasm of protectiveness for them veered through him. They seemed to huddle in against each other, and him, afraid to be in such a spot, afraid even of the play, for the playwright was sometimes reckoned scandalous, though of great talent.

"Don't worry, Mother," he whispered to the older woman, "I'll see no one insults you."

"Oh, you're a kind young man," she whispered back. "God will reward you."

"And God did reward me," Blya said, lying looking into the face of beauty, "for my foolishness and ignorance."

The play quickly absorbed all his concentration. It was a work of delicacy and grotesquery, mingled like swansdown and broken glass. One moment there was astonishment, then laughter, then marvel, then pity—then romance that drifted like a lovely scent to the acrid residue of an austere terror and a deep sorrow. The playwright had stipulated he preferred that no interval should be observed, but even so a slight one was inevitable. Such scenery as had been managed had to be rearranged. During these minutes, the younger of the two women seated by Blya, murmured that she felt unwell. Blya heard, and looked about as both of them got to their feet. He asked if he could assist them in any way, but hoping, he afterwards acknowledged, they would refuse. He did not want to miss one iota of the play.

Refuse they did. The mother said lightly, "Oh, don't be concerned. She's subject to these fits. A turn in the air will put her right. Perhaps you would save our place if anyone tries to take it?"

Blya said he would. They, very modestly, their heads bowed, slipped away. They were careful, he saw, to disturb no one.

"They did not return. But no one tried to steal their place. I admit I thought of them, once or twice, during the first dialogues of the new scene, but then I forgot. How callous I was—or am. I'd be the same now, perhaps. Or not. How can I tell? Besides, *now* I would have learnt a sort of lesson in such things."

Not until the play's end, when Blya stood up, intellectualy reeling, to wildly applaud, did he abruptly recollect his neighbours. Then he suffered a vague pang. Going out, he had a dismal idea he might find them in the snow, the girl prone, the mother bending over her, at her wit's end. But only his upright, hale, fellow theatregoers congested the outer thoroughfare. Neither woman or girl were anywhere to be seen.

"Maybe no one can believe this. Perhaps you, perhaps *you* of all persons, can credit me. I had also *forgotten* the money the angry priest gave me. It was so—unsuitable to my life, you see, as I had already lived it. And I'd crammed all the notes into the pocket of my coat. Like a fistful of rags. It was only when I put my hand in there to find a coin for a drink that instead . . . that instead I found nothing at all. And then I *did* remember. And then I stood astounded on the roadway, more crazed than when I had been given my father's fortune, with people jostling by me, and a carriage rushing along, striking sparks from the hoofs of the horses, the driver bellowing and swearing that I was in his way."

The modest women had competently robbed him, as the priest had not. Every note had been lifted (his own small stash of coins also), by the skill of the mother's almost fairy fingers. He had not felt anything of it, only her trusting warm closeness, and the chilly gap after she was gone. Probably they had seen him get the money in the first instance, and followed him, sliding into the theatre on some pretext. How cool she had been, to sit on there with him all through that initial scene, his life, as it were, in her pocket.

Blya and The Swan lay supine, looking at each other.

He said, "Because of that robbery of all my unlooked-for inheritance—which otherwise then, obviously dried up like a withered plant—I had nothing. I therefore struggled a while, selling what slight possessions I had. But soon enough I was ejected from my lodging and from the University. Do you know, I've often thought, my parents died when they did out of a sort of inertia. Their miserly tendencies had hastened their deaths certainly, but they had been miserly on my behalf. There's an extra parody to it, is there, that all their self-denial, meant to make of me such a supreme scholar, ended by rendering two thieves so happy? But really I believe they died simply because they thought I would no longer need them. Nor, despite any previous hope, they me."

Then Blya blushed. He had crassly spoken of the easy death of human things—to *her.*

But she did not seem to notice.

How lovely she was. What did anything else signify? He could lie forever by her, gazing on her. This was simple, too.

And nothing of any of it could matter to her.

Yet, her eyes were so luminous and holy.

"We are all," he said, "trapped and enslaved by the webs of others. And by the extravagant and stupid structures of events. If I had never gone to see that play, that work of genius and fire and fear—I shouldn't ever have ended up in penury, and so on the Heroic Vlova Bridge, and so—here, now. Did I say, the drama was by the writer Strindberg? It was called *The Ghost Sonata.*"

Somewhere beyond the dark, yet low-lit cavern which contained them, another bell chimed over the river. Surely soon the dawn must break, the day of Christ's birth.

Abruptly Blya Sovinen sat up.

"Darling," he said. "Come with me now. Come back with me to the roof of the house."

Inevitably, he thought, she rose as he did. At the door, with a sombre tactfulness, he held it wide for her to pass. They went up the steps, he guiding her away from the pool of vomit, again as if it could mark or trouble her.

She made no sound, nor he. Behind other doors, drowsy mutterings and long, rattling snores, coughing and bed-shifting rolls, and bad dreams. Not a single waking note.

When they reached the attics, he entered first, now guiding her through the ironically ghostly stockings, beside all the sleepers there spread on mattresses, sighing and moaning in sleep.

They came to the hidden door behind a curtain, and the treacherous, ladder-like stair.

No one woke. He had known they would not. Some other sorcery was on the tenement, perhaps only that of tiredness, eating, and strong drink.

She—*blew* up the ladder. Thistledown, smoke rising. He was agile in only a mortal way. He closed the exit behind them.

– TWO –

How altered now, the city of the sleeping night.

Not a candle showing anywhere, only the isolated torches, dull as embers, and the greenish ebb of lanterns along some individual streets. Yet the snow itself was gleaming up, one entire white lamp, into the sky's indigo and star-streaked eye.

When she had finally met with people who themselves possessed great physical beauty, the indifference and apathy of The Swan were penetrated. For she saw they must be as she was, less than human. It had not happened often. In the household of the aristocrats there had been a kitchen girl of porcelain delicacy. And among the generation or so of tenants in the slum, once or twice, others shone out. One was an exceptional elderly man with long, silvered hair, and the features of a pagan god. But he died one evening. Another was an infant, a marvel, but *he* coarsened as he grew up. Both had disconcerted The Swan, for how could progression to proper humanness, let alone expiry, have happened? (Her own expiry she did not consider. She had not, anyway, been able to expire completely.) Orena was a member of this order, fair and blindingly pretty. But Orena became Olcha, waxing gross and amoeba-like, flowing over and absorbing the energies of any who approached too near.

Blya, though, had a beauty which inevitably struck and resonated on the awareness of The Swan. His beauty, in fact, was very much a male equivalent of her own—although neither understood this. Of them all, therefore, it stood to reason, the shackles he could lay on her were infinitely more mighty.

She had not fought against them. She never fought.

Yet as she heard him tell his short story, The Swan felt something move inside her, uneasy but almost sweet. Perhaps it was only the clank of the chains slithering to a more comfortable position. Blya, too, it was obvious to her, had been also demon-got, as had she. And like her he must have had to camouflage himself and take care to be tolerated among others. He, too, would have been always alone.

If her own story was precisely as Blya had read it from her, surely no one could be entirely certain. But the premise that a monster had sired her he, naturally, had never believed. More likely some oaf of another forest village had lain with the mother in the field. The woman then manufactured horrible webbed prints in the earth with a stone, to save herself a beating or worse. The slight science Blya knew informed him that two foul compounds, when mixed, could occasionally by some fluke produce a miracle—a flawless gem, an unusually coloured flower, a perfect child.

As they stood on the roof of the tenement together, The Swan looked closely at Blya Sovinen.

Her deductions had always been oblique. And now, too, they were quite strange. Bound by the chains he had refashioned, she did not guess, the ghost, that what currently held her so tight was neither coercion or compassion. Instead, she had begun to be in love with him. That was all it was. But she, so endlessly, greedily loved, did not know what love was. It filled her, and she could give it no name.

She watched his every movement, even the blinking of his eyes, the lashes rising and falling and rising. She *watched* him— as others watched *her.*

From her hand, the small dish with its golden, miniature pike, her symbol, had vanished.

If she had breathed she would have held her breath, hanging on the turn of his head, the shape of his eyes when again they regarded her.

His story of himself had moved her to the quick, the soul. For they were of a kind, and she grasped his suffering better than her own.

What, what would he do now?

Blya Sovinen beckoned The Swan. They moved to the parapet, and then he stared down. The yard lay far below, packed with an ungiving snow, like adamant.

"Listen to me, my Swan. If human obsession traps you here—if *I* trap you here—I'll let you go."

In snowlight, her face clear as ice—almost—*alert?* But she spoke. "How can you?" As a living woman might.

"Our boiling lives snare and bind you. All of them, but worse always, the *new one*—the fresh blood. This time, me. The enchanter's spell . . . *our* spell. Everyone wants to keep you, because you are beauty and *otherness*; you're the sudden fortune the thieves must never be allowed to steal. But they do. Oh, I bless those wretched women, since they sent me here. Let them become saints. All you've known, darling, my Swan, is to be gripped. But I—shall deliberately let you fall." Blya Sovinen's own face was filled with a radiance, as if the white flame of the snow had entered into him, or it was only the flame of madness, but a flame it was. "We hug life and you, we live for you and make you *suffer* this life, when you should be free of it. When you should be in Heaven." He put out his hand, and gently stroked her long dark hair, not feeling a strand of it, making no impression, as if *he* were the ghost, not she. "But I," he said, "I'll die for you. Watch, beloved. See how it's done—" And turning from her in one movement he leapt clear over the low parapet, his arms flung high, his face now tilted up exalting to the sky above, blind and insane with love, love's other side like the dark of the moon. Three heartbeats in the air, a bird in flight. Then the crash upon the iron earth. Everything of him broke apart at once—bones, body, blood. Carapace. Out of him the force of life erupted, cast back like a spray of unseen flowers and leaves.

Dead, he lay there on the yard. He had expected mere nothingness despite his words. For though he had been taught to believe in God, and in an afterworld, these hopes had died away like everything else, leaving only their disconsolate husks—to which, from sympathy, he showed respect. Dead then, Blya Sovinen. A shattered instrument, its music expelled. And she?

In the sky, wheeling, a slight snow purling past, soft and no longer cold. Below, the city, and the vast flexible river, broad-bordered with ice, and the ships at anchor strung with faint lamps, and the bells tinkling from the amber somnolence of the Gethsameen. And there in the east, a ribbon the colour of a ripe peach. Perhaps sunrise was still possible . . .

"How beautiful it is," she said.

"Are you here?" he said. "Am I?"

"When you fell—when you struck the ground—something hit me like one of my mother's blows—and then something else seized me," she said, "like two gigantic hands, and flung me outward. Am I the same as I was?"

"No, my love. Not at all. Am I?"

"No, my love," she said. "Not at all."

"There's no need," he said, "I think, no need to loiter here any more. We have no names. We speak without language and exist without any form we have ever known, or if we know, then we had forgotten. And both of us—love?"

"We both of us love."

"Shall we then—?"

"Shall we," she said, "go there together?"

Above the river, something like two stars coming undone, spinning, flashing away into—into— And in the river, under the ice, the glint of rapid gold, some alchemy sinking, a coin or a fish. Or nothing. Nothing at all. Or perhaps—

"How bad the house feels," Olcha said. She stood in her night-gown, a faltering candle in her grasp, looking up the vault of stairs. "Empty," she said. To her horror she wept. All through the tenement they were waking and beginning to weep, sobbing and crying even in dreams. Zergoi cuddling his triangular guitar, Yori clutching a pair of shoes, Mariasha and Zophi and Timara running from room to room, Stavin smashing his pocketwatch, as if to stop time, Koresh howling like a wolf, Ossif tearing at his hair. The world exploding apart and pieces flying upward in the storm. The mansion walls ran water as if it, too, lamented. The water soaked through the floors. It was the purging of a grief long withheld, from which few are exempt. At last, at last, it was mourning.

Dartmoor! Now doesn't the very sound of it conjure visions of hounds and howlings, dark deeds and daring detectives, and one of the latter in particular in a deerstalker hat? Down here in Torquay, Devon, on England's southwest coast—the so-called English Riviera (we have palm trees!) and the next county east of Cornwall and Land's End—I live on Dartmoor's doorstep, as it were. Indeed I can drive into the heart of Dartmoor in just forty-five minutes.

And the Tors are real just as described: these massive out-crops carved in an age of ice, many with their individual myths and legends, and some with genuine macabre mysteries attached. Of course, Tumble Tor isn't one of the real ones—or maybe it is but I'm not offering up its real name because the topography of the countryside around isn't precisely the way I have it. As for the rest of my descriptions, however—the names of various towns, villages, and of course the Tors—they're all there in or around Dartmoor, and all are very real and solid.

As to why I wrote this story: well, let's be honest, that's simply because Marvin Kaye offered me one quarter of a proposed

Ghost Quartet. And since ghosts have always left something of a hole in my body of strange stories, I took him up on his kind offer and decided to fill the gap with "The Place of Waiting." If you like it, please write and tell me. If you don't, write and tell Marvin!

Brian Lumley
Torquay, Devon

I have loved Shakespeare's plays since my days as a theatre undergraduate, when I learned to get my head into his characters and my mouth around the blank verse. I have taught his plays to literature students, directed actors in performing his plays, and even fiddled with some of his scripts so they'd be fresh and funny to modern audiences despite the way the language has changed since he wrote them. (See my adaptations of *Romeo and Juliet* and *The Taming of the Shrew* at www.hatrack.com.)

I don't like all the plays equally. *Coriolanus* simply doesn't speak to me. In fact, none of the Roman plays do. But the play that bothers me the most—because I don't much care for it and think I should—is *Hamlet.*

Of Shakespeare's great tragedies, I love *Lear* and *Macbeth; Othello* at least I understand. But *Hamlet?* I have little interest in a dithering hero; nor am I much inspired by revenge plots. Yet I keep hearing that this is the greatest of them all.

So I analyzed the story to see what it would take to make me care about it. "Hamlet's Father" is what I came up with. I'm fully aware of the fact that I have just messed with the play that many consider the greatest ever written in any language. But Shakespeare stole his plots from other people; and nothing I do is going to erase a line of his great work or diminish his reputation in any way. So why not?

If you think it's blasphemous to fiddle with Shakespeare's work, then for heaven's sake don't read this story. I leave his version in shreds on the floor. But my body count is just as high, as long as you don't expect me to account for Rosencrantz and Guildenstern. I figure Tom Stoppard took care of them for all time.

Orson Scott Card
Greensboro, North Carolina

Back in 1989, I went to Edinburgh to act in two shows in that city's International Fringe Festival. The first day that I had free from the rehearsal schedule, I took an exploratory walk about Old Town and discovered The Tron on the Royal Mile a bit to the east of St. Giles Cathedral. The place was pretty much as described in my story, though its dimensions are as remembered and not necessarily what they are in reality.

To the best of my knowledge, no supernaturalist society holds meetings at The Tron, though Mercat Tours did and probably still does conduct ghost walks through parts of Old Town, and some of them would end up at The Tron, where, with the aid of a wee dram, visitors were encouraged to share their own ghostly experiences.

I patterned the character of Mike after the bartender at the Royal Scots Club (RSC), where our performances took place. I don't remember his name, but he did resemble Edward Woodward, and he did tell me Tam Connery was a local bouncer who he once personally tossed out of the RSC. The real "Mike" indeed loved Laurel & Hardy. He said Stan liked to play the famous Old Course (golf) at St. Andrews; his "nineteenth hole" was not The Tron, but the RSC. "Mike" learned that I'd been president of the Founding Tent of the Sons of the Desert, and once he did, every evening at the end of whichever show I was in, I'd come upstairs for a Whisky Mac, and "Mike" would say, "Put yer money away, Yank, this one's on me."

The ruined cathedral in the story of Ian Napier's brother was based on the one I visited in the town of Dunkeld; it is close to Birnam, both the town and the woods famous for its role in Shakespeare's Scottish play. The house near the Royal Botanical Gardens in Lily Watson's story was torn down quite some time ago. The events that took place therein constitute one of Edinburgh's more famous ghost stories.

Melinda Lawrence is loosely patterned on my dear friend and fellow author Carole Buggé, who once visited Glencoe and indeed found it quite an unsettling experience.

The Glencoe massacre involved complicated politics that I could not introduce without undue prolixity. Those interested may search the Internet for details; the complete lyrics of Jim McLean's haunting ballad may also be read there.

Marvin Kaye
New York City

The novella is set in a city of the parallel Russia, as may be fairly evident. Having written two previous parallel-city quartets (Paris/Paradys and Venice/Venus), I've for some time had in mind a third quartet set in a metropolis called Petragrava—which is a cross between Moscow and St.Petersburg.

Petragrava therefore is the unnamed city in the novella. Russian literature (in translation) and music have ensnared me since about the age of ten. I was about fourteen, though, when I first saw a TV production of Strindberg's unnerving, hilarious, insane, logical and entirely wonderful play, whose title is most frequently translated as *The Ghost Sonata*. It has appropriately haunted me ever since, and I have in fact read it far more often than watched it in performance. Although this story of mine offers only a strange counterpoint to the play, some of the *Sonata*'s elements of surreality, despair and faith very much threaded through my inspiration.

Tanith Lee
St. Leonard's on Sea, East Sussex